PRIME-TIME SHUFFLE

Here's the story:

A nice, sentimental guy holds a bunch of kids hostage.

A hotshot TV reporter is in there with him.

No one knows how long it will take for this renegade reporter to push the guy with the gun over the edge, but whatever happens, the lives of these two men will never be the same again.

It's a show that has captured the attention of millions, in living rooms and bar rooms from coast to coast. Every day the suspense builds and the ratings go right through the ceiling.

The only question is, who's really running the show . . . ?

MAD CITY

MAD CITY

by J. H. Marks

Based on the Screenplay by
Tom Matthews
Story by Tom Matthews
& Eric Williams

A SIGNET BOOK

SIGNET
Published by the Penguin Group
Penguin Putnam Inc., 375 Hudson Street,
New York, New York 10014, U.S.A.
Penguin Books Ltd, 27 Wrights Lane,
London W8 5TZ, England
Penguin Books Australia Ltd, Ringwood,
Victoria, Australia
Penguin Books Canada Ltd, 10 Alcorn Avenue,
Toronto, Ontario, Canada M4V 3B2
Penguin Books (N.Z.) Ltd, 182–190 Wairau Road,
Auckland 10, New Zealand

Penguin Books Ltd, Registered Offices:
Harmondsworth, Middlesex, England

First published by Signet, an imprint of Dutton Signet,
a member of Penguin Putnam Inc.

First Printing, November, 1997
10 9 8 7 6 5 4 3 2 1

Prologue

The day began like any other day in a town much like many others across the country. People woke up and turned on the television to see the sun rise in the logos of morning talk shows. Instead of stepping outside to see if it was raining or snowing, they watched the weather report. No longer did neighbors meet at the end of driveways and shout good morning while picking up the newspaper to learn what had happened around the world overnight. Instead, they watched twenty-four-hour news programs. Nor did they lean over fences or sit around kitchen tables to catch up on what was going on in the neighborhood. They now had gossip on a global scale courtesy of Oprah, Ricki Lake, Regis and Kathie Lee. Phone calls about evening arrangements were no longer necessary; it was easier to consult *TV Guide* and plan to meet up later with their favorite prime-time characters.

But on this particular day something unexpected was to happen. Before Ted Koppel led America in its collective good night, one event would grab the television consciousness of the nation and demand absolute attention.

America had always been a nation on the move, and its wanderlust found expression in channel surfing with remote "clickers." But even the most dedicated flipper would have been stymied by the intensity of prime-time coverage one story was about to receive.

What was truly remarkable about the event that began this early morning was the perfectly unremarkable setting where it all took place. While programming experts dictated that viewers preferred glamorous locations such as Manhattan or Melrose Place and irresistible characters who combined unnatural beauty and wit—this show openly defied the rules.

The production starred neither cops, doctors, nor young, sexually frenzied models, but everyday people who went to work and then home again. The site of the performance was a suburban sprawl of little distinction. As far as demographics went, the community of Madeline, California, which was about to become the center of obsessive national attention, owned barely a blip on market-share charts.

Chapter One

In another place, someone might have been suspicious of the two men standing outside the Foothill Federal Bank. The structure itself looked invulnerable. Built in the twenties, the bank's design suggested a fortress. People depositing their life savings here would sleep comfortably at night, assured that no one could easily break in. Still, the two men standing outside the bank moved quickly and with purpose as they assembled various pieces of sophisticated equipment. Maybe in a bigger town they would have been taken for high-tech thieves preparing an armed assault. But in quiet Madeline, California, no one gave the men much notice.

Madeline was neither urban, entirely suburban, nor rural. Rather, the seventy-five-thousand-person town was representative of the new American frontier—where suburban communities grew beyond their borders and paved over the fruit groves and bean fields of what had once been family farms. Madeline was a community without a rationale for its existence other than its proximity to the freeways that led to "real" places like San Jose or San Francisco.

The people of Madeline loved the town for its quiet streets, safe schools, and the large homes with relatively low mortgages. It was a nice place to raise kids—at least that's how parents felt. Their children, on the other hand, though usually well behaved and respectful of their elders, were less than thrilled by Madeline's small-town atmosphere. While the town boasted of a sixplex movie theater, all the fast food anyone could want, and a faded Woolworth's soon to be replaced by a Gap, Madeline could not compete with the thrilling images of urban life cable brought into the living rooms of their amicable but dull town. Kids, and anybody else seeking excitement in Madeline, were more than likely to be disappointed by its generic motif.

When one of the men waiting outside Foothill Federal finished checking their equipment, the other man—aggressive and intense—barked at him to do it again. Max Brackett had no equipment of his own to prepare, but watched the front door of the bank without blinking an eye. Obviously in charge and used to enjoying a position of authority, Brackett looked misplaced in sleepy Madeline. Brackett's immaculate blue blazer and tie stood in contrast to his accomplices' T-shirts and jeans. His clothing may not have been expensive, but he wore his jacket and tie vainly. His clothes signaled that he was the one in charge— the center of attention with his lean features and passionate sense of focus. The man working for him was paunchy and soft. He fooled around while waiting for the action to begin.

Though Brackett was a few inches shorter than the other man, a passerby would not have thought so. Brackett's persona towered over his confederates, and they were eager that he should be pleased. Maybe they liked him. Maybe they didn't. But it was apparent that Brackett knew more than they did about whatever they were doing—and his subordinates had a

grudging respect for him. It was clear that Brackett
was an aggressive city person, more likely an East
Coast city person, a fighter about to go into the ring,
a terrier about to chase an especially hated cat.

Max Brackett glared through the doors of Foothill
Federal, saw something, and yelled at his guy to take
up his assigned position. A moment later, a distracted
middle-aged man named Ralph Burns stepped outside
and then jumped with fright as Brackett and his crew-
man descended upon him. Max Brackett and his man
were not robbing the bank, but it looked as if they
were mugging the bank president.

Max Brackett and his man were not thieves. As
they surrounded Ralph Burns, the startled man was
momentarily relieved to see they were not carrying
weapons but a video camera and sound boom. But
when Max violated the banker's personal space, going
nose to nose with him and shouting the question,
"Any comment on the possibility of your indict-
ment?"—Burns felt certain that a mugging would have
been preferable.

The bank that had been built to make its depositors
feel safe from criminals sneaking in from the outside
had been violated from within. Brackett figured there
was no architect alive who could design a bank to be
safe from the people who ran it. He laughed quietly
and allowed himself a self-indulgent moment in which
he saw himself performing a civic duty—catching the
bad guys who otherwise would have escaped
undetected.

But Burns had no relevant comment for Brackett
other than to beg off. "Please, I have to go to the
hospital. My wife is very ill." Burns wanted to get to
his car, but Brackett and his man had him trapped.

From years in the news business, Brackett knew the

value of working with large crewmen. Sheer bulk could be as valuable as journalistic brilliance. Burns was not going anywhere until Brackett got the shot he wanted. Assuming a look of restrained moral outrage, Brackett intimidated the cowering banker and got the tape he needed. "A lot of people are going to be ill when they find out their savings are gone. What about them, sir?"

There was no answer to this question, and Brackett knew it. Instead, he got precisely the reaction he wanted as he stepped out of Burns's way and let the man convict himself in front of the television audience. In a gesture universally recognized as an admission of guilt, Ralph Burns hid his face with his hands and slipped past the camera through the space that Brackett had given him. If Brackett had been a movie director, he could not have choreographed the action more expertly.

Brackett gestured for the cameraman to tape Burns as he fled in his car and then stepped into frame to wrap up his report. "Mr. Burns may have had no comment for KXBD, but he may be compelled to find his voice for the district attorney." Brackett's eyes blazed with self-righteous triumph. He stared directly through the camera lens and into the eyes of the audience that would soon be watching this report. When he had enough tail trim, Brackett called "cut," and his expression of moral rectitude slipped into a self-satisfied grin of accomplishment. He had nailed the son of a bitch, and now he had to get the story on air. Brackett knew he still had a battle to fight.

Chapter Two

KXBD was the Madeline affiliate of the Continental Broadcasting Network, better known as CBN. While KXBD was extremely proud of its relationship, and CBN logos filled the bottom right-hand corner of many of its local broadcasts, chances are the legendary network barely knew of the affiliate's existence. CBN had been around since the beginning of broadcasting. In the early days the network "created" radio along with competitors NBC and CBS. In the forties families tuned in to CBN for news of their fathers and brothers as they fought the great battles of the Second World War. During the fifties CBN introduced the country to television. In the sixties more people watched Neil Armstrong walk on the moon on CBN than the other networks combined because their legendary anchor, Earle Waters, was the "best newsman in America." And in the nineties people watched the prime-time Gulf War unfold as it was described to them by CBN's current star anchor, Kevin Hollander—a self-acknowledged legend in the making.

A tiny affiliate in a nowhere town did not mean much to a hallowed organization like CBN other than to show advertisers how vast its empire was. KXBD was a station where occasional novices might cut their teeth as they began the long climb toward working for the network. Sometimes a rare has-been might show up to finish off his career. Most of the people at the station were easygoing and if they never enjoyed the glory of the big story, they also never suffered the despair of the fall. They went to work every day, put out a respectable product, then went home to their families. As Brackett drove into the KXBD parking lot, he winced at the futility of working for a station in a community where people actually took pride in how little went on.

Later, after a rushed edit, Brackett showed his piece to news director Lou Potts. Brackett was proud of his work and assumed that the mild-mannered Potts would recognize the effort for what it was—top-notch, hard-hitting investigative reporting. Balding, chubby Lou Potts was interrupted by a phone call and asked Brackett to replay the closing seconds. Brackett grinned as he watched his cut of the report. It was a good piece of work.

Lou Potts had put in his time at KXBD, having worked at the station for the twenty years it had been on the air. Prior to that he worked at another CBN affiliate in Sacramento, the state capital. For years Potts hoped that he would be recruited for major market cities like San Francisco or Los Angeles. He had even entertained the idea of moving to New York or hooking on with a foreign bureau. But the call never came, and he had never bothered to take the initiative himself. For all of his younger fantasies, Potts was a small-town guy and had settled happily into his routine. Now, he was sitting here in an editing bay with a guy from another part of the country with a completely different way of doing business—and attacking someone Potts had known for years.

"We're not using that," he said. "It's conjecture. Circumstantial."

This didn't make Brackett happy. What the hell did Potts think news was? Brackett had an exciting story in a community where nothing ever happened. How could Potts say no? What did he need to run a story? Brackett wanted to tell this rube what he thought of him, but knew that would accomplish nothing. Instead, he took a deep breath and tried to explain how wonderful the bank scandal story was. "But I've got an exclusive. We can take this guy down. Break it wide open. Let him answer the questions."

Potts wanted nothing to do with it. He had known Ralph Burns since he had moved to Madeline. Burns had given him the mortgage on his house and helped him finance his daughter's college fund. Brackett, on the other hand, knew nothing about Burns and simply wanted to shed a little blood to make himself look good. Worst of all, Potts knew that Burns's wife *was* in the hospital, as he said, and the long-range outlook was not good. Burns had serious problems, and Potts was not the kind of newsman to kick someone who was down. "I know this man. His wife has cancer." Potts knew that the video of Burns running to his car was incriminating, but he was not about to convict a man without due process. "We say he had no comment, and we finish our piece. We don't ambush him in front of his place of work."

Brackett could not believe what he was hearing. The first time he might have heard wrong, but the second confirmed his worst fear. The stakeout was a classic form of journalism. The stakeout had brought down presidential aspirants and others deserving exposure for wrongdoing. It was the meat and potatoes of their business. Eliminating the stakeout from television news would be like building a car without an engine.

Brackett tried, but could not contain his disgust. "Oh, if the guy's a swindler *and* he's pathetic, we leave him alone. Excuse me, I thought this was a newsroom; I didn't realize we were in the business of handing out pardons."

Wrong strategy. Potts didn't appreciate being the butt of Brackett's sarcasm, and his decision was now irrevocable. "Recut it. Without the ambush."

Potts walked out of the room, having put Brackett in his place. Maybe Brackett had once been something special, but now he was just another reporter who worked for him. He would do what he was told, and he would conform to the way things were done around here. At KXBD reporters adhered to what Potts understood as the fundamental law of journalism. His reporters told the story as it happened. They did not influence it in any way.

Brackett understood the nature of hierarchies, but never liked them much. More often than not they rewarded people like Potts for simply persevering instead of excelling. Brackett tried halfheartedly to keep his cool, lost the battle, and then pursued the news director out of the station's editing suite. Brackett knew that he had been doing great work for KXBD, and that gave him license to push things further.

Brackett followed Potts into the station's newsroom. Unlike the exciting network sets that look like NASA Mission Control, the KXBD newsroom was a modest affair. On-line computer services had replaced teletypes, but the old units still had not been moved out. Half a dozen reporters and producers worked on ancient IBMs, their attitudes relaxed. Nothing new was going to happen today, and the staff knew they would be home to watch the six-thirty broadcast from New York in their own living rooms. If the newsroom buzz of legend was the excited voices of people working under pressure on life-and-death stories, then the sound at KXBD was more of a polite murmur.

Brackett had done too much for the station to be treated like someone who didn't know what he was doing.

"Why do you keep trying to rein me in?" he asked. "I took you from three share to a nine, single-handedly."

"Shares" were a percentage of the all-important Nielsen ratings. Stations set their advertising rates based upon what percentage of the television-watching public was tuned in to a particular show. In more sophisticated markets local news was a big moneymaker. This was not the case in Madeline. But jumping from a three share to a nine was still a major accomplishment. It represented a threefold increase in revenue, and even if Potts didn't seem especially concerned about advertising dollars, Brackett knew that the station manager would be.

Potts knew he could not argue with the facts—more people were watching their broadcast now than ever before. But it was not the kind of thing you lorded over your superior in front of a crowd. Sure, Brackett helped, but Potts believed in a team sensibility, and could not stand a prima donna. Potts was pissed off, and Brackett's arrogance gave him the ammunition he needed. He turned to the news staff, all of whom were pretending not to have heard a thing, and said, "Excuse me, whose week was it to kiss Brackett's ass for saving the station?"

Brackett was no more popular in the newsroom than he was with Potts. Most of the KXBD reporters and producers resented Brackett's habit of showing them up. They resented his condescending attitude. They knew he looked down on them and thought they were just a step above amateur. Maybe he had worked at the network once—but he had fallen—and there was nothing less appealing than someone down on his luck still arrogant from past glories. The staff laughed, and one longtime producer puckered up her lips in the direction of Brackett's posterior.

Bob Martinez enjoyed a good laugh at Brackett's expense. Martinez had grown up in California's Central Valley. His family had been poor, his parents immigrant sharecroppers from Mexico. They never learned to read or write and were especially proud of their son who had been the first in the family to go to college and now made a good living as a journalist for KXBD. Martinez had endured a tough youth and found himself tempted to take Brackett down a rung or two. But that was not his style, so he grabbed an assignment folder and headed for the door. Better to just get out of the guy's presence and stay out of trouble. Martinez had a report to do and figured this would be a good time to get to work.

Potts had other ideas, however, and grabbed the file from Martinez's hands. "Bob, you going out to the museum?"

In the ten years Martinez had known Potts, he had never seen him so mad.

Martinez just nodded and wondered what Potts was about to do.

Potts turned to Brackett and handed him the file. "Mr. Brackett will be taking that assignment."

Brackett opened the file. It did not look like much of a story.

Potts gave him the background with a dose of

friendly irony. "The state laid off some people out there—it's a great story. I think you'll relate to it."

Martinez went back to his desk and watched the fireworks along with the rest of the staff. Brackett was furious. "I'm not done with my edit," he said.

But Potts was not in the mood to argue. He went on with what he was doing as though Brackett had never opened his mouth. "It's covered, Max." As far as Potts was concerned, the battle was over. Crossing the cramped newsroom, he called out to a young woman who was examining a video camera, "Laurie, roll some tape while you're out there; maybe we'll run it tonight."

Laurie Callahan was new to the news staff, straight out of UCLA. Beautiful and fresh-faced, her cheerful enthusiasm had quickly won over the veteran staff. Laurie was a hard worker, polite, and a team player. Potts had known her since she was a child. And even if she got the job thanks to a bit of nepotism, Laurie had surpassed everyone's expectations. She was a good kid, the sort of young woman any parent would have been proud of.

Laurie waved at Brackett. She was delighted to be assigned to work with him. Brackett ignored her and followed Potts into his office, shutting the door behind him. Potts's office was not lavish. Framed photographs illustrated the news director's decidedly local career. Pictures of Potts with Caesar Chavez, Governor Pete Wilson, and an older photo showing him lost in a crowd of reporters surrounding then candidate Reagan. Most prominent were framed pictures of his wife and three children. Brackett had been in this office dozens of times and had never commented on Potts's family—as most of his staff regularly did. Potts was sure that Brackett had never even noticed.

It was still morning, and Brackett was already giving Potts a serious headache. He didn't want an argument. He didn't want a lesson about the nature of journalism. He wanted Brackett out of his face, out of his office, out of the station, and on assignment at the natural history museum. But here he was, ten o'clock in the morning, and building toward the second fight of the day with Brackett.

"Lou, you know I'm right," Brackett said.

The news director did not want to hear it. "Not here. Not on my shift, Brackett. There's a line I will not cross."

Brackett tried to retract his fangs a bit and be more reasonable. He needed to explain that television news had changed since the seventies. "You don't cross the line, Potts, you move it. It's our job to tell people the truth." Brackett's tone had softened, almost begging Potts to understand. The ambush of the banker had to stay in.

But Potts would not buy it. Lines in journalism did not move. Right and wrong had definite boundaries. "We cover people. We affect their lives . . . you . . . I think you're hotdogging."

Brackett looked as though he had been punched. Potts watched as Brackett winced and took a step backward. Lou Potts was amazed. Though he might be a hardened newshound, Brackett was still sensitive to an accusation of not being professional. Tell him he was a son of a bitch, insult how he looked, how he dressed, even challenge his mother's lineage—none of it seemed to matter to Brackett. But say to his face that he was something less than a serious reporter and you took the wind out of his sails. Brackett was still in a fighting mood, but it was now a defensive battle.

"Got me all figured out, huh, Lou? I'm just some

slick East Coast character. No ethics. No standards, just show biz!"

Brackett saw Potts's look of surprise. The news director bought the performance hook, line, and sinker.

The truth was Brackett did not give a shit what people thought of him. But he also knew the value of acting as though his feelings could be hurt. He had stolen the moral highground from underneath his sanctimonious news director. Brackett had no choice but to take the assignment. Nevertheless he knew Potts would feel bad about insulting him, giving him useful ammunition for another battle that was sure to come.

Just as Brackett expected, Lou Potts felt guilty about taking a low shot at one of his employees. He tried to backtrack and make things right. "Max, I'm not saying that."

Brackett looked like a man whose great disgrace had been uncovered. He was the repentant sinner maintaining his dignity before the preacher who was trying to save his soul.

"Sure you are. And who knows, Lou, maybe you're right." Brackett knew that Potts would appreciate a sense of wounded stoicism. He gave the news director a steely look and turned to leave. "I got a museum to cover."

He was out the door and down the hall before Potts could properly apologize to him. The news director felt like a jerk and promised himself that he would make things right with Brackett one day.

Chapter Three

The van made its way through downtown Madeline, and Brackett felt disdain for the place. How on earth had he ended up here? How could people live in a place like this? Didn't they know there was a real world out there? Brackett had lived in various places during his network career: New York, Saigon, Beirut, and London. He laughed to himself when he added Madeline to the list. After the thrill and excitement of world cultural capitals, Madeline was no more than a mall without a roof. Homogenized. Well planned. Sanitized. Climate controlled. No crowds on the sidewalks, and everybody, well, so nice. It made Brackett slightly nauseated and anxious.

But several years back, KXBD had been the only station to offer him a job, so he had no choice but to move there. If Brackett was ever to reach the network again, his journey would begin here in this small town where nothing ever happened. It did not seem a likely prospect. Brackett could finish out his career covering nonevents at local museums, civic groundbreaking ceremonies, seasonal features, and the occasional crime of passion. Brackett swore to himself at the possibility of serving a life sentence in Madeline.

As Laurie Callahan drove the news van, Brackett flipped through the file on the natural history museum and then tossed it away. Were they kidding? Is this really what Lou Potts considered a story? Some guy losing his job because of budget cuts? No, it's worse than that, Brackett realized; even Lou did not think this was a story. The assignment was pure filler. If for some reason they had trouble filling out the thirty-minute broadcast, they would slip this piece in. Otherwise, it would never see the light of day. Brackett knew too well that the natural history museum was not a story or an assignment. It was punishment and humiliation.

Brackett stared out the window and watched as wholesome-looking people went about their lives. While he wallowed in his misery, Laurie interrupted. "I hear they make things up just so the newspapers will be heavy enough not to blow away. You know. The news in Madeline."

Brackett halfheartedly replied that she was funny, and went back to staring out the window.

Laurie seemed like a nice enough kid, but her perkiness made Brackett uneasy. He noticed that on the sidewalk several young mothers and their kids sat at a table outside an ice cream shop. A healthy, prim high school student brought them a tray full of ice-cream sundaes. If Brackett's life had been a television program, he would be flipping channels right now.

But at least the girl driving the van realized that they were operating in the boondocks. The previous week Brackett worked with a another kid just out of college. They had covered the fiftieth anniversary of the Good Neighbor Restaurant and interviewed the ninety-year-old couple who ran the place, Lars and Sonja Dahlberg. The college kid treated the piece as though it was an election night exclusive with President Clinton. Afterward, Brackett took him down a few rungs—and the kid had taken to slinking away from him whenever they passed in the station corridors. At least this new girl was smart enough to know that what they were doing was not much.

Laurie glanced at Brackett and could not ignore his complete disgust with the situation. She understood, at least she thought she did. It was not difficult for her to sympathize, even though she was at an opposite place in her career from the veteran reporter. Laurie was in her early twenties and looked younger. Her beauty reflected her Madeline upbringing—upbeat, good-natured, and guileless. Laurie's four years at UCLA did not seem to tarnish her with big-city attitudes, and she had chosen to return home to start her career. Laurie's father was Lou Potts's dentist, and she had interned summers at KXBD, knowing there was a job for her when she wanted it.

Brackett glanced at Laurie with disbelief as she slowed at a crosswalk and smiled to an elderly couple who were moving across slowly. At that moment he knew she was singularly unsuited for journalism, and he thought she resembled nothing more than a cheerleader playing dress-up.

Laurie noticed Brackett observing her and wanted to make a good impression. They had not worked together before, and his history as a former network reporter was exciting, if intimidating. Laurie wanted Brackett to know that if some of the other young people at KXBD did not remember him, she certainly did. Laurie understood that a man like Brackett could teach her a lot. Wanting to acknowledge his experience, she said, "I guess layoffs are not news to someone like you."

Gritting his teeth, Brackett watched a cop stop to chat with a group of high school kids who were clearly happy to talk. This place was too much. He turned back to Laurie. "Happens every day like the sun coming up. I'm supposed to roll tape on that, too?"

Laurie was surprised to find the veteran reporter responsive, if sardonic. Still, she did not agree with him and did not bother to censor her opinion. "I guess it's news if you're the one getting laid off."

Brackett appreciated her chutzpah. Most kids just out of school would have listened to his cynical declaration and become flustered. She could hold her own in a conversation with an adult, even if she was an idealist. Brackett thought Laurie did not quite understand the situation and decided to explain things. "Sure. It's news. But nobody cares unless we make them care."

That was the power of the job. There were a million stories going on every day across the country, but only twenty-two minutes of news per broadcast a night. A person's story was only news if a journalist decided to make it news.

Brackett gauged Laurie's reaction, thought she understood, and went on. "Why do you want to become a journalist?"

She fired her answer back at Brackett without hesitation. "Because I love it."

Brackett straightened in his seat. It had been a long time since he had met someone like her. For most of his adult life Brackett moved in a realm where people never said what they really meant. He was used to having to translate a person's words. Brackett didn't even believe that people like Laurie—innocents—still walked the earth. Maybe something about the valley where Madeline was located protected the town from the corruption of the outside world.

Brackett felt like a scientist coming across a species

long thought to be extinct. Suddenly, this attractive, if slightly too decent, young woman interested him. He wanted to know more.

"Aiming for the network?" he asked.

Laurie laughed out loud. San Francisco had been as far as her daydreaming had gone. Or at least that was as much as she would openly admit. Laurie was pleased, however, that Brackett had not just tossed out another cynical observation. He had asked how she felt. This was a crack in his heavily shielded personal armor.

"I'm not that ambitious," she replied.

Laurie should have stopped there, but she was used to talking without editing her thoughts, so she just went on, perhaps a bit too far. "How about you? Did you ever want to be an anchor?"

Brackett reacted as though someone had stabbed him with something sharp. "An anchor! Some pretty boy who sits there like a schlub, reading stories people like us have chased down!"

But there had been a time when Brackett wanted to be an anchor. Of course that had been during the prime of his career when anchors were still the best, most experienced of the reporters: Walter Cronkite, Huntley and Brinkley, John Chancellor. And while the big four were still top newspeople, the ranks of anchors beneath them had become prettified. Whether it was the diminishment of the requirements for the job or the realization that he would never be given the opportunity to sit at an anchor desk—Brackett's opinion of the job had sunk very low. But Brackett's memory was stirred by the fresh-faced, admiring young woman, and he had to turn away from her, unwilling to admit his own failure.

As they drove the clean streets of Madeline, Brack-

ett thought back to other roads he had covered. He
remembered the panicked streets of Saigon during the
Communist takeover in '75—when he had been a cub
reporter making a name for himself. Brackett thought
back to the chaos and danger of Kabul as rebels battled the Soviets after the invasion of Afghanistan in
'79. He savored memories of the genial campaign trail
during the re-election effort of Ronald Reagan in '84.
He remembered the bombed-out streets of Baghdad
during the Gulf War. And now he was stuck in Madeline, where people did not dare to jaywalk and what
was worse—they did not even want to. A wave of
melancholy overwhelmed him, and he turned back to
a respectfully silent Laurie. Brackett offered her the
wisdom of a grizzled veteran who had lost his place
and taken a terrible fall. "Someday you'll find out
what it is to own a story so powerful that millions of
people will not just be affected, but shaken. Thanks
to you."

Laurie was delighted that she was having this conversation with *the* Max Brackett. She hoped that over
the next months Brackett would be willing to be a
mentor to her. Laurie was willing to work hard and
study at the foot of this faded master. Laurie believed
in herself in a quietly unaggressive way and knew that
if Brackett shared his experience, she could begin the
long journey that led to being a successful, responsible
journalist. Her eyes were open wide, and she wanted
to know exactly what it was like to have reported the
kind of story that Brackett was talking about.

Brackett knew the young woman was hooked. She
was an ingenious kid from the cornfields. The worship
in her eyes and voice was a comfort to his inflated
ego. Lovely Laurie Callahan would be easy to impress,
and she might provide him with just the sort of distrac-

tion he needed while being stuck in this remote outpost of CBN's broadcasting empire.

Brackett got a little carried away as he described what it was like to have an important exclusive. "It's like I'm holding a rock in my hand, and I'm standing in front of the biggest picture window ever. And then I let it go. And at that precise moment, I am at ground zero as history changes course. And I am there alone, because I found the story."

Brackett watched as Laurie nodded with reverential understanding. Then, as they drove past a Dairy Queen and a Chuck E Cheese, Brackett realized that he had laid it a little too thick. This was not Beirut during the civil war nor even Los Angeles during the riots. In contrast to his current assignment, the picture window analogy seemed ludicrous. It made him look pathetic—holding on to a part of his life that had been lost. Brackett figured he better stop trying so hard. "Of course it's nothing compared to covering the financial woes of a suburban minimuseum."

Chapter Four

The Madeline Museum of Natural History had been built in the twenties, a time when Madeline had been a prosperous farming town and its citizens wanted to create an aura of dignity for their rural community. The building had a Victorian sensibility and was solidly constructed with the best Vermont granite, boasting a two-story display hall, stained glass, and turrets that served no purpose other than to satisfy the peculiar architectural tastes of the local benefactors. It was a public building similar to many others of its era—designed to create a sense of past and permanence in a newly settled land.

Once a point of civic pride, the natural history museum was now mostly a relic of the past, much like the fossilized exhibits inside. The parking lot was empty, and the only indication that the museum was open was a large yellow school bus from Foothill Elementary school parked outside.

Laurie got out of the news van and began to assemble the video camera package. After hooking on the battery belt, she put on a headset with earphones and a microphone. Then she performed a quick sound check. After making sure the camera lens was clean, Laurie performed a few more preparatory rituals and was ready as Brackett stepped out of the van, carrying a clipboard with notes.

Laurie was surprised that Brackett seemed so relaxed. Most KXBD reporters made more of a show of readying themselves for a serious journalistic endeavor. Brackett simply sauntered toward the museum as if he were going out to grab a cup of coffee. Laurie followed, and Brackett gave her the lowdown on how he expected the shoot to go. "We'll get the curator. She'll yammer on about how the museum will somehow carry on despite the budget cuts, blah, blah, blah."

Laurie was a little put out by the veteran reporter's derision. When she had first seen her name on the assignment board, Laurie readied herself for an in-depth human interest story, something that would fill people's eyes with tears and make them reflect upon their own place in society. She had been taught that there were no small stories, only small reporters. Laurie believed that the health of a cultural institution reflected the well-being of society itself. While she was well aware that their assignment was not an interview with the president of the United States, she felt it had value.

But here was Max Brackett treating the story with barely veiled contempt. She listened silently to Brackett's harangue. "We'll get a couple of locals, saying how they can't picture this city without its museum, blah, blah, blah. You grab some shots of the mummies they've got in here, the dead ones, then I'll buy you lunch."

As Laurie thought about Brackett's dismissive attitude, she was struck by a novel thought. For the first time, she looked at her career in a new way. A solid opportunity suddenly seemed pretty low rent. Laurie

Callahan understood that working for Max Brackett was going to be an illuminating experience, and she had better pay close attention.

At the steps leading into the museum, Brackett and Laurie were greeted by a friendly young security guard who was scrubbing graffiti off the side of the building. Cliff Williams was a large African American with a full mustache and a shaved head. Brackett said hello, catching Cliff by surprise, and continued talking before the guard even had a chance to turn around. "We're looking for the curator."

Cliff turned to Brackett and Laurie with a smile that grew into recognition. "Hey, you're that TV guy."

Brackett was used to being recognized in Madeline. It was amazing that even a small market job like KXBD reached enough people to confer a modest version of celebrity. Such was the power of television. Brackett was quick with a smile—you never knew, this guard might be good for an interview. "That's me, 'that TV guy.' Are you the 'museum guy'?"

Cliff had worked at the museum for years, but was not sure that he could be given such a lofty title. He laughed, pleased that a famous reporter could be such a regular guy, and explained, "I'm the guard. There used to be two of us, but the other guy got laid off."

Brackett assumed a look that said he understood the problem and sympathized. He nodded, saying, "We heard you're having some financial problems."

Cliff agreed. "Yeah, you never know who's next."

Brackett liked Cliff's response and said, "Hey, stick around. I'd like to hear you say that on camera."

That sounded good to Cliff. His wife and his daughter would love to see him on the news. He said, "Really? All right. You'll find Mrs. Banks right inside." They all shared smiles as Cliff checked his neatly pressed blue uniform to make sure it was clean enough for his interview and Brackett and Laurie headed inside.

Entering through the lobby, Brackett and Laurie found themselves in a modest but well-maintained building. Marble floors with inlay work shone immaculately, and Roman columns rose to support the roof. Large floor-to-ceiling windows kept the foyer bright and cheerful, while the exhibit rooms were lit with the dim illumination that highlighted display windows. Intricate metal work rose in a flourish over doors, and perfectly polished brass banisters followed a stairwell to the second floor. Well-dusted globular lamps hung from the ceiling and gave the structure a somber atmosphere.

But Brackett was most impressed by two towering dinosaurs that guarded the lobby. A nasty-looking skeleton of a tyrannosaurus rex eyed a wary, fully fleshed, plump brontosaurus. Brackett thought this was the best possible lesson for visiting schoolchildren to learn. Even in the slightly fossilized, musty atmosphere of a museum, the law of the jungle existed. He had rarely seen survival of the fittest so effectively portrayed. The little brats should take a long look at the display and think about it when they went home.

Then Brackett noticed something else that inspired his admiration. Above the dinosaurs, looking down upon the competition between the eaten and the eater, flew a long-winged pterodactyl. Brackett admired the prehistoric bird's distance from the fray. It saw the life-and-death struggle, but was not affected by it. The ancient bird could fly away unharmed or wait to feast on the scraps the killer left behind. Brackett felt a dim affinity for the ancient creature.

Overall Brackett was surprised. It might not be the

Museum of Natural History in Manhattan, but this was pretty good for Nowheresville, California. He gave the building a perfunctory look around. To the right was a room dedicated to Indian artifacts, and a diorama illustrated the lifestyle of the local Miwok Indian tribe. To the left of the entrance foyer a room displayed discoveries made during the twentieth century, including major scientific breakthroughs, natural phenomena, and the requisite mineral display cases.

Brackett quickly came upon the museum curator. Mrs. Jill Banks was a trim, beautiful woman in her late forties who wore her hair blond and her suits well tailored. A constant, hovering presence in the museum, she descended upon Brackett and Laurie almost immediately after they had entered her building. Television news crews were not the normal visitors to her museum, and she wanted to know what their intentions were.

As Brackett explained their story, he thought Mrs. Banks was more attractive and tailored than a suburban curator ought to be. Her clothes and immaculate grooming were not paid for by the salary from a small nonprofit institution. After a few minutes of conversation, he learned that Mrs. Banks was a tightly wound mechanism from one of Madeline's leading families. Her proprietary attitude toward the museum came from her great-grandfather, the institution's founder. Mrs. Banks's intentions were good, but her attitude crossed the border into the priggish realm of the schoolmarm.

Despite Mrs. Banks's general disapproval of television, she quickly realized that an interview about the museum's precarious financial condition could be good for the institution. If being on the news could help at all, she would pull herself together and go on the air.

And when Brackett told Mrs. Banks that she was especially photogenic and would make an appealing spokeswoman, Mrs. Banks felt convinced that this would be the right thing to do.

Laurie set up the camera in front of the Miwok Indian diorama while Mrs. Banks ran to the ladies' room to check her hair and makeup. While they were waiting, Brackett encouraged the visiting schoolchildren to mill around in the background during the interview. Their harassed young teacher, Kelly Rose, tried to focus their attention on the various displays that were pertinent to their studies, but could not compete with the lure of television.

As Mrs. Banks returned and the interview began, she never noticed how the business of television overwhelmed the thoughtfully planned, dramatically produced world of dinosaurs and other natural history. Brackett watched the kids as Mrs. Banks spoke, and was once again impressed by the power of his medium. The curator's talk was mundane. The interview was as dull as any he had ever conducted. Yet the kids could not take their eyes off the camera, the interviewer, and the interviewee.

Something stronger was at work here.

Mrs. Banks droned on. "The Miwok Indians have a rich history in this area, and we currently have on display one of the largest collections of Indian pottery ever assembled by a museum of this size."

Brackett stifled a yawn and tried to enliven the conversation a bit. "There are those who say that it's not financially responsible to pour money into a dying institution."

Mrs. Banks was not one to suffer fools lightly. "There are those who say if we do not learn from the past, we will be doomed to relive it."

It was not the most original idea in the world, but Brackett had to grudgingly admit that Mrs. Banks had just given him a good sound bite.

With fifteen minutes to go before the noon news, Lou Potts rushed his anchorman onto the set and wanted to tape a wrap-up with Max Brackett at the museum before the show began. The piece was not going to air today, but the sooner it was on the shelf, the better.

Laurie set up the satellite dish, and Brackett's interview was simultaneously taped by her camera and beamed back to the studio, where it would be recorded for a later broadcast. From the KXBD studios, anchorman Mort Dohlen, fifty years old and fighting a losing battle to shed a few pounds and to keep his hair, spoke to Brackett on the chroma key screen behind his desk, a large blank, blue screen in the studio. On TV the blue screen would be replaced by an oversized version of Brackett's face, and it would look like the two men were having a conversation. When the piece was eventually shown, it would cut from Brackett's interview with Mrs. Banks to a concluding comment from Dohlen.

The anchorman's repartee was hardly inspired, but it was good enough to pass for wit on the local news. "Max, I see some dinosaurs there. I guess the fear today is that the museum may share the same fate as those mighty beasts."

Brackett indulged Dohlen's tortured chitchat without a trace of glibness. He responded with a brisk "That's right, Mort," and knew that he had given the station what it wanted. As Dohlen thanked him, Brackett held a tight smile until the bright light on Laurie's camera blinked off. Immediately, Brackett switched off the microphone in his hand and was about to turn off the backup pinned to his shirt when he was distracted by Mrs. Banks's anxious smile. To reassure her, Brackett voiced a standard compliment on her television technique. "You're good. You must have done this before."

Mrs. Banks was pleased that she had done well, but had never been on the air previously. "Heavens, no," she said. "It's just that I feel so strong about this museum. My great-grandfather founded it, you know."

Brackett was ready to move on, and was not particularly interested in Mrs. Banks's family history, although she appeared to be more than willing to talk with him further. He had what he had come for, and it was time to go. Brackett wished Mrs. Banks luck and thanked her for her time.

Mrs. Banks knew she had been dismissed. Nonplussed, she spun around, spotted a kid who was smearing greasy hands over a display on "Grains of the World," and shot him a glare that stopped him cold. She tried to get the children's attention. Now that the excitement was over, it was time for her to finish their tour.

Brackett waited a moment while Laurie checked the tape to make sure there were no problems. A nine-year-old schoolboy called Mrs. Banks's attention to a mistake the museum made in its presentation of small dinosaur models. "Hey, that's a allosaurus chasing a chasmosaurus! . . ."

Mrs. Banks did not like being shown up by children, even if they were right. She had a tour to finish, and she wanted these kids to move on to the next exhibit. "Children, in the next room you will find a stuffed dodo."

The boy was certain he was right and astonished

that no one was paying attention to him. "I mean, one's Cretaceous, the other's Jurassic! How come they're together?"

Brackett watched as the curator disregarded the boy and moved the other kids along. Brackett felt an instant affinity for a kid who was telling the truth—but who was ignored by the establishment.

Again, the educational insights the financially troubled museum offered its young visitors stirred Brackett: "Survival of the fittest" and "Truth is not necessarily going to win you any friends." Both lessons before noon. Maybe this backwater museum did have something to teach the children of Madeline after all.

Brackett watched the pint-sized whistle-blower sulk behind the rest of the class as they moved into the next room. Then he listened as Mrs. Banks's reedy voice echoed through the building. He shared a look with Laurie and said, "She sounds like something out of *Masterpiece Theater*. Go outside and get ready for my stand-ups. I've gotta take a press leak."

Laurie offered him a game smile to show she was not offended by his stupid joke. Brackett was annoyed by her cheerfully indomitable spirit and stalked off toward the men's room.

Meanwhile, Laurie secured her equipment, crossed underneath the hungry tyrannosaurus rex, and made her way to the museum entrance. Awkward with her video pack, Laurie tried to dodge a tall, nervous-looking man carrying a large canvas bag as they each tried to cross the threshold simultaneously. Her evasive maneuver did not work. It did, however, lessen the blow as the two collided.

The tall man spoke softly and asked Laurie to excuse him. Laurie stepped to the right just as he stepped to his left—and once again they blocked each other's path. Laurie joked, "Care to dance?"

But the tall man was only serious as he politely refused her offer. "No, thank you." Then he stepped around her and walked into the museum.

Laurie was not impressed by his sense of humor and watched him as he proceeded inside.

Something odd and contradictory about the tall man, though a nervous smile suggested a nice enough guy, hinted at something darker. Laurie stood in the doorway and watched as Mrs. Banks noticed the tall man walking toward her. The uptight curator looked more anxious than ever as she stepped away from the children and confronted the newcomer, wary but determined. Laurie did not give the situation any more thought and walked out of the building. She had work to do, the setup for Brackett's introduction to the story.

Brackett stood at the urinal in a chilly bathroom decorated with spotless white ceramic tile. He ran through his stand-up piece in his head, coughed once, and heard a good echo. Knowing he was alone, Brackett tried his opening out loud. "I am standing here in front of Madeline's museum of natural history, where this celebration of the past has collided with the hardships of the present." Brackett looked at himself in the mirror and could not believe that he really was here doing this inconsequential piece. What the hell had happened to him? Could this really be *his* life? At long last, this had to be the end of the line, didn't it? The toilet of an obsolete museum in an anonymous suburban sprawl, doing a community interest story. Another, less traditional opening came to mind, and Brackett gave it a shot to see how it sounded. "I am standing here in front of Madeline's museum of natural history, blowing smoke rings out my butt. Why, you might ask? Because I'm good at it." As he pissed, Brackett looked down at his open fly and began an impromptu interview. "You, sir. You look like a fine young man. What's your comment on this situation?"

In the news van, Laurie strapped on a new battery belt and put her headset back on. As she did, Laurie could hear Brackett's "exclusive interview" from the museum bathroom.

"I'm pissing away my life? Well put. This is Max Brackett, reporting live with his fly open."

Clearly, Brackett had forgotten to turn off his body mike, and Laurie was embarrassed to listen in. She switched off the audio feed and went back to work.

Chapter Five

The tall man carrying the large canvas bag who passed Laurie in the museum doorway was Sam Baily, late thirties, good-looking with thick brown hair, long Elvis-like sideburns, and an infectious smile. He wore a neat blue uniform with a tie, and the patch on his blazer identified him as an employee of the natural history museum.

Actually, Sam was a former employee of the museum. His job had been eliminated in the budget cuts. In fact, it was his firing that brought Brackett over to do his report. Sam's face was a study in contrast, combining elements of strength that bordered on anger and gentleness that verged on regret. His blue eyes blinked quickly, and the hesitant way he carried himself suggested someone who was in familiar territory rather than a person about to enter a new, possibly unchartered, realm.

In contrast to Mrs. Banks, Sam Baily appeared to be a man of simple tastes and average intelligence—but no more. If Mrs. Banks's designer-suit attitude spoke of old money, authority, and graduate degrees, Sam was an off-the-rack guy who worked hard at low-level jobs and never seemed to get anywhere. At the same time, Sam never had any great ambitions and had always been satisfied with a steady, quiet life.

While Sam was a large man, his size was not inherently threatening. In fact, something about the way he moved gave him an aura of innocence. Maybe it was the candid grin or his slightly loping gait, but as he walked underneath the dinosaurs, he clearly resembled the doomed victim more than he did the predator. Still, what was most remarkable about Sam Baily's presence was that there was nothing remarkable about him at all. He was a regular Joe, a guy who lived a quiet life and tried to do the right thing.

But today was not a normal day for Sam Baily, and before the sun set in the evening news logos, remarkable, unpredictable events were to happen. Although he had walked the halls of the natural history museum countless times, today, right now, everything seemed different to him. Mrs. Banks, whom Sam had greeted thousands of morning before, now seemed like a stern cross-armed woman who intimidated him with her sophistication.

Sam's voice was pleading. "You have to listen to me—"

Mrs. Banks did not agree. "Sam, I don't have to do any such thing—you shouldn't be here. I told you before—there is nothing more that I can do."

Sam did not want to believe this was truly the last word on the matter. If she wanted to, Sam was sure that Mrs. Banks could find a way to take him back. Her refusal to even discuss the matter made him angry. But he shifted nervously on his feet, as though he was not entirely committed to his anger. Sam had thought the matter through over and over. He had discussed it with his wife and his friends. And he had come up with an idea. It wasn't perfect, but it was better than nothing. "Please, Mrs. Banks, please just listen. I'm willing to take less money."

Mrs. Banks was not normally a patient woman, and the stress of the situation just aggravated her short fuse. "Do you have a hearing problem? It's completely out of my hands."

Sam stepped back as though he had been slapped. He had known Mrs. Banks for years, and he had never been spoken to like this. Worse yet, he realized she was hardly in an accommodating mood. He could shrug off her rudeness if it had been over a minor matter. But this was his job. This was how he paid the rent and fed his kids. She couldn't be this dismissive about something as important as his job. Sam was speechless, but did not go anywhere.

Mrs. Banks had a museum full of wild children, and she did not need the extra nuisance of dealing with Sam Baily right now. She felt bad when she had to let him go—but that was the real world. If the savings from cutting his salary was the only way the museum was going to carry on, then the sacrifice had to be made. She liked Sam, as much as she liked any of the people who worked for her. But it infuriated the curator that he was interrupting her day, trying to reopen a dead issue. "You're wasting both of our times," she said. "Now you must leave. Right now."

Mrs. Banks had a great deal of experience dealing with recalcitrant children and knew that firmness was the key to success. In her mind, Sam had always been something of a child, and that worked both to his advantage and disadvantage. She had always liked his straightforward, uncomplicated ways. He knew his job and did not ask a lot of questions—he simply went about his business. Mrs. Banks knew that Sam was dedicated to his job, even in the unlikely event heroism had ever been called for. But the museum's most serious disaster had been a burst waterline in the women's bathroom. Sam had led an orderly evacuation of the building and then gone back in to mop up—hardly heroic action, but devoted work nonetheless.

Though dedicated to his job, Sam did not get carried away. He did not feel like a bigger man because he wore a uniform. It was hard to imagine that a guard in a sleepy museum could enjoy a power trip, but Mrs. Banks had seen it happen. Instead, Sam had a laid-back style and dealt with misbehaving schoolchildren better than anyone else in the museum. Sam never had to get mad because he had a natural affinity with children—and they felt the same.

If Mrs. Banks had thought through her actions more carefully, she might never have grabbed Sam's elbow. It's not just the present-day legal ramifications, but the way in which it triggered Sam's temper. As soon as Mrs. Banks made contact, something in him snapped. Nothing serious, but after a lifetime of being told what to do, he was tired of being pushed around. His reaction was not considered, but instinctive. Sam twisted Mrs. Banks's arm, shook off her grip, and pushed her away. Under different circumstances, Sam would never have reacted so angrily toward anyone—even someone he had reason to dislike. But today was not a normal day, and Sam yelled at the startled woman as he escaped her grasp, "Let go of me!"

In the men's room, Brackett was finishing his business and self-pity session. As he zipped up his fly, Brackett thought he heard a commotion in the main part of the museum. He grimaced, realizing that he was a down-on-his-luck newsman trying just a little too hard. He knew that nothing of note could have occurred. Maybe one of the schoolchildren had gotten sick and not reached a trash can. Maybe one of the students had sassed the pretty teacher. Maybe Brackett should go out there—set the kid straight—and look like a hero to the embattled young woman.

Brackett never remembered having a teacher quite so alluring as the one standing in the display hall. He envied the fourth-graders and wondered if his old war stories might be able to charm the young lady into some extracurricular activity. Laughing with disgust, he not only saw himself as a desperate journalist, but also a lonely, middle-aged man. Brackett flushed the urinal, and the sound drowned out the noise from outside. He was ready to go back to work. He could wrap up the piece in front of the museum in a few minutes. Then, maybe he could take Laurie Callahan out for lunch and get her drunk. It was just a little after noon, and the night beckoned.

Brackett washed his hands and started out the door when something made him stop dead in his tracks. In the main room of the museum, he saw a man unzip a large canvas bag and pull out a rifle. The weapon should have endowed the man with deadly machismo, but somehow he did not look comfortable. Mrs. Banks looked at the armed man with astonishment—not yet afraid, but uncertain whether or not this was a bad joke or a real threat.

And then things began to happen so quickly that Brackett could not decipher what he was seeing.

A wave of laughing, shouting schoolchildren raced past the armed man—entirely unaware of his presence. They charged toward the building's exit. Their voices were shrill, and the tension that had suddenly filled the room rose quickly to another level.

Sam was caught by surprise. He had been hoping—illogically—that the sight of the gun would force Mrs. Banks to listen to him while he pleaded his case to keep his job. It was not much of a strategy, but he was not much of thinker. As the kids swarmed past him, Sam panicked, uncertain about what he should do—but sure that something needed to be done. His first thought was that the kids could get him into further trouble before he solved things with Mrs. Banks. Then he thought that the schoolchildren might help him get his job back. Sam wheeled around, pointed his rifle at the kids, and shouted as loudly as he could, "Wait! Everybody stop!"

Mrs. Banks had so far been annoyed by Sam's interruption of her day and then irritated by the bad taste of his joke. But once he threatened the children, she gasped with shock. Sam's voice rang out like a shot through the building—echoing harshly against its stone walls. The children stopped where they were and recoiled with fear. Everyone stood still and stared at Sam—not knowing what was going to happen next.

Sam had no better idea than the rest of them. He had no plan. He was not even sure why he had the gun with him. Sam had not planned to use it, or even to show it—yet he had taken it because it made him feel more powerful. Sam looked back at the kids, surprised to see fear in their eyes. No one had ever looked at him like that before. He did not like the feeling, and it did not make him feel any stronger. Sam wanted to tell the kids to relax—he had no plans to hurt them—this was all some weird misunderstanding. Sam had come by to get his job back, not to cause trouble.

Still, since he was carrying the gun, he knew that he was expected to take control of the situation. He was agitated, but understood that the next move was his. "All right. Everybody over here," he said.

Sam waved his rifle at the kids and their teacher,

corralling them toward the hallway near the men's room. Kelly Rose, the teacher, tried in vain to hush her students. Some of the kids were on the verge of tears, while others thought they were part of a game, laughing and joking as they listened to the guy with the gun.

From inside the men's room, Brackett watched in disbelief. As the gunman herded the hostages toward him, Brackett closed the bathroom door until it was open just a crack. He kept one eye on the gunman— thrilled to be in the middle of this developing story.

Sam told the kids to stay where they were, then walked back toward Mrs. Banks. His manner was quieter now. He was holding a gun, but he was asking for an audience. "Gimme five minutes. That's all Mrs. Banks." It was not much to ask. It was too bad she had not agreed to talk to him before he had been forced to pull out the gun.

Mrs. Banks could be domineering, stuffy, a pain in the ass, but she was not easily intimidated. They were standing in Mrs. Banks's museum, and what happened there was her personal responsibility. Like Sam, she took her job seriously. "I sincerely hope you are not pointing that gun at me, Sam," she said.

Sam's fuse was short, his nerves increasingly frayed. Christ, even when he aimed a gun at her, Mrs. Banks acted as if she had the upper hand. Sam's fury rose again. "Be quiet!"

But Mrs. Banks would not be quiet. "If this is supposed to be a joke, Sam, I just lost my sense of humor. And you won't be smiling when the police arrive."

Sam couldn't believe Mrs. Banks wasn't fazed a bit. She kept right at him as though he were powerless.

Sam yelled back, hoping to drown out the sound of her voice. "Shut up! Just be quiet! Give me the keys!"

Mrs. Banks reluctantly gave Sam the keys, and he rushed over to the museum entrance and locked the doors.

Brackett knew that with his detour into the men's room he had just fallen into the best story to hit peaceful Madeline, California, in its monotonous history. A museum full of fourth-grade hostages. This was a network story if there ever was one. All he had to do was get it on air—somehow. From his vantage point, literally in a toilet, Brackett saw the breaking story as his ticket out of network exile. He had to be careful, however. The story would have to develop as it needed to. He quietly pulled the door shut and got ready to do what he did best.

Chapter Six

With the door closed, Brackett's heart raced as he inserted his earpiece and whispered into the microphone pinned to his shirt, "Laurie! Laurie!" But for some reason the mike was dead. After trying to call her again, Brackett looked around the men's room frantically—and was relieved to see a pay phone on the wall. Brackett searched through his pants pockets for loose change and found nothing. Without the price of a phone call, the story was unfolding and he could not reach the people he needed to talk to. If he didn't come up with a solution—and fast—he was going to miss his ride out of Madeline.

Outside the museum, no one had any idea what was going on within. Laurie stood next to the news van and videotaped the building in preparation for Brackett's opening and closing segments. He was taking longer than she expected, and Laurie hoped he had not become sick. Laurie turned off the camera as she heard her cellular phone ring inside the truck. Laurie lowered the equipment from her shoulder and went to answer it. Maybe it was Lou calling to give them an afternoon assignment. Laurie flipped open the cell phone and said hello in newspeak, "Van." An unfamiliar voice was at the other end, a telephone operator. "Will you accept a collect call from a Mr. Max Brackett?"

Laurie was puzzled. Brackett had some unusual work habits, but he was not known for his sense of humor. Was this a joke? Was someone from the newsroom pulling her leg? Why on earth would Brackett place a collect call to her from across the museum parking lot? Prank or not, Laurie thought it best to go along. You never knew. "Uh, sure, I'll accept it—Max?"

Brackett sighed with relief as Laurie accepted the call. As soon as the operator hung up, Brackett dove right into business. "Laurie, listen to me. There is a man with a gun in here."

Back in the van Laurie wanted to laugh. What was he up to? Was this some bizarre test or initiation ritual? Laurie was truly confused. "Where are you?" she asked.

Brackett tried to keep his voice to a whisper, but his adrenaline was pumping him into high gear. "I'm in the museum!"

Laurie looked out the van window—everything seemed perfectly normal. Her first thoughts were to get help. "I'll call the police."

Brackett knew a rookie's response when he heard it. Calling the police was not the first order of business, not at all. In times like this an experienced crew and producer were mandatory. But Brackett knew that he would have to make do with a youngster raised in the malls of Madeline. He corrected her brusquely. "You first call Lou. We have to go live. *Then* call the police." When Laurie started to protest, Brackett spelled it out for her. "We've got some news going on here, Laurie. Don't blow it."

Laurie found herself in the midst of a breaking

emergency, and for a moment she was flustered. After taking a deep breath, she realized that this was it. She did not yet know what was happening inside the museum, but it was clear from the tone of Brackett's voice that whatever it was—it had potential.

A man with a gun. It could be a life-and-death story. And she was the one person in position to get the news out to the rest of the world. Some newspeople like Lou Potts spent their entire working careers covering school board meetings and traffic accidents. Laurie Callahan had been on the job for less than five months and had stumbled into a story that would certainly lead the six o'clock news. Brackett even wanted to break into the noon news and do a live feed! It had to mean something. Laurie enjoyed the rush of excitement and knew she was in the right business and that she was going to do whatever was required.

Back at the station, Lou Potts sat in a small, windowless conference room and held the daily budget meeting. A screen showed Mort Dohlen delivering the noon news, but the sound was turned off. Lou washed down a chunk of sugary donut with a swig of stale coffee that had been left on the burner for too long. If the pressure of making tough financial decisions did not kill Potts, he figured that someday the KXBD coffee would.

At the moment, he was discussing the possibility of extending shifts a few hours so that the station could let one production crew go. He did not want to lose anyone, but management sent down word that cuts had to be made. Potts knew that if he refused, he would be fired and replaced by someone who would do what the executives wanted. With a mortgage and two daughters to send to college, Potts did not have the luxury of principle.

Potts almost choked on his coffee as the door to the conference room was opened unceremoniously. A young reporter barged into the meeting and stood there breathlessly. Potts appreciated enthusiasm, but it was more welcome in appropriate situations. He could only imagine what this intrusion meant. Maybe the highway department budget, or another local merchant had sold out to a national chain. The reporter just barked out her scoop. "Lou! It's Laurie. It's urgent!"

Lou winced at the kind of trouble Brackett might have stirred up in a natural history museum. Dinosaurs found in downtown Madeline! He would have to talk with Brackett about exploring jobs with shows like *Hard Copy*. Lou picked up the flashing telephone in front of him. "Laurie?" The others seated around the conference room watched as Potts listened. His demeanor grew darker. His eyes narrowed, and he told the others what was going on. "It's Brackett again . . ."

Stuck in the men's room, Brackett rocked on his heels impatiently as he waited for Laurie to patch him through to Lou Potts. Endless moments later, Potts was on the other end of the phone, growling, "Whaddaya got?"

Brackett was no more interested than his boss in pleasantries. He got right down to business. "Gunman—he's got a rifle and a canvas bag." Brackett paused, peered out through the crack of the door, and made sure that the gunman could not hear his conversation. So far so good. He returned his attention to Potts. "I'm guessing there's more firepower. He's holding two adults and some kids."

No one talked about calling the police. Potts first

thought was how quickly they could get on air. "Okay, Laurie, how fast can you power back up?"

Laurie was already on her way out of the van, balancing her cell phone and her video equipment. "I need five minutes," she answered.

In the men's room, Brackett slammed his free hand against the white tiles. "Too long." Five minutes in an emergency was an eternity. In five minutes all the kids could be dead, or the gunman could have surrendered. In five minutes another station might have arrived at the scene, and Brackett could lose the exclusive.

Lou Potts put the call onto speaker phone and let his staff listen in. Potts was clear on what he wanted to happen. "As soon as you're up, Mort'll throw it to you, Max. And listen to me, Max, we don't know what you've stumbled into. There are kids involved. No grandstanding."

Brackett took mock umbrage and needled the news director. "Lou, have you ever known me to grandstand?" It was a joke, but a barbed one.

Carol Dempsey was an associate producer for the evening news. Potts told her to get word to the control room to prepare for a breaking story. Carol charged out of the conference room and bolted across the newsroom. Reporters, technicians, and support staff looked up as Dempsey ran out of the newsroom and down the short hallway into the station's broadcast nerve center.

Ernie Demetrius sat in the director's chair and talked calmly to his board operator—instructing him to get ready to shift back to camera one for a shot of the anchor desk. Weatherman Ronnie Thunder was wrapping up the week's forecast and was segueing back to Dohlen. On Ernie's word the board operator switched from a graphic to a shot of the two men framed together. Ernie whispered over his headset to Dohlen, telling him that the teaser going into the commercial would be for the upcoming sports segment.

On a normal day the control room was a tense place. Live broadcasting inevitably had its pitfalls—TelePrompTers going down, videotape playback synched to the wrong story, anchors mikes short-circuiting. Usually news directors spoke in soothing, reverential tones—as if quiet could stave off the possibility of disaster. Ernie's hushed voice could have been that of a clergyman offering submissive prayer to a deity.

Carol Dempsey burst into Ernie's sanctuary with the news of Brackett's hostage situation. All hell broke loose. After spilling his Coke and getting ready to read Dempsey the riot act, Ernie listened to the details. Immediately, he understood the complications and began to plan how he would direct the live feed from the museum. This story might be a phenomenal pain in the ass, but at least it would get his blood flowing. Ernie exchanged an excited look with the board operator and began to feel like a newsman. The hushed whispers were gone. Ernie shouted into his headset to a surprised Mort Dohlen that the rest of the broadcast schedule was scrapped as of this moment—they were going to take it on the wing.

On the set of the noon news Mort Dohlen was finishing his tired repartee with Ronnie Thunder. Like everything else in Madeline, the prediction of placid weather was no surprise. Ronnie Thunder was paid to be more of a clown than a meteorologist. But Mort Dohlen was not known for his wit, and his joking banter was often painful to watch.

But today, as Ronnie Thunder laughed hysterically

at his own one-liners, Dohlen's earnest face betrayed a certain puzzlement. His hand went to his earpiece, and he focused on unexpected instructions from the control booth. Dohlen's expression showed pleasure and fear as he turned to face a TelePrompTer that was now frozen on an obsolete sports hook.

Dohlen stared through the camera lens and into the eyes of the thousands of viewers at home. His jaw was set, his manner grave, and his eyes intense. People watching the news could read his facial cues and knew that something serious was happening. As he tried to ignore Ernie's nearly hysterical voice shouting into his ear, Dohlen's solemn baritone was steady, "We go now to Max Brackett who is inside the museum of natural history with a hostage situation."

Inside the control room, Carol Dempsey shuffled quickly through a stack of video loops. Finding one labeled "Brackett," she pulled the box and tossed it across the room to an engineer who immediately pulled the tape from its container and threaded it onto an empty one-inch tape machine. Simultaneously, a second engineer frantically pounded the keys of a chyron, a machine that created type for video images. He hesitated for a moment—did "Brackett" have one "t" or two? Lou Potts came in and watched as the board operator pushed his throttle stick, and a live image from outside the natural history museum appeared over the shoulder of their anchorman. Ernie shouted "Go!" into Dohlen's ear, and he spoke as he was told. "Max, can you hear me?"

Before Brackett could respond, Ernie ordered the board operator to roll tape with Brackett's video and to bring up the lettered print. Potts checked the on-air monitor and saw a still photograph of Brackett appear in the upper right-hand corner of the live feed.

A moment later, the title "KXBD Correspondent Max Brackett" appeared just beneath his picture. Brackett's voice could be heard over his picture. "Yes, I can hear you, Mort."

Brackett stretched the cord from the pay phone as far as he could and peered cautiously through the crack of the doorjamb. From his vantage point he could see the schoolchildren huddling in a corner of the museum lobby, being comforted by their teacher. The gunman was tense and kept his rifle aimed at the group. Brackett spoke quietly into the pay phone and tried to keep the excitement out of his voice. "I am inside a men's room, no more than fifty feet from where an armed man is holding about twenty hostages, most of them children."

Outside the museum, Laurie listened to the report as she tried to catch her breath. She had barely managed to set the camera up on its tripod in time to go on the air. Anchorman Mort Dohlen was asking Brackett questions. "Max, do you have any idea what his motives are?" Brackett had no idea what Sam wanted, but reported to his audience that the gunman was increasingly agitated.

Brackett was absolutely right. Sam was wired. Thoughts flew through his brain more quickly than he could process them. He was not sure what to do next. All he had wanted was to talk to Mrs. Banks, and now he had a lobby full of hostages. Sam was not sure how he should behave, but being in charge made him think he ought to be vaguely threatening.

The students were gradually becoming aware that the man with the gun was not joking around. Some turned to their teacher, Kelly Rose, to ask what was going on. Kelly did her best to keep her children calm, but was becoming frightened herself. She looked to

Mrs. Banks, who still managed to convey authority, even though she was as much a hostage as anyone else. But Mrs. Banks did not return her gaze, and instead glared at Sam.

The children's fear was contagious, and soon their anxious voices and crying reverberated loudly through the building. The noise bothered Sam and pushed him closer to the edge than he had ever been in his life.

Mrs. Banks's anger was building up to a dangerous level. She knew that she had to do something to take control of this predicament. Just what that might be, she was not sure. But this was her great-grandfather's museum and now her responsibility. Was Sam serious about what he was doing? She had never suspected this unusually gentle man would ever turn violent. Could this be a joke—far beyond the normal boundaries of good taste?

Joke or not, Mrs. Banks knew that she intimidated Sam. She hoped that he would respond to a firm voice. "Think about what you are doing. We're in the presence of children, for God's sake!" This time, however, she did not try to grab his arm.

Sam was not listening to her, however, and cocked his head in the direction of the rest rooms. He was certain he had heard something. Sam knew the ins and outs of the building and was well acquainted with the employees' schedules. Was someone hiding over there in the men's room? Or was it just a noise that old buildings made? Mrs. Banks was not making it any easier for him to hear by continuing to talk at him. Sam asked her to be quiet. Then he kept his rifle trained on his hostages as he backed out of the lobby toward the rest rooms.

Meanwhile, Brackett moved away from the door in order to continue his conversation with Dohlen over the phone. Brackett began to sweat as he heard footsteps moving cautiously toward his position. He stopped talking abruptly, hugged a wall behind the bathroom door, and covered the earpiece of the telephone with his hand to muffle Dohlen's latest inquiry. "Max, do you have means of escape?" Brackett wished to hell that he did.

In the studio, Dohlen waited a moment for a reply. Hearing nothing, he asked his question again. Getting no response, Dohlen began to worry. Had something happened to Brackett? Dohlen began to lose his anchorman's cool, the fear in his voice obvious. "Max? Can you hear me?"

The airwaves were silent. A sick feeling rose in Lou Potts's stomach, and he shared a worried look with Ernie. Sure, Brackett might be a pain in the ass— even an egotistical son of a bitch—but no one wanted anything serious to happen to him.

The subject of their concern flattened himself against the cold tiles of the bathroom as Sam Baily stepped partway across the threshold of the men's room. Sam peered quickly around the rest room. It was a lucky break for Brackett that the pay phone was hanging on a wall directly behind the door. Had it been placed elsewhere, Sam would have spotted him easily. As it was, the gunman was only inches away from him. Brackett was protected only by the width of a wooden door. If Sam bothered to look more carefully, it would be all over. Brackett did not breathe and began to think how ridiculous this all was. He had survived war zones and natural disasters. Was he going to die here—in a suburban toilet?

Apparently not, at least not yet. Sam saw nothing suspect and left the bathroom, closing the door behind him. With so much going on, he was not sure of anything. Sam convinced himself that he must have imagined the noise.

The airwaves were still silent, however, and no one knew whether or not Brackett was alive or dead. Laurie felt a chill in her spine, horrified that something might have gone so terribly wrong. A moment later, Laurie heard Brackett's voice reasserting itself over the air. "Mort, I'm not sure how much longer I can keep this line open." Laurie smiled with relief.

Then a new danger presented itself. Laurie watched as Cliff Williams, the graffiti-cleaning security guard, walked up the steps toward the front door of the museum. Apparently, he was still working on the grounds and had no idea that there was a crazed gunman indoors.

Laurie knew she had to stop the guard before he walked into a deadly trap.

Chapter Seven

Sam did not listen to Mrs. Banks. Instead, he told her to shut up. In the years that she had known him, he had never even raised his voice to her. Then he had run off to check out a noise in the bathroom. Was he hearing things? Was he delusional? Mrs. Banks prayed that if Sam was still the man she knew, she could talk him out of this insane business before it was too late. But if he was hearing things, that would be a frighteningly bad sign. Mrs. Banks wanted to converse with Sam, hear him talk and see if he was still rational.

Mrs. Banks watched as a jittery Sam made his way back to his captives. He had not found a source of the noise and looked worse for the trouble. Sam was now sweating profusely, his adrenaline flowing. He was jumpy and Mrs. Banks changed her strategy. The firm approach had not worked. Now she was determined to soothe his frayed nerves. "Sam, I want you to be calm. Let's reason this out together."

Sam looked at her blankly. For a moment a half smile crept over his face. Then he resumed his stern look. He knew he had to look like he was in command. But Sam was secretly pleased. Mrs. Banks was offering to talk. That was all Sam had wanted in the first place.

But now there were a few other things going on. It

was more complex than just sitting down for a chat as they should have done several days ago. The kids did not help matters much. They were loud and getting louder. What were they worried about? He was not there to hurt anybody. He had never hurt anybody in his life, and no matter how angry he got, Sam Baily would never hurt a child.

Still, Sam hoped that if the situation did not get any worse he and Mrs. Banks could find a way to keep his job. Nothing terrible had happened yet. Maybe it could all be forgotten. They could tell the kids it had all been a joke—a scheduled part of the field trip. Mrs. Banks would go along because she did not want bad publicity for her museum. Who would send their kids to a museum where visitors were taken hostage by gunmen? The teacher might be harder to convince. On the other hand, she looked like a sweet young woman. She would understand he had been under a lot of pressure lately. Sam's family depended upon him. Maybe if he took her out for a beer, he could explain himself, and she would agree to forget the incident.

As long as nobody made this out to be a bigger deal than it was, everything might turn out fine. More than anything, Sam wanted Mrs. Banks not to blow this whole event out of proportion. "No, Mrs. Banks, you be calm," he said. "I have something to say here—"

But the woman cut him off midsentence. She was not listening. As usual, Mrs. Banks was giving orders, making demands. Some things never changed. Who had the gun here and who was a hostage?

While Mrs. Banks saw the advantage of pacifying Sam, she was still enough of the schoolmarm that she could not tolerate outrageous behavior. Sam had gone over the line and he needed to be scolded like a misbehaving little boy. "Well," she said, "I'm not listening as long as you're holding that thing. I'll tell you that much."

Had she said something different, something more conciliatory, the whole problem might have been resolved there and then. For at the moment, Sam wished more than anything that he could just go home. All Sam wanted was for his life to return to normal. "Mrs. Banks . . ." He was holding a rifle, and yet he was pleading.

The museum curator was frightened but unfortunately her fear seemed just fussy and annoying to Sam. She interrupted Sam again, refused to talk, and offered him no respect. "No, why should I? This is absurd."

Her arrogance infuriated Sam, and he raised his rifle, pointing it into her face. "Shut up!" he shouted.

Laurie had no idea what was happening inside the museum. She could hear Brackett breathing heavily over the phone as if something was making him nervous. But she did not know anything more than that Brackett might not be able to keep the line open.

What she did know was that she had to stop the security guard before he walked in unaware upon a lunatic gunman. Without a second thought, she simply reacted. "Hey! Stop!"

But Cliff did not hear her from her van across the street, and when he arrived at the top step, he reached for the door.

Inside, Mrs. Banks did not want to shut up as Sam was shouting at her to do. Instead, she reached the end of her patience and thought it was time the ridiculous affair came to an end. Sam could wave around his rifle as long as he wanted, but she was certain that he could never be a bona fide threat, certainly not a killer. As Mrs. Banks looked around the room, it was clear that Sam was the most frightened person there.

Mrs. Banks swatted the barrel of Sam's rifle out of her face as she would have shooed a fly, and reprimanded him. "Get that thing away from me!"

Her reaction was precisely what Sam did not need to hear. What enraged him most was Mrs. Banks's attitude—not fearful or even hostile. Mrs. Banks was simply—dismissive.

At that confused, infuriating moment the front door to the museum rattled loudly as Cliff tried to get inside.

Every nerve in Sam's body exploded with the unexpected noise. He spun around reflexively, faced the intruder at the door, and fired his rifle impulsively.

KXBD, the CBN affiliate in Madeline, California, had an exclusive. A man had just been shot on live television. Cliff Williams fell the instant he was hit by Sam's bullet—and slid down the granite steps of the museum toward the sidewalk. His body came to a stop, and he lay there without moving as a puddle of blood grew beneath him.

The hostages began to scream.

Sam was silent and held the gun in position—still aimed at the door. Had there been someone there, or had he just heard the kids milling about? Had he just fired the weapon? Looking at the door he could see nothing that proved that he had done so. But the screaming of the children and the reverberating echo of the gunshot suggested that he had indeed pulled the trigger.

Sam froze in place. He had not meant to shoot. Luckily, it did not look as though he had caused any real damage to the door. Angry with himself, he determined to be more careful in the future. Sam hoped that no one outside heard the shot. A passerby might get the wrong idea and call the police. If that happened, the whole equation would change.

Back at KXBD, Lou Potts listened to the gunshot over both Brackett's and Laurie's audio feeds. After a stunned moment of disbelief, Potts swung into action.

"Cut the feed! Now!"

Inside the control booth, the director killed the line from the remote. For a moment, KXBD went to static, and then the startled face of anchorman Mort Dohlen returned to the air. Dohlen had never participated in an event like this and tried to get Brackett's take on the matter. "Max? Can you hear me?"

Brackett could hear Dohlen. As he tried to pull himself up to peer through the bathroom's transom, he was uncertain about what had just happened. "Mort? Was that a shot?" Brackett could not see a thing other than the ceiling of the lobby and the gleaming eye of the hovering pterodactyl.

Dohlen filled him in. "Yes, someone was hit, Max, in front of the museum. I didn't get a good look at him before we pulled the plug."

Brackett did not believe what he was hearing. "What asshole pulled the plug?"

Dohlen began to sweat with embarrassment. "Max, we're still live on the air."

The brutal and accidental shooting of Cliff Williams was broadcast live and unedited to thousands of homes in the Madeline area. The tiger was out of its cage, and try as they might, the people who planned to ride it were in for a rough trip.

Chapter Eight

At the Madeline Police Station, the 911 emergency operators were accustomed to certain kinds of calls—car wrecks, fires, medical emergencies, even confused callers dialing for directory information and pressing nine instead of four.

Gladys Wu was finishing an eight-hour shift and then stayed at her console because her replacement had called in sick. Wu had worked the 911 emergency system for the better part of a decade and thought she had heard it all. But now, tired and with her guard down, Wu took an incoming call. "911, what is the nature of your emergency?"

A breathless caller tried to spit out words, but was too shocked to explain coherently. "I just saw a shooting on TV."

Wu's job was fraught with intense pressure, and now punchy from too many hours fielding the distress calls of her community, Wu could only offer a surprised "Where?"

"On TV. A guy was shot!"

Gladys Wu lost it. She had not heard everything after all. The caller had seen a shooting on television? Wu remembered statistics showing that an average American child witnessed literally thousands of shootings in film and on TV by age ten. Wu began to laugh, first a chuckle, then her laughter erupted. Gladys was laughing louder and louder. She tried to let her puzzled colleagues in on the joke. "A guy saw a shooting on TV!"

No one was laughing inside the museum. Instead, the kids were nearly hysterical as Kelly overcame her own fear and tried to quiet them down.

Mrs. Banks stared at Sam with horror. She had never expected him to pull the trigger. Mrs. Banks had considered the rifle something of a prop. She could no longer comfort herself with that illusion, however. He was in worse shape than Mrs. Banks had thought. Accordingly, everyone stuck in the museum was in more danger than she had anticipated.

Sam chided himself for losing his cool. If he wasn't more careful, he might get into some real trouble. Here he was trying to get his job back as a guard— to protect the museum—and he had just shot a hole in the front door. Sam ambled over to the entrance to see how bad the damage was. A small bullet hole would not be such a big deal. If Mrs. Banks was willing to cooperate, he could replace the pane of glass himself once he got his job back.

Sure enough, the hole in the glass was smaller than a quarter. Sam figured he could get a new pane at a hardware store for under ten dollars and they could all forget about the whole thing.

Sam peered through the bullet hole and blinked with confusion. He looked through the door itself to get a better view and was staggered by what he saw. A man lay at the bottom of the museum steps. It took a moment, but then Sam realized what he had done. Everyone in the museum could hear him call out, "Jesus, it's Cliff. I shot Cliff."

*   *   *

Sam and Cliff had worked together for years and were good friends. Cliff was the senior of the two at the museum and had warmly welcomed Sam to the staff when he signed on. Since then their families spent a good deal of time together, sharing trips to the beach or watching the two men as they played side by side in local sports leagues. Sam saw Cliff lying in an expanding pool of blood and realized he had shot a man who was closer to him than his own brother.

Sam was immobilized by the gravity of what he had done. Inner fury grew and rapidly approached explosion. As the noise of the crying children began to overwhelm him, Sam's rage detonated. He roared at Mrs. Banks. "This is your fault!" Then whirled around to the schoolchildren and yelled at them to be quiet. The hostages assumed that he was furious, and did not recognize his anguish.

The pandemonium allowed Brackett to get back in communication with Lou Potts. The reporter was ready for a fight. Potts had pulled the plug on the live feed. Currently, KXBD was showing only an increasingly panicked Mort Dohlen, who had a lot of air time to fill and not a lot to say. Brackett hissed as loudly as he dared into the pay phone, his tone heated, "Lou, this is the story of your career."

In KXBD's studio, Lou Potts watched Dohlen try to tell an incomplete story. His mind was made up the second he told Ernie to kill the feed. There were journalistic standards to live up to. Television had become sordid enough without showing actual murder. Maybe another station in another market would want to make a buck by stooping into the gutter, but that was not how things were done in Madeline. People did not want to see their neighbors being shot down in cold blood. But Brackett was not listening, and Potts felt a need to justify himself. "A man has been shot on our air; he could be dead."

Brackett was not surprised. Spend enough time as a newsman in a place like Madeline, and you had to lose your edge. Here Lou Potts had a major breaking story, and he did not want to even show the pictures. The story had happened. It was fact. How could you turn down such a godsend? "Lou! They didn't pull the plug when Oswald was shot or the Challenger blew up."

Potts had to concede that Brackett had a point, but stalled for time. He watched Dohlen, who was handling the crisis as well as could be expected. But all the anchorman could do was present the same facts over and over again. A gunman in the museum. While Dohlen tried to tell the news in a fresh way, the repetition grew absurd. Potts knew that something had to change. Still, there were important principles to be considered. "They don't need to see the blood, Max. Our viewers know what's going on."

Brackett disagreed vehemently. Potts was violating a sacred law of television news. "You're giving them radio. We've got live pictures, and you're giving them radio."

Potts winced—as a television man that was the ultimate insult. He had worked all his professional life in TV and to be challenged at such a fundamental level was excruciating.

Brackett could sense his boss weakening. "Lou, this is going to turn into a big thing. And if we don't report it, I guarantee you that in a matter of minutes everyone else will."

Brackett helped Potts see his way through the ethical dilemma. The news director's crisis of conscience was quickly eased by the commercial pressure of the market share.

Mort Dohlen got instructions through his earpiece, turned to face camera one, and brought his viewers up to date. "And now . . . we have reestablished our live hookup to the museum. Max Brackett, are you there?"

Potts checked the on-air monitor and sighed with relief as the live shot of the museum's exterior filled the screen. Brackett's voice could be heard behind the image. "Yes, Mort. I am still here. If I could have our cameraperson zoom in on the person who has been shot."

Dohlen and Potts looked at the picture from the live camera and waited to see it close in on the wounded man. They waited a moment, then realized that the camera was going to remain static. Dohlen filled Brackett in on what was happening. "Max, the camera is not responding."

Stuck in the bathroom, and frustrated that he could not exert more control over the situation, Brackett wanted to know what the problem was. "Laurie? Are you reading me?"

Back at the station, and all over the region for that matter, people watching KXBD could see a figure creeping up the museum steps toward the wounded man. Dohlen let Brackett know the latest. "Max, excuse me, but I see someone else approaching the wounded man. I can't quite make them out . . ."

Dohlen and Potts both leaned forward to get a better look at their monitors. As the figure reached the fallen man, they recognized Laurie Callahan. She had left her camera and bravely drawn closer to Cliff Williams. Dohlen's words shot out of his mouth with surprise and delight. "It's our cameraperson, Laurie Callahan."

Hearing this, Brackett rolled his eyes and tapped the phone receiver against his forehead with exasperation. What kind of amateur hour was this? A breaking news event and the cameragirl runs off to play Florence Nightingale? It was indulgent bullshit. Not only had she violated the journalist's first rule, not to become involved in a story—but she risked the whole exclusive by abandoning her post.

Across the region wherever KXBD's signal reached, thousands of people called friends and family members to tell them to watch Channel Six. Live, right in front of their eyes, a young woman risked her life during a hostage crisis by going to the assistance of a wounded man. This was better than any syndicated cop show. People could actually get blown away at any moment, and there was no censor.

Laurie reached Cliff, who was conscious but groaning with pain. She grabbed his hand, and he smiled, realizing that someone had come to help. There was no time for many questions, however. Laurie worked quickly. "Can you walk?" Cliff was dazed and not sure whether or not he could. Laurie reached around his waist and helped him to sit up.

Smeared with Cliff's blood, Laurie wanted to get him out of the line of fire as rapidly as possible. As she waited for him to catch his breath, Laurie expected to hear the sound of another rifle shot. But the gunman did not open fire again. Was he willing to let her take the bleeding guard for medical attention? Using all her strength, Laurie pulled Cliff to his feet. Then they carefully made their way to safety behind the news van. Cliff moaned with every step, but still managed to thank Laurie for risking her life to help him.

Sam peered nervously out the window, visibly relieved that Cliff was able to walk away. If Cliff moved, albeit with assistance, then he could not be that badly hurt. Sam prayed that he had only grazed his friend with the errant bullet. His first thoughts focused on Cliff's well-being. Then Sam realized that Cliff's welfare was now directly linked to his own. If Cliff was not badly hurt, then Sam would be in less trouble than he feared.

As the paramedics led Cliff behind a van, Sam saw Laurie look back fearfully. Sam wanted to yell to her not to worry—he did not want to hurt anyone—but the words never came out, for his focus shifted when he read the logo on the side of the truck—KXBD ACTION NEWS. Sam's eyes then darted to something else standing next to the truck—an unmanned video camera pointed at the museum. Sam pulled back from the small window, kept his gun trained on his hostages, and moved into the carrel that passed for a guard's station.

Switching on the tiny television atop a desk, Sam flipped the dial to Channel Six, KXBD. He was amazed to find an image of the museum's exterior on the air. Looking carefully, Sam could make out the bloodied steps leading to the front door and the tiny window that he had peered through. Sam frantically leaned over the counter of the security desk and gaped out the window. He saw the news van and camera as they stared at the museum. Sam found himself stuck in a hallucinatory moment as his attention darted between the monitor on the desk and the electronic eye that held him in its gaze. For a moment Sam was trapped in a never-ending pattern of the observer and the observed.

Sam grew more agitated, aware that somehow he

was no longer in sole possession of his identity and destiny. The news camera that stared at him showed Sam off to hundreds of thousands of viewers. It was an influential participant in the events that were unfolding, taking away Sam's ability to define himself and offering him to the world according to its own agenda.

Before Sam could think this through, however, something else more immediate caught his attention. A reporter was describing the situation at the museum as escalating in seriousness. Sam watched and listened as Brackett reported from the men's room. "Mort, this situation has shifted dramatically with its first casualty. A line has been crossed." Brackett's voice betrayed his growing sense of tension. "We've got a dangerous situation here."

Lou yelled a question through Dohlen's earpiece, and the anchorman asked, "How are the children?"

Brackett stared apprehensively through the crack at the doorjamb, watching as Kelly and Mrs. Banks tried to comfort the students.

At the security desk, Sam divided his attention between the news on TV and watching his hostages. Sam listened as Brackett reported, "They are all together in one corner of the museum lobby. The museum curator and the teacher are tending to them." Sam looked back at the two women as they took care of the children. The reporter was accurate in his description. How could that be? How did the reporter know what was going on inside the building?

Sam looked around the lobby as Brackett began to tell the world that the students were upset and clearly frightened. Sam was beginning to get angry. This reporter was making him look bad. Sam had not come into the building, looking for hostages. What troubled

Sam most, however, was the question of how the reporter knew what he was talking about. Sam had to discover the reporter's trick before he was made to look any worse in front of the television audience.

Sam scanned the museum for any vantage points that he might have missed. He was not sure why, but he still suspected that there was something wrong with the men's room. He had checked it out earlier, but it was the only possible place where someone could be hiding. Maybe he should have checked the stalls. Sam held his rifle at waist height and started angrily toward the men's room.

Brackett pulled away from the doorway and put his back against the wall. Even though his voice was just above a whisper, he wanted to make sure that the gunman did not hear him. Brackett had live air now, and he had to fill it. The situation in the lobby was static for the moment, so he began to talk about other hostage situations that he had been involved with, hoping to supply some resonance and insight into the current crisis. "It reminds me of the—"

The door to the men's room flew open. Sam swung the door shut and spun around the room—looking for an enemy—and quickly found Brackett up against the wall, holding the pay phone receiver to his mouth. Their eyes met, and for a moment they held each other off with their respective weapons—rifle versus television audience. Terrified as he was, Brackett's journalistic instinct took over, and he was determined to stay on the air. Thrusting the receiver forward like a microphone, Brackett stared into the face of the gunman and went for the story. "Max Brackett, KXBD News. We are on the air . . . Can you tell us why you are here."

Confronted by this unwanted presence, Sam lashed

out in a gesture more of frustration than deadly intent. Using the butt of the rifle, Sam drove the receiver out of Brackett's hands. The telephone unit was smashed to pieces as well as the reporter's sense of invulnerablilty that came from controlling an interview. Brackett stared into the infuriated eyes of the gunman and felt the sort of fear he had not known since Beirut. The man staring back at him was a volatile piece of work. Max Brackett began to be concerned that his own obituary might lead tonight's evening news.

Chapter Nine

In the KXBD news studio, Mort Dohlen stared at the locked-off shot of the museum entrance and listened as Brackett's voice was replaced by an ominous dial tone. Dohlen was frightened. Could Max Brackett have just been killed on the air? Dohlen prayed Brackett was alive. "Max? Can you hear me?"

Off Main Street in Madeline, a crowd was gathering in front of Supertronic Electronics. A bank of televisions in the display window were all broadcasting the live news event. Ten images of Mort Dohlen looked concerned and repeated their plaintive question. "Max Brackett, are you there?" The people watching the televisions were of mixed ages. But even the older viewers had their noses almost pressed to the glass. No one spoke, but there was a palpable sense of excitement. Could something like this really be happening in their hometown?

Several miles away in the museum parking lot, the frenzy was about to begin. A wailing police car nearly collided with a news truck from an ABC affiliate as they both raced to the scene. Right behind them, an ambulance pulled up. Two paramedics jumped out and immediately began to examine Cliff's wounds. As he was led to the ambulance, the wounded guard smiled his thanks to Laurie.

As Cliff was driven away, Laurie went back to her camera, took it off its tripod, and began to capture the scene for KXBD. At the same time, a television reporter from KCAL jumped from his truck, and a newsprint reporter from the Madeline *Daily Record* ran out of his battered car. Both converged upon the police car and surrounded Sheriff Alvin Lemke as he surveyed the location.

Sheriff Lemke was a lifer in the Madeline Police Department. His father had been on the force, and Lemke pinned on a star after a tour of duty in Vietnam. Some thirty years later, Lemke had grown comfortably middle-aged while patrolling the streets. He watched as his small town had grown into a large bedroom community for San Francisco. Having served overseas, Lemke could hardly be called provincial. He was, however, old-fashioned and had dedicated his life to preserving the small-town feel of Madeline. His hard work combined with the wealth of the community had kept the dangers that came with urbanization away from his streets. Lemke had no desire to be a big city cop, racing around in speeding cars and catching killers. He preferred a quiet life, and enjoyed the boredom and frustration that younger cops hated. Lemke had spent years trying to keep Madeline a boring place, and the citizens were grateful to him.

The *Daily Record* reporter shoved a notepad in Lemke's face. "Sheriff Lemke, what are your plans?"

Lemke stepped around the overexcited young journalist and growled his response, "No comment. Outta my way." Lemke had never mastered the modern art of public relations and walked up to the scene with a practical swagger. The reporters were left wanting more.

All around Madeline, people watching TV wanted

more, too. People who turned on television for some
company during lunch found themselves entranced.
Some who had places to go, didn't. Even some who
just argued with their spouses and were set to walk
out the door watched the story unfold.

About five miles away, near the eastern edge of the
community, a nine-year-old girl sat in her terry cloth
robe and bunny slippers as she endured a bout with
the flu. Dee Williams had stayed home from school
when her mother found she had a temperature. Before
he left for work, her father had promised to bring her
some chicken soup and magazines that evening. Dee
had enjoyed the morning cartoons and was waiting for
the interminable news broadcast to end so she could
watch her soap operas. Dee browsed the comics section of the local paper and barely paid attention while
Mort Dohlen brought his listeners up to date. "Our
cameraperson has informed us that the victim's name
is Clifford Williams. Mr. Williams is a security guard
at the museum."

Dee lowered the funnies and stared at the television
screen while whispering her surprise. "Dad?" Channel
Six cut away from their grimly visaged anchor and
replayed the videotape of Cliff being shot on the museum steps.

Lou Potts had resisted the idea of rebroadcasting
the shooting when it had been suggested by one of
the producers. He had been subsequently convinced,
however, by a young executive who rushed into the
studio from the corporate offices. The shooting of Cliff
Williams had been altered—it was now shown in slow
motion—to underscore the tragedy, or so the executive explained. Potts knew that it was more truly
meant to tweak the ratings and was appalled by the
idea of manipulating the picture. But he also knew

that the thirty-year-old suit had the power of employ-
ment over him. Potts frowned, but told the broadcast
director to go ahead.

Dee Williams watched with disbelief as her father
took the bullet, slowly fell backward, and slid down
the steps. She screamed at the top of her lungs,
"Mom!"

Some time later, and far across the country, other
people were watching the same disturbing image. A
group of men and women huddled around a small
television monitor in the worldwide network headquarters of the Continental Broadcasting Network.
They watched with a combination of awe and admiration as their backwater affiliate KXBD broadcast the
images of an ongoing hostage crisis. It was the sort of
story that made newsmen, broadcasters, and advertising executives take notice.

Meanwhile, across the studio floor, silver-haired anchorman Kevin Hollander wrapped up a human interest story on a surfing Doberman pincher from Texas.
Although only in his late fifties, Hollander was already
a broadcasting legend. From Vietnam to Watergate to
the fall of the Soviet Empire—Hollander brought the
news of the world into the living rooms of millions of
American homes. He was beloved around the nation
for his humor, decency, and most especially for his
distinctive—and well-practiced—sincerity. While his
clean-cut all-American boy looks had aged into a gray-
ing personification of the trusted father figure, he was
still number one in the ratings. The formula for his
gargantuan success was straightforward—Hollander
sold integrity on the nightly news—along with various
laxatives and stomach-soothing medicines.

At the moment, however, Kevin Hollander was annoyed. He had a news program to deliver, and he had been distracted by the clustering buzz surrounding one of the studio monitors. Hollander was a highly paid newsman, and during his nightly broadcast he expected to be the center of attention. If the support staff was not entirely focused on him, then they were not doing their jobs as well as they should.

When the broadcast went to commercial, Hollander unhooked his earpiece, got up from his desk, and hurried over to see what the hell was going on. Two senior editorial staffers, Al Merton and Dennis Frank, were watching as well. Both men were in their mid-thirties—Merton was tall and thin, Frank short and chubby. Both men had risen quickly through the ranks of the news business, and they had done it the old-fashioned way—they sabotaged the competition, stepped over their "corpses," and genuflected before their superiors.

Hollander tried to maintain a dignified approach, although he was seething. "What's up?" he asked.

A junior staffer filled him in. "Hostage crisis. Fed in from our affiliate in Madeline, California."

Dennis Frank tried to listen to the angry voice over his cell phone, but found it difficult with the noise in the studio. He plugged an ear with a finger as Al Merton told Hollander the good news. "Guess who the reporter inside the museum is. Max Brackett."

The crowd around the monitor registered their familiarity with Brackett's name. Some laughed. Some shook their heads. All were jealous that Brackett had control of what looked to be a great story. Hollander's was the only subdued reaction, and his face looked as though he had tasted something sour. One staffer laughed. "I knew that bastard would turn up somewhere."

Merton knew this would grow to be a national story and turned to Hollander with a plan. "We should use this for your tease at the top of the hour."

Hollander wanted no part of the story. "With Brackett involved? No way."

Frank flipped his cell phone shut. He had heard the interchange and had his own contribution to make to the conversation. "You'll say, 'The situation is still unfolding. Tune in this evening for a full update.' That's a tease if ever I heard one."

Hollander reacted with a personal anger, but tried to make it sound professional. "Wait a minute! We have no idea what the circumstances are, and you're just going to drop it into my newscast?"

Frank did not get excited and never raised his voice. But he answered Hollander in such a way that the anchorman was reminded that the broadcast did not actually belong to him. "It comes from above."

Hollander could only frown, realizing that he had been overruled. He may have been the network's top anchorman, but he was still a hired hand.

The stage manager shouted to get their minds back on business. "And we're back in ten seconds . . ." He began his countdown.

Having beaten down his anchor, Frank needed to stroke his star so that he would not be angry when he went back on the air. An anchorman's credibility depended to no small degree upon his equanimity in the face of a crisis. Viewers expected their anchormen to be calm and collected. If Hollander had an attitude while telling the Madeline story, people would get the wrong idea. Frank put an arm around Hollander's shoulders, led him back to the set, and cooed condescendingly, "Kevin, it's a guy. Getting shot. It's good television and no other net has it."

All around them staffers scrambled to be ready
when they went back on the air. The stage manager
was down to "Five, four . . ."

Hollander had lost and wanted to register his dissat-
isfaction. If something went wrong, it would not be
his fault. "Brackett can't be trusted," he said. "You
remember what he did."

Merton dusted the dandruff off Hollander's shoulders as he sat him back down at his anchor desk.
"Actually, that was before my time." The younger
man did not want to be tarnished with the brush of
that old scandal. The stage manager was down to two
seconds and pointed to Hollander.

It was show time.

Hollander glowered for a moment as the countdown
continued. He had been a newsman before Merton
and Frank had been born. Still, you had to be flexible
if you wanted to survive, he thought. Merton and
Frank exchanged a worried look. But Hollander was
a professional, and as the stage manager got down to
one second, the anchor's face relaxed into his world-
famous, slightly bemused smile. His sympathetic expression told his viewers that he knew it was a crazy
world out there and he commiserated with their cha-
grin. But he was not upset by it. He was stable—rock
solid—the unfrightened captain on a ship in stormy
seas. Somehow—particularly if you watched his broadcast regularly and bought the products that sponsored
his show—you might just survive.

Chapter Ten

Back in Madeline, a jittery Sam watched the local news while also keeping focused on Brackett and the other hostages. A grim Mort Dohlen was assessing the events so far. "Now that the gunman has shown a willingness to use firepower to make himself heard . . ." Sam yelled back furiously at the TV, "It was an accident, moron!" There he switched the TV off, backed toward the door, and looked out at the growing commotion in the parking lot. A crowd of police cars, news trucks, satellite dishes, and curious citizens stared back at him. Sam was astounded by what he saw—how had things gone so deeply wrong? Sam became slowly aware that this was not something that would go away, something that could be handled with a verbal reprimand or a note attached to his work record. Everything was snowballing, and he was over-whelmed. Sam yelled to the onlookers, "All I wanted was my job back!"

It was as much a plea as it was an angry voice of defiance. Sam slammed his hand against the window-sill as his frustration veered again toward violence.

Brackett squinted with incredulity. He thought the gunman had just said something that could not possibly be true. While it was a risk to talk to someone as enraged as the gunman, Brackett's curiosity superseded his discretion. "You're doing this to get your job back?"

Brackett realized he should never have said a word, when Sam spun around with the rifle aiming right at Brackett's heart. "Yes. I did this to get my job back. What did you think?"

What staggered Brackett most of all about Sam's reaction was not the gun pointed at his chest. As a journalist he was used to life-threatening situations. While a person never grew entirely comfortable with the notion of imminent extinction, Brackett knew that more often than not a threat was a bluff.

What Brackett had not expected was Sam's confusion. The gunman's face was not contorted in any way. Nor did he snarl like the proverbial cornered animal. Instead, he seemed upset that people might think bad of him. Sam was offended that the police were ascribing him a malevolence he did not deserve. Despite holding a dozen children hostage, Sam Baily maintained an innocent bearing as though he were the one being wronged.

Sam spun around and pointed his rifle toward the parking lot. Outside an army of police and media were settling in for the siege. "Look at this! They're not going to give me my job back now."

Now Brackett's mouth almost got him killed. All his life he had been a wiseass. His nature, and unfortunately his tongue, had little instinct for self-preservation. Countless people had listened to acerbic comments from Brackett and felt the urge toward unrestrained violence. Of course, usually nothing ever happened. Men like Lou Potts and Mort Dohlen reined in their anger and ignored their colleague as best they could. But at this particular time and place, Brackett said the wrong thing to the wrong person. "No, you're not going to get your job back this way—not unless you were really good at it."

Sam lost it. Pivoting on his heels, he stalked across the lobby toward Brackett and shoved the rifle at the reporter's body. Sam was suddenly both afraid and furious. Smarter people always lorded their superiority over him. He was tired of it. He did not appreciate sarcasm coming from the man he believed escalated an incident into a catastrophe. He screamed at Brackett, even though they were only a few feet apart, "This is all your fault. Everybody knows I'm here because of you!" Sam did not move any closer, but his hands began to tremble violently.

At that moment, Brackett expected to die. But even during the most trying circumstances, Brackett's caustic outlook prevailed. He was not afraid, just sardonically amused. Brackett enjoyed the irony that after surviving some of the most brutal warfare of the last thirty years, he was to die in a backwater natural history museum. His killer would not be a deranged fundamentalist terrorist, but a hapless security guard, and he would die before an audience of elementary school students and two rather worn dinosaurs.

Brackett briefly imagined the network's obituary report, momentarily awed by his lengthy list of accomplishments. No doubt Kevin Hollander would deliver the homage in an appropriately reverent voice. Brackett was so moved by the grief that his colleagues would feign that had he been one to cry, tears would have poured down his cheeks.

It was a high price to pay to get back on the network. But that had been Brackett's goal for the past few years, and he was not about to screw it up now by begging for his life.

The security desk telephone rang and interrupted

Brackett's reverie. Brackett watched as the gunman was instantly transformed. He was no longer enraged, but a terrified child who had been caught misbehaving. Sam kept the gun trained on Brackett, but did not move. The reporter watched the gunman stare apprehensively at the ringing phone.

Brackett had an idea.

He knew this was a tricky situation, but the lure of working for the network again gave him courage. Perhaps his return to CBN would not have to be limited to an obituary.

Brackett stared at the gunman and saw that he did not know what to do. If he picked up the ringing telephone, he would not know what to say. Sam Baily was desperate for guidance. And because of his need—Max Brackett knew that the gunman could be encouraged to follow directions. If he could orchestrate events, Brackett knew that this hostage affair could become one of the triumphant moments of his life.

He spoke quietly. So quietly, in fact, Sam was not sure the reporter had addressed him at all. Brackett tried again. "If you tell them everyone's okay in here, you'll buy yourself some time."

Sam's anger flashed, and he glared at the man who had revealed him to the world. Just like Mrs. Banks— here was someone else telling him what to do. "I'll tell 'em if they don't back off, I will shoot someone. Starting with you. Throw your body out the door," he said.

Brackett had second thoughts about his scheme and wondered if he had grievously miscalculated. He took a long look at the gunman and decided that Sam was only parroting dialogue from television and the movies. Still, it was an effort to remain calm. If he misjudged the gunman—if the gunman was not the basically decent person that Brackett thought he was, then things could get ugly quickly. Brackett offered more advice and tried to keep the gunman calm. "Oh, I wouldn't do that."

Sam's reply was hostile, but it also left the door open for more conversation. "Why not?"

Brackett wanted to scare the gunman. If Sam was frightened, he would need someone to turn to. But Brackett did not want to push him so far that he began to despair. "That will make everybody jumpy. They might do something we'll all regret."

Sam understood. Once again his fierceness vanished. He lowered his rifle and looked at the reporter with anticipation. Sam did not want to die and did not want to kill anyone. The reporter seemed to grasp this. Sam now recognized Max Brackett from the local news and was moved that such a famous man actually gave a damn about his welfare.

Sam Baily did not know it yet, but he had just found a new best friend.

Brackett knew about incidents like this, and it gave him something to work with. He was pleased to see Sam soften, and immediately played his hand. By assuming the role of ally and offering advice, Brackett knew he could win the gunman's loyalty—and then demand exclusive rights to the story. "Remember the incident in Torrance two years ago?" he asked.

Torrance was a suburb south of Los Angeles where Brackett had been sent to do a human interest story on a Madeline girl who was a *Baywatch* lifeguard. Brackett had missed an exit on the San Diego Freeway and found himself in Torrance, where he asked directions in a car dealership. Luck being a factor in any journalist's career, Brackett found himself the first reporter on site when an angry customer stormed the showroom with an automatic weapon.

Sam remembered the affair. "In that car dealership?" He remembered discussing it with Cliff.

"I covered that story. Four people died. Including the gunman."

Sam saw that Brackett knew more about what was going on than he did. If the reporter advised him not to threaten the schoolchildren, Sam was going to listen. He looked at the ringing phone with distrust and then answered it with a tentative hello.

In the parking lot, Sheriff Lemke was pleased to make contact. "This is Sheriff Alvin Lemke. Am I speaking to the man responsible for this situation?"

Sam assured him that he was, and Lemke asked for his name. But Sam's mind was elsewhere. There was only one thing he wanted to know. "How is Cliff? Is he all right?" Cliff was not all right and had been rushed to the local hospital. Hearing this, Sam tried to set the record straight. "I didn't mean to shoot him. It was an accident."

True or not, Lemke considered this good news. At least the gunman was not a raving psycho. His apology meant that he understood right from wrong. The gunman's regret at having shot an adult might well mean that he had no stomach for killing children. Lemke wanted to pacify the gunman and then talk him into surrendering. "Well, if you were to give up right now, we might take that into account."

"I don't think I'll be doing that."

Bringing this terrible day to a close had real appeal to Sam. The thought that he could stop the madness right now was something he wanted to believe. He wished that somehow he could go home tonight and have dinner with his wife, Jen, and their two children. If Cliff was okay, then Sam knew his friend would not press charges. Cliff would understand it was all an accident. Still, Sam had his doubts. The police were already there. How could they let him go?

Lemke had not thought the gunman would give up that easily. But he wanted the man to think he was reasonable. It had been worth a shot. Now he was all business. "I see. What are your demands?" he asked.

Demands? Sam had not formulated any specific demands. He covered the phone's mouthpiece as his mind raced to figure out what to say next. Brackett watched Sam carefully and saw his confusion. Quietly and gently, he insinuated himself into the conversation. "What did he say?" Sam told him that the cop wanted to know what his demands were.

"So tell him."

But it was not that easy. Sam concentrated on the question as best he could, but no demands came to mind. Nothing. As Sam thought furiously, he saw Brackett scrutinizing him. Nothing angered Sam more than that sort of condescending stare. It was the same way teachers, employers, and other adults looked at him all his life. Sam's humiliation came out in aggressiveness. "What are you looking at?" he demanded.

Brackett realized he should have tried a more comforting approach, but he was simply flabbergasted. "You do have some demands, don't you?"

Sam knew never to let anyone guess that he did not know what to do. It was clear, however, that Brackett knew the score. Sam abandoned any pretense of control. "I don't know. I never meant this to happen."

Brackett tried to figure Sam out. The gunman just stood there, paralyzed by his confusion. Brackett decided the time had come for some specific coaching.

"Look, just tell them you'll talk when you're good and ready. And no bodies out the door."

This made sense to Sam. He picked up the phone again and talked to the sheriff, his attitude firm, but not especially threatening. "I want everybody to back off. I'll talk when I'm good and ready."

Pleased with Sam's performance, Brackett smiled his approval.

Having asserted his authority, Sam felt a thrilling rush of power. He slammed down the phone for emphasis, realizing this new sensation.

His euphoria did not last long, however. Concerned, he turned back to Brackett. "What's next?"

Brackett did not let Sam down. He knew the drill. "You get yourself some demands."

But all Sam could say was, "Like what?"

"Well, there's always money."

Sam looked offended by the suggestion, and Brackett began to suspect that Sam did not fully comprehend the notion. He spelled it out for him. "Yeah, you know, money? Ransom."

"I don't want money I didn't work for!"

Brackett had witnessed a lot of strange things and tried to grasp the contradiction standing before him. Though no psychiatrist, he fancied himself a student of human nature. Still, he was forced to admit that Sam Baily was confounding. But Sam had to make some sort of demand, even if he did not really mean it. "Ask for a fast car, a Greyhound bus, a Lear jet. You have to have a demand. If you don't, they get very nervous."

Of course there *was* something Sam wanted. Why had he come to the museum in the first place? Annoyed and confused by the intimation that he had mercenary intentions, Sam remembered his original goal as though struck by a god-sent epiphany. He blurted out his demand with conviction. "I just want my job back!"

Perfect. If Brackett believed in a Supreme Being, he would have fallen to his knees with thanks. Sam Baily's uncomplicated need was something any audience could respond to. All across the nation people were worried about job security. Sam merely expressed their collective fear in an extreme fashion. Brackett had the first building blocks that he needed to create a sympathetic image for Sam.

Still, Brackett's normal inquisitiveness made him ask why Sam had taken such drastic action. "Did you really think you were going to get it back at gunpoint?"

Sam threw up his hands in exasperation. That was where he really screwed up, wasn't it? If only he had left the gun at home. "I just wanted her to listen to me!" He had never planned to pull the gun out of its canvas case. Sam had just thought, perhaps the mere suggestion of a weapon would encourage Mrs. Banks to hear him out. Otherwise, she might well dismiss him out of hand—as she did.

"Maybe I should just give up." Things had turned out badly. Sam knew he was in serious trouble—but at least no one had been killed. Perhaps he could earn some goodwill by releasing the children and just getting the whole damn thing over with. Sam Baily was a defeated man, ready to call it quits.

As Sam's hostages looked at him with hope, Brackett felt entirely different about surrender. He did not want the gunman to make any hasty decisions. "Well, that's your only viable option." That was for public consumption. The curator and the schoolteacher heard him, and he was happy to have covered his ass.

If Brackett had said nothing more, the hostage crisis might have ended immediately. Sam was not a man used to standing up for himself. He was more accustomed to being kept down. His first significant expression of defiance had spun tragically out of control. It was time to take his punishment and trust there would be some sort of life for him when this mess was concluded.

But Brackett also had a private message for Sam. He gestured for the gunman to join him by the window, where they could talk without anyone overhearing their conversation. "There are different ways to give up, Sam. It could make the difference between a long prison term and a slap on the wrist."

At no point prior to the crisis had Sam thought of the ramifications of his plan. All he expected to do was talk with Mrs. Banks. He took the rifle along in a spontaneous, ill-conceived gesture of despair. Prison had never occurred to him. Once the police had arrived at the scene, Sam was worried. But to hear Brackett talk about jail was shocking. The idea that he would serve time for losing his job infuriated him. "I can't go to prison!" he shouted. "I can't support my family in prison!"

Brackett had not expected such an outburst of hopelessness tinged heavily with the threat of violence. He thought Sam was more passive. Realizing Sam was dangerously unpredictable, Brackett became anxious, but not alarmed enough to encourage Sam to give himself up. Instead, he calmly pointed to the gathering crowd outside and began his seduction. "Look out there."

The parking lot was becoming a frantic circus. Along with police, media, and paramedics—a growing mass of local people had gathered. Some were there to offer sympathy, and assistance if necessary. Some were there to enjoy the excitement. Some were parents of the hostage children, clearly in distress.

Sam stared at them with awe. No one had ever noticed Sam Baily before, and now that they did—it was for all the wrong reasons.

Brackett whispered into Sam's ear with a conspiratorial tone that passed for wise counsel, "See those people? Not the cops. Not the news media. The people. That's public opinion; it's a powerful force." Sam was not sure what Brackett meant. He saw a crowd of people waiting for his next move, and he became deeply afraid. Brackett continued with his lesson. "But here's our problem. Those people? They hate your guts. You're holding kids hostage. They think you're some kind of a nut."

That was exactly what troubled Sam. "I'm not! I mean, not usually," he said. "Jenny always says that I don't think."

Jenny was Sam's wife and mother of his children. For years Jenny Baily had encouraged Sam to think things through before he acted. In the past he tried, but when the pressure was on, he reacted impulsively. Sam could not think about Jenny right now, however. That would be too painful.

Brackett saw the pain of a man who had been tripped up by a fatal flaw that he had worked hard to overcome. For a moment, Brackett sympathized. In the past, he had tried to beat his own Achilles' heel. He shrugged. People could not escape something so fundamentally a part of themselves—even if they wanted to. Brackett assumed a convincingly paternal tone. "Right. You're not crazy, and you're not a terrorist. You're just an ordinary guy who popped his top. You think some of them haven't lost a job, or don't know somebody who's lost a job? They'll understand you. If they get the chance."

Hearing this, Sam felt a lot less alone. Sure, he had overreacted and messed up. But according to Brackett, there were a lot of people who would sympathize with his mistake. Maybe he was not going to lose everything today after all. Sam looked at the crowd in the parking lot in a new light as Brackett continued his pitch. "The one thing you might want to do before you give up is let those people know what you're about."

Sam thought that was a great idea, but how could he share his story while he was trapped inside the museum? Brackett offered a method. "If I had my camera, I could interview you. You could tell the people what's going on in your head. I think they'd like to know."

Brackett saw that Sam grasped the value of his suggestion. Brackett felt that everything was starting to come together.

One of the schoolchildren sneezed, and Sam looked over at them. They were just a little older than his kids. With a possible resolution to the crisis in sight, he began to feel guilty for frightening them.

Brackett saw the emotion in Sam's face and knew he could get something out of it. He needed Sam to do something concrete. For if he talked Sam into a television interview, he had no way of knowing if he could get it on the air. Television and law-enforcement authorities normally frowned upon giving terrorists and criminals air time. If Brackett could offer the freedom of a hostage, he would ease his way onto the air by making the authorities a deal they would have difficulty refusing.

"Sam, as a good faith gesture I would want you to release one of the kids. They do something for you, you do something for them. Okay?"

Sam had no problem with Brackett's recommendation. He had more hostages than he wanted anyway.

Chapter Eleven

Sheriff Lemke was the center of attention as he talked with the gunman over his cellular phone. Members of the press, onlookers, and family members all wanted to hear. At the moment there was not a lot of progress. The sheriff, not impressed by the gunman's idea, said, "I cannot put a hostage taker on TV."

Inside the museum lobby, Sam kept his eyes on Brackett as he spoke with the cop. Sam was not watching the reporter in fear that he would run or posed a threat, but because Brackett coached him thoroughly on the negotiation. Brackett warned that the authorities would not just give him an interview for the asking. His initial request rejected, Sam raised his offer, as instructed, and made the deal more appealing. "As a good faith gesture, I will let one child go. Once Mr. Brackett has put me on TV I will consider releasing the others."

Sheriff Lemke shot back, "Let everyone go first."

Sam was not prepared for a counteroffer. He covered the mouthpiece and whispered to Brackett for help. "He says to let everyone go first." Brackett did not say a word, but gave Sam a theatrical scowl to encourage him to get tough with the cop. Sam understood, gave Brackett a complicitous smile, and then overdid it by screaming into the phone like a madman, "Look, don't fuck with me, or—"

Brackett grabbed the phone from Sam before he dug himself a hole neither man could climb out of. "Sheriff, this is Max Brackett. Look, I know the rules about these things but—"

Lemke interrupted him. The sheriff had been seriously disturbed by the gunman's outburst—he was afraid things were about to melt down. "Mr. Brackett, is he listening?" Brackett lied and told Lemke that Sam was not listening. The sheriff wanted to know if the gunman was aiming his weapon at the reporter—was he talking under duress?

Brackett did his best to soothe everyone's nerves. "No, sir. Listen, I think I can guarantee that Mr. Baily is sincere in his offer. I also think things are going to become increasingly unstable in here if you don't grant him this air time."

Sam listened, frightened by what he heard. Brackett saw his fear and smiled to show that he was talking purely for effect. Sam relaxed a bit.

Lemke could not relax, however. It was against all the rules to put a criminal on the air. On the other hand, he could see the parents' torment. If one child was set free—if his kids had been among the hostages—wouldn't that be worth it? "Brackett. I don't like to do this."

Brackett tried to reassure the cop. "I know you don't."

Lemke looked around and decided. "All right. But I want this over with quick. Do you understand?"

Brackett understood. He had just been given the exclusive of the year—possibly the opportunity of a career.

A few minutes later, as Brackett started outside to

get a video camera for the interview, Sam followed
him to the door, awkwardly holding the rifle and his
large canvas bag. Brackett assumed the bag had held
the gun, but he could see that it was still full of something. He needed to know what it was before he went
out and met the police. "They're going to want to
know exactly what they're dealing with. What's in
the bag?"

Sam hesitated as though he were embarrassed. Then
he unzipped the bag, revealing countless sticks of dynamite. Brackett was truly startled. "Jesus. What are
these for?"

Brackett began to think the situation through from
an entirely new perspective. If this guy had gone out
of his way to horde all these explosives, he might not
be the fool he was making himself out to be. Sam
responded as though he had a perfectly reasonable
answer. "My brother-in-law uses 'em to clear stumps
from his farm." Brackett was not completely reas-
sured. Then Sam realized that his explanation was incomplete. "I wanted Mrs. Banks to believe I was
serious. I thought they might impress her."

Brackett did not experience pangs of conscience
often. He was a driven journalist who did not mind
bending the rules if the story occasioned it. There
were, however, still some standards he followed. The
dynamite was a problem. He looked at the schoolchildren and sought Sam's reassurance. "Everybody's
going to be okay in here, right? The kids, and you,
and this?"

Sam could see that Brackett was worried about the
explosives. "I just want to get outta here."

Sam stepped forward to open the door for Brackett.
The reporter pushed him away. "You might want to

stay away from doors and windows," he said. It took Sam a moment to understand.

He swallowed hard, but felt a little better knowing that Brackett was looking out for his well-being. Then Sam was troubled by another possibility. "How do I know you're gonna come back?" Maybe Brackett had arranged this interview business so he could escape.

The reporter almost laughed. He answered the question as honestly as he knew how. "Because you are the best show in town."

Sam hesitated. He wanted to say something but could not quite get the words out. Brackett waited and then gestured for Sam to hurry up. Sam asked a favor. "I wonder if you could check on my wife. This is gonna set her off big time."

Brackett was thrown for a loop again. He could not remember the last time he had been surprised so many times on one story. Maybe he did not know everything there was to know after all. Here was a guy holding hostages—and he was scared his wife was going to be angry with him. What a world. "Sure. The press'll be all over her. I'll put out the word that you want her to talk only with me. If that's okay?"

"Sure. She's never going to forgive me for this."

After giving Sam an encouraging pat on the shoulder, Brackett stepped outside and closed the door behind him. Sam looked out the window, saw the siege, and then looked back at his captives. Without Brackett there to advise him, Sam began to feel lost.

Not at all sure what to do, Sam went back to the security desk and turned on the television. He watched a live broadcast that showed Brackett outside as the sun began to set. Sam switched the channel, wondering what else was on, and found another live news report showing Brackett walking toward a group of policemen. Sam smiled when he saw how much coverage his story was getting. If he had been asked why he was happy, however, he could not have answered. The truth was that all these people were there because of him. He had done something, and for the first time in his life people had been forced to take notice. Sam was worried, confused, and scared. But he also tasted a kind of power that he never imagined—and that gave him energy to go on.

Brackett strutted down the steps of the museum like a prize fighter entering a ring, certain of victory. His confidence was obvious, and Sheriff Lemke crossed his path, demanding to know what was going on inside.

Brackett savored the moment. He was the source, and everyone relied on him. "His name is Sam Baily, and he's got enough dynamite in there to level the place. Don't piss him off."

Lemke was astonished. The explosives changed things drastically.

While Lemke recovered from his shock and contemplated his options, Brackett walked around the sheriff and addressed a gathering of worried parents. Without consciously planning to do so, Brackett let various camera crews encircle him. He maneuvered so that the yellow school bus from the ill-fated field trip made an effective backdrop. Brackett spoke as though he was in charge of the crime scene. "Your children are fine, and we're doing everything we can to resolve this situation."

An irritated father was confused. "And who the hell are you?" he said. Brackett identified himself, and the parent became furious. "Well, that makes sense. The police don't have any control, so some newsguy is running things."

The angry father had unintentionally hit a nerve.

Brackett corrected him quickly. "I'm not . . . I'm not running anything."

But the father had support from other anxious parents. Encouraged, he thought it was time to save his son if no one else was going to try. "So what happens if I decide to walk up to that door and get my son?"

Brackett knew that would be disastrous. Who knew what reaction that would elicit from Sam. "That wouldn't be a very good idea." The angry father wanted to know what he meant. But Brackett could not tell him that Sam Baily might well give up if confronted by an angry parent.

And that would ruin his wonderful scoop.

Fortunately, Sheriff Lemke had gathered his wits and reasserted himself into the confrontation. "Sir, if you walked into that museum, you might get your fool head blown off your shoulders. Now let's break this up and back off."

Moving away from the worried parents, Brackett headed toward the KXBD van as reporters shouted questions to him. He enjoyed the attention and the envy. After being down on his luck for some time, Max Brackett had the world where he wanted it. Laurie met him before he reached the truck and whispered into his ear, "Don't talk to the press. Network's orders. We're going national from now on."

For an instant, Brackett was infuriated. He had found the story. Who the hell was CBN to tell him what to do? This was, after all, the same network that dismissed him, saying he was no longer fit to be a national correspondent. Brackett felt the bile build in his chest. He briefly considered turning to someone from ABC or CBS and offering them his exclusive. Then, after reconsidering, Brackett realized his vindication only counted if he could beat Kevin Hollander on the anchorman's home turf. He grinned at the hovering reporters and decided to stick with CBN. "Sorry, guys. We're exclusive. Turn us on and you'll learn everything I know."

Arriving at the van, Laurie handed Brackett an earpiece, fixed his hair, and then put the camera package onto her shoulder. Brackett mussed his hair mildly, hoping to convey the image of someone who had just survived a traumatic incident. A member of the support staff turned on Brackett's wireless microphone and gestured to him. The red light shone on Laurie's camera. Brackett gave the television audience a stoical look. He looked brave—intrepid even—but fully aware of the terrible circumstances he was reporting. He would tell them the bad news, but he would not enjoy doing it.

Back at the station, Mort Dohlen saw Brackett's image come up on the live feed, and he welcomed his associate back onto the air. "Max, it's good to see you safe. This is a remarkable job you're doing."

Soon the images of Max Brackett flew into the homes of ordinary Americans at the speed of light. He was a welcome sight to most viewers, and they were captivated by his performance. Max Brackett had been in the middle of a terrible hostage situation, and now was filling them in on the details. This was better than the prepackaged news and more compelling than anything else that might go on the air that evening.

In one midtown Manhattan building, however, Brackett's extraordinary reporting was not welcome. Kevin Hollander sat at his darkened broadcast desk and watched the feed coming in from Madeline, California. Merton and Frank were standing behind Hollander, also watching the report. Important decisions had to be made, and Frank was considering the options. "Should we fly Broyles in if this thing takes a hold?" Roger Broyles was a leading CBN national correspondent who covered the best stories.

Merton opened his cell phone and punched the speed dial button for the director of the news division. "I'll ask, but what for? Brackett was born for this story." Merton began to talk quietly on the phone.

Frank watched Brackett reporting from the hostage site. He could not help but love what he was seeing. "Look at him. He's a pig in shit. Did anyone ever feel him out for anchor work?"

Hollander was watching the same monitor but his reaction was decidedly different. "That's an anchor? Look at him. I wouldn't even buy a new car from him."

Merton had been put on hold and added his two cents' worth. "He'd never sit at a desk. He wanted to be where the bullets were flying. Then, of course, he got too hot to keep around after your little incident."

Hollander's blood pressure started to rise. He could not believe the bullshit he was hearing. "Little incident? Are we all suffering from memory loss here?"

Merton was not listening, however. He thought Brackett was doing a terrific job. "He's older now. Maybe he's mellowed out."

Kevin Hollander saw a real problem headed his way. Brackett was riding the kind of story that made careers and sometimes even resurrected them. He swore and turned away from his two staffers, perceiving a threat in their admiration of his fallen rival.

Frank raised the volume and watched as Mort Dohlen interviewed Brackett. ". . . and yet I understand that you are going back inside the museum."

"Mr. Baily has agreed to that."

Dohlen could not help but brag on the air. "So KXBD will be the exclusive conduit of information."

Brackett ignored the anchorman's showboating and kept the focus where he wanted it. "But the important news is that in exchange, Mr. Baily has agreed to release one of the children."

Sam flipped off the television and looked at his young hostages. Which child should be set free? Sam could not make up his mind and turned to their teacher. "Maybe the girl in the glasses . . . ?"

At twenty-five, Kelly Rose found herself in the kind of crisis she could never have imagined. This was her second year of teaching, and she had bonded firmly with her classroom of fourth-graders. They, in turn, were equally in love with her. Kelly was uniquely enthusiastic. Her eagerness made for creative lesson plans. Her students learned to enjoy education instead of just tolerating it.

Having grown up in Madeline and having attended the same school where she now taught, Kelly had looked forward to the trip to the natural history museum. Any sort of field trip was a luxury in an era of fiscal parsimony, but the young teacher had lobbied the principal aggressively and organized a car wash to raise the money for the short bus trip.

During Mrs. Banks's welcoming lecture, Kelly had begun to worry that she had miscalculated. The kids were bored. But Kelly attributed their reaction more to the curator's stolid speech than to the students themselves. She planned to take her students through the museum item by item on her own when Mrs. Banks finished. She knew she could show them something more than the older woman could.

And then madness had erupted in this most unlikely

of places. Now the gunman was demanding her advice as to which child to set free. Kelly might have been a young and inexperienced teacher, but she was not going to let her kids see her intimidated. Warily, but firmly, she answered the gunman's question about releasing Marie Sanchez. "You're asking me?"

Sam was. He thought he was doing something nice, but was surprised by the teacher's reaction. He tried to explain. "But I have to pick one."

Kelly was disarmed by his unthreatening approach. She had seen him shoot a man and yell wildly over the phone. Yet, as he talked to her now, he seemed reasonable and even apologetic. Kelly decided that her best bet was to soothe his nerves. She adopted the steady tone that she normally used to a misbehaving student. "Do you have any children?"

Sam had two.

"Could you bear saving just one?"

She was right. Sam could not deny it and began to feel ashamed. How would he have felt if someone had taken his children captive? But something made him uncomfortable. He was the guy who lost his job. He had been the victim. And now, suddenly, he was the bad guy. He could see that in the young woman's eyes. Kelly Rose was putting on a brave show, but she was scared of him.

Kelly saw Sam hesitate and knew she had broken through. He looked embarrassed. Kelly was familiar with that look, saw it often on students who had done something wrong, but felt misunderstood. Maybe she could end the crisis here and now by reasoning with him. "Let them all go. That's how you'll get the people to sympathize with you."

Sam would have loved to say yes. He would have

been happy to let this nice young lady go and even Mrs. Banks.

Kelly stared at Sam and tried to encourage him to do the right thing.

But Sam was confused. If Brackett had been inside the museum at that moment, Sam would have asked for help in ending the standoff. Without the reporter's advice, however, he did not feel comfortable making a decision on his own.

Chapter Twelve

Brackett was still on the air, wrapping up the latest live segment. ". . . and hopefully that will soon be followed by a resolution." The camera light went off, and Brackett moved out of its eye and back toward the truck.

Laurie bounded over to Brackett, her feelings well beyond that of mere admiration. "Max, we scooped everybody!" Laurie was genuinely thrilled and wanted Brackett to be as delighted as she was. She felt like hugging him and jumping up and down. They were riding a story that was destined for the network.

Brackett was unexpectedly tense. "What the hell was that stunt?" She had no idea what he was talking about. Brackett explained, "The wounded guard. What did you think you were doing?"

"I was rescuing him!"

Brackett cut her down with a harsh reprimand. "You are a journalist covering a story. You do not become part of the story."

Humiliated by the man whose approval she so desired, all Laurie could manage was "But he was hurt."

Brackett was not a man given to nurturing. He was, however, a trained observer and instantly realized that he had been too tough on the young woman. Brackett needed Laurie. He knew she could not perform to her full abilities if she was upset. Taking her gently by the shoulders, Brackett tried to win her back. "You could've gotten killed. I need you with me and in the loop."

While he knew Sam would never have taken a shot at Laurie while she rescued Cliff, the explanation served his purpose. Laurie was comforted, and she smiled back at him. Brackett was pleased. She was now ready to go back to work.

A crew member climbed out of the news van and offered Brackett the phone. Lou Potts was calling from the station. Brackett said, "Lou? Having fun?"

Lou Potts was not having fun. And as much as he may have disliked Brackett, he was calling to perform an ethical obligation that came with the job. "As your boss, I have to tell you that you don't have to go back into the museum."

Brackett was familiar with the speech and knew that Potts was flying on autopilot. Brackett cut Lou off before he could finish his sermon. "Yes, I do have to go back inside. You know I do." What kind of newsman would stay away from something this good?

Potts was exasperated; this was turning out to be a hell of a day. "Jesus, Max. I send out for a piece of fluff and you come back with a hostage situation."

Potts may have been expressing aggravation, but Brackett took his comment as a compliment. "I guess I'm just not one of those fluffy kind of reporters."

Potts knew that all too well and sighed. He asked for the bottom line, and Brackett filled him in. "The guy's a straight arrow. Probably feels guilty when he jaywalks. Loses his job, flips out, now he's the Terminator."

"What does he want, Max?"

Brackett thought a moment—approached the question from a few different angles—then continued. It was remarkably simple. "His job. To be heard."

Potts thought of the long night ahead of them and was not happy. "And we're stuck in the middle," he said.

Brackett's disgust was apparent. No wonder Lou Potts had never made it to the majors. "Hey. You don't want him, fine. I don't have a contract with you. I'll go to another channel."

Potts might not have objected to that idea. He much preferred going home at the usual time, having dinner, and going to bed. But it was too late for that. "The network called. Looks like you're back in the big saddle, cowboy."

For most people it would have been an unlikely reaction. As the lives of a dozen children and two innocent adults hung in the balance—and just prior to walking into a volatile standoff—Max Brackett celebrated quietly. The network had called, and he was going to appear again on a national feed.

After years of wandering in a professional desert, Max Brackett was back. He vowed never again to let anything detour him from his rightful place in the broadcast hierarchy.

Chapter Thirteen

Some time later, Brackett was loaded down with camera equipment and food as he made his way back into the museum. At the top of the steps, he turned to the crowd and paused just long enough to strike a heroic pose. The mass of onlookers were impressed. The veteran news media, however, knew a ham when they saw one, and all swore silently.

Sam was relieved to welcome the reporter back into the lobby. As Brackett set his gear down, he was all business. They had to keep the show moving, "Okay. Who gets to leave?"

The two men scanned the schoolchildren, all of whom looked deserving of release. Forced to make a decision, Sam pointed to a blond girl named Michelle Berger. "Maybe her."

Brackett was pleased by the choice. The kid was photogenic, practically an angel. He could already hear the television audience gasping as this all-American embodiment of childhood innocence darted down the museum steps to freedom and into her parent's arms.

The liberation of little Michelle Berger might be precisely the thing he needed for an Emmy.

Brackett's mind raced with the possibilities. There

was a lot to organize, and he was trying to stay several
decisions ahead.

"Good. Now let's give them two kids."

Sam did not understand. Had Brackett gone over
to the other side? Could he no longer be trusted?

The reporter could see distrust growing in Sam and
took him through his reasoning. "Look, you shot a
black man. Some people are going to make an issue
of that. You show kindness to a black kid, and it'll be
harder to play the race card against you."

Sam was stunned by the logic of the idea, and he
beamed at Brackett with undisguised admiration.

The scene played on television just as Brackett had
hoped. Two lovely little girls, Michelle and Bonnie,
one white and one black, ran down the steps of the
museum, holding hands and yelling for their mothers.

What could not be seen on television, however, was
that once the two kids passed the cameras, they were
effectively cut off from their parents by an impenetra-
ble mass of media personnel. Intimidated by the lights,
noise, and reporters shouting at them, the two little
girls stopped where they were, and their joy turned to
confusion. Their mothers could not make any headway
through the crowd, either. Separated by a jostling
group of journalists, crew people, and bulky equipment, the mothers and daughters could not reach
each other.

Brackett, Sam, Mrs. Banks, Kelly, and the remaining children observed the bedlam. When Michelle
and Bonnie began to cry, Sam herded his hostages to
another room, turned off the television, and went to
join his captives.

A half an hour later, Brackett had set up his camera
in a corner away from the hostages. Sam stood in a

rigid pose, trying to look at ease and failing miserably. He answered Brackett's questions haltingly and with earnest conviction. "I came in about twenty minutes late. See, we won a softball game the night before and had a party afterwards, so when Mrs. Banks said she wanted to see me—"

Brackett interrupted. "Skip the party." The party was irrelevant. Better not to give the other side any ammunition.

Sam did not understand. He had nothing to hide. "It's true. I had been partying."

Brackett patiently explained his reasoning to Sam. "Is that why you were fired?"

Sam said that was so.

Brackett steered him back on track. "Then let's not give that impression. Just start with 'Mrs. Banks asked to see me . . .'"

Sam shot an indignant look over at Mrs. Banks, who watched the interview from where she was standing. "She's not the type to ask. She tells. It's like the dinosaurs. Her great-granddaddy put 'em up and that's good enough for her."

Sam would have gone on about Mrs. Banks's failings, but that would have made him seem resentful. Audiences could accept honest, passionate anger. There was something heroic about a man standing up for himself. But Brackett realized bitter resentment was less appealing. It would make Sam appear to be an angry malcontent.

Brackett interrupted and directed Sam back onto course. "Hey, Sam. Let's not get lost in the details."

Sam listened and took a moment to collect his thoughts before continuing. "So she called me in and said the museum couldn't afford to pay two security guards, and they were going with Cliff. Cliff's been here longer. I tried to tell her I was willing to cut my hours or something, but she wouldn't listen."

From her post several yards away, Mrs. Banks was listening. Despite being armed and possibly dangerous, Sam was still Sam, and try as she might, Mrs. Banks could not hold back any longer. "Sam, did it ever occur to you that I might be here to deal with problems a bit bigger than your personal economics? That my job is running a museum, not running my employees' lives?"

Brackett noted the curator's audacity. She did not back down from a fight. Commendable under normal circumstances perhaps, but at the moment pretty damn stupid. Not that she was necessarily wrong—she made a good point. But her irritating manner overwhelmed any argument. Brackett was relieved when Sam did not become upset. Instead, he stood up for himself with hurt nobility. "You would not see me."

Mrs. Banks corrected him. "At that particular moment."

"No. Don't turn it around."

Mrs. Banks had never said that she would be willing to talk to Sam at a later date. She had fired him regretfully, but with no room for further discussion. And here she was trying to make herself look good on TV.

Sam was riled, but Mrs. Banks did not restrain herself. "You only want things your way."

Sam blew his top. He shouted at his former employer with a child's defiance, "No. You're wrong!"

Brackett jumped between the two of them and tried to cool things down by ushering Mrs. Banks to a far corner of the museum. "Mrs. Banks, why don't you make sure these buffalo are grazing properly."

A stickler for detail, even when her life was being

saved, Mrs. Banks could not help correcting him. "Bison—not buffalo."

If Brackett had a rifle in his hands and had toiled for someone like her over the years, he would have been sorely tempted to empty a few rounds in her direction. Brackett discovered new appreciation for Lou Potts and sympathy for Sam Baily.

But Sam was glowering in the curator's direction, so Brackett distracted the gunman by turning his attention back to the interview. He asked, "What did you feel? At the very moment you were let go?"

Sam gave the question some thought, and his anger dissolved into a weary smile. "You know that trip meter on your car, where you push that button and—zip—the miles go back to zero? I swear I saw one of those in my head. I couldn't tell my wife. I've been dressing for work every day like a fool. Then I'd hide out at the movies, all day. Killing time, eating popcorn and thinking."

Brackett thought that was good material, the odometer an effective image. People would understand. He was pleased, for he had not expected a guy like Sam to be so articulate. Brackett wanted more. "And today, you came back here. What did you want?"

All Sam wanted was for Mrs. Banks to listen to him. Fair enough. But now Brackett had to ask the big questions. "Did you want to hurt her?"

"Not really . . ."

Brackett winced at this answer. "Not really" wasn't good enough. Sam's response had to be an absolute no, I did not mean to hurt anyone.

Noting Brackett's reaction, Sam edited his reply. "I mean—no."

Sam was catching on. Brackett pushed a little harder. In truth, it was not much of a risk because if

Sam screwed up the answer, Brackett could simply edit the tape and ask again. But he knew the audience demanded hard questions if they were to believe that they were watching an honest interview. "Come on, Sam, you grabbed a gun and a bag full of explosives. Why?"

That was a tough question Sam could not answer. Frustrated, Sam tapped back into his overwhelming sense of futility and fury. "I don't know!" he shouted.

Not good enough. No audience in America would believe him. Brackett shot back at him, "You have to know. What was going through your head?"

"I was thinking about my babies."

Jackpot. Extreme behavior in the defense of family was forgivable, even sympathetic, possibly admirable. Brackett was pleased. "That's good. What about 'em? Tell me about your babies."

Sam stopped performing and responded from the heart. "What was going to happen to them if I lost my job? I could lose the house."

Excellent material. Most people in America shared the same fear at some point. Brackett gestured for Sam to go on.

Sam did. "And I could lose my benefits. How I'm s'posed to protect them. I guess that's what I was thinking about."

"And what do you want?"

"I just want to be left alone! I want everybody out there to go away and I want to forget this ever happened."

Brackett was not sure how this would play with viewers. Would they scorn Sam's naiveté or like him for it? Brackett stared at Sam and saw that he was for real. The reporter hated to admit it, but for some strange reason Sam's innocence made him want to protect him.

Still, the drama needed to be clear. Sam had to make specific, attainable demands that were easy to understand. "Ask for a million bucks or a plane to South America," Brackett said. "You might get that. But they won't just let you walk away."

But Sam had no ulterior motives and would not budge from his position. He was not there for money or to escape. All he wanted was to go on with his life as it had been.

While Brackett and CBN had an exclusive with Sam Baily, there was nothing to stop other networks from pursuing the story by different means. As Brackett taped the interview inside the natural history museum, other stations and other reporters tried to track down anyone who ever had anything to do with the crazed gunman.

Sam, his wife, Jenny, and their two daughters lived in a modest section of Madeline. Their neighborhood was made up of neatly kept, mainly single-story homes built just a little too close to each other, some with porches, most with kids and animals on the front lawns.

A small army from the press camped out on Sam Baily's lawn. No one inside Sam's house had responded to telephone calls or the doorbell. So the media tracked down neighbors and put them on the air as instant experts regarding the tortured mind of the crazed Madeline gunman.

As television lights obscured the night sky, Maria Diaz of CBS affiliate Channel Two straightened her turquoise jacket and checked over her notes. As the segment producer called the countdown, Diaz gazed solemnly into a video camera and began her report. "I am in front of Sam Baily's house, and I am joined by Trevis Bartholomew, his best friend."

Bartholomew stepped forward eagerly, thrilled to be on camera. Wearing a reversed baseball cap and an unbuttoned flannel shirt, Bartholomew looked like a California version of a hillbilly. While he and Sam were neighbors, the two men would never have been mistaken for friends. Sam Baily did not have a lot of money, but he had a certain integrity—even when he was holding a dozen schoolchildren hostage. Conversely, Bartholomew was standing in his own neighborhood, doing nothing against the law, but was a substantially less likable figure than his "crazed gunman" neighbor. Grinning with delight at his new found celebrity, Bartholomew addressed the world. "That's right. I know Sam real well. We've been fishing and stuff."

Behind him, neighborhood clods waved to the television audience—proudly celebrating the good fortune of one of their own. Diaz tried to ignore them and encouraged her subject to give her the answer she wanted. "What's he like? Is he weird or what?"

It took some time for the question to permeate Trevis Bartholomew's thick skull. But after looking dully at Diaz for a while, he realized that she was expecting him to give her something juicy. Bartholomew was happy to cooperate if it meant he stayed on camera for a while longer. "Well. He is kind of weird, you know?"

Inside the Baily home, Jenny and her mother, Betty, peered outside at the circus ruining their front lawn. Jenny was an attractive thirty-three-year-old who wore her blond hair up, and dressed in sensible clothing from discount stores. Holding her baby daughter,

Sally, in her arms, Jenny watched the delight in four-year-old Joey's face as he marveled at the commotion. He could never understand what was going on, and she did not bother to try to explain. She herself could barely comprehend the disaster that had befallen the family. Her mother, Betty, looked around the simply furnished but comfortable home and shook her head. It would never be the same.

They returned to the couch in front of the television and watched as another reporter, Bill Peterson from the NBC affiliate, interrupted Maria Diaz's interview and began one of his own. "Does he have a temper?" Peterson asked.

Bartholomew was beginning to catch on. He did not actually have to know anything specific about the subject. The reporters told him what they wanted to hear by inserting the answer they desired in the question. Feeling like an old pro, Bartholomew gave them what they wanted. "A temper? Yeah, I've seen him have a real temper . . ."

Peterson continued. "So you'd call him dangerous?"

Bartholomew laughed as a friend began to make obscene gestures and goofed off for the camera. "Dangerous? Well. You know. Whatever. Sure. Yeah."

Betty swore quietly and Jenny turned to her. "He is not Sam's friend," she said.

Jenny and her mother watched as a reporter walked past Bartholomew and approached the front door. A moment later, Jenny and Betty were flustered by the reporter's pounding on the door. Simultaneously, the noise could be heard over the TV. Joey thought it was really something. "Mommy, look! We're a TV show."

He did not understand why his mother broke down and began to cry. The noise at the door—and from the TV—increased the tension even further. Something had to change. Betty looked for a way to quiet things down. "Maybe if we talked to a few of them." She thought it was a reasonable idea. If the reporters were tossed a few tidbits, they might be satisfied and lessen their assault.

But Jenny had spoken earlier to Brackett on the phone and had agreed to give him exclusive rights to interview her. "No! Mr. Brackett said to talk just to him. He said it would be better for Sam."

Neither Jenny nor her mother understood why talking only to Brackett would make things better for Sam. They had never been in a spot like this before, and they decided that if Sam had befriended this reporter, they would do whatever he asked. If they had to, they would sit in the house all night and take the onslaught as best they could. But the baby started to cry, further frazzling Jenny's nerves. "How could Sam do this to us?" she cried. "How am I going to face everybody at work tomorrow?"

On TV, behind the gloating Bartholomew, Jenny could see a reporter cross her lawn and try to peer in through the living room window. Jenny lost her composure. "She's standing in my flowers. Oh, well, that does it!" Racing over to a window, she called out to the intrusive reporter, "Excuse me! Could you not stand in the flowers!"

The reaction was not what she expected. Instead of being cowed with embarrassment or at least slightly courteous, a wave of reporters stampeded across the lawn. Joining their colleague, trampling Jenny's flowers, they stood beneath the window, looking up at Sam Baily's wife—hungry for an interview, an anecdote, a scrap, anything.

Across town, another interview subject was being targeted. The news director at KCTE had pulled Nat

Jackson off an interview with the mayor of San Francisco and sent him to the Madeline hospital, where Cliff Williams was undergoing emergency surgery. Nat was a reporter who brought intensity and intelligence to his work. More important to the news director, however, Jackson was African American. The news director wanted an exclusive with the wounded security guard and any family members, and she had an angle on the story and thought Jackson was the man to close the deal.

After hearing that Cliff had been shot, Diane Williams had called her mother to baby-sit while she rushed to her husband's side. Now, hours later, she knew little more than when she had arrived.

Diane Williams was married to Cliff for ten years. They had met in Sacramento when he retired from the army after injuring his back during a training exercise. Diane had been Cliff's physical therapist, and they had moved to her hometown of Madeline shortly after their engagement. Diane still worked for the Veterans Administration, but had taken the day off to care for their daughter, Dee, who had been hard hit by the flu. Diane had never imagined that anything serious could happen to Cliff on the job. He had survived five years in the military, so she never worried about him when he left for work in the morning. Now she wished she had been more anxious. Maybe Cliff would have been more attentive and not now undergoing surgery to have a bullet taken out of his stomach.

Diane Williams had wanted nothing to do with the press when they converged upon her at Mercy Hospital. The staff provided her a refuge in a tiny, but private, waiting room. The persistence of the press, however, finally wore her down. They stood outside the waiting room, knocking on the door and peering inside whenever possible. When the hospital public relations representative recommended that she talk to one reporter, she had given in and agreed to talk to Nat Jackson, whom she had watched for years on TV. Jackson consoled her, offered sympathy when she cried, and opened his interview with softball questions. Diane felt comforted by his presence and began to relax.

When Jackson saw that his subject was softened up, he began the line of inquiry that interested his news director. "Your husband was kept on at the museum. The man who was let go—a white man—came back and shot him. Do you think race had anything to do with that?"

Diane was almost as surprised by the question as she was when she heard that Cliff had been shot. The whole idea that Cliff's shooting was a racial incident was entirely out of left field. Diane was almost speechless. After looking at the reporter to see if he was serious, Diane knew she had to respond. "Cliff and Sam were friends. Sam didn't blame Cliff for what happened. At least . . . I don't think he did."

Diane stumbled over her words, then stopped talking altogether. Nat Jackson had planted a seed in her mind, and suddenly Diane Williams was no longer sure of anything.

Chapter Fourteen

It was no exaggeration to say that most of Madeline's citizens had forgotten that there was a natural history museum in their community. Once a landmark of civic pride, the museum had lost the battle for Madeline's attention to shopping malls, television, and other distractions. That night, as working people came home, many flipped on the evening news and were reminded of the venerable institution in their midst.

What they saw, however, was something quite different from what Mrs. Banks would have preferred. The genteel institution had been transformed into a surreal scene of chaos. Police barricades cut off the museum building from the parking lot. A long line of police cars, trucks, and heavily armored officers created a fortified front surrounding the perimeter. Just inside the ring of cops was a burgeoning army of media: newspeople, trucks, vans, satellite dishes, and various support staff. Overhead a police helicopter monitored the situation from the air. Hovering above the police chopper was a news helicopter that allowed the television audience to scrutinize the official observers.

The scene was particular to the last decade of the twentieth century. Never before had audiences been witness to breaking news stories with such ease. Oswald's assassination had been a lucky fluke. Thirty years later the networks had dismissed their patrician embarrassment to embrace the value of live disaster. Since then, the Gulf War had been packaged for television, high-speed chases were a regular staple of some stations, and fallen football stars were pursued in the hope of capturing a suicide on the air. One network even broadcast a special showing a collection of the decade's greatest disasters—including helicopter and plane crashes, fires, and real people dying live on tape.

Disasters were now entertainment, in which audience members could participate; catastrophe had become interactive. Such was the state of the American Dream that citizens were willing to participate in nightmares—if only to be noticed for a moment. Numbed by years of confessional talk shows and voyeuristic news, America lost its sense of shame. The fifteen minutes of fame once sought by the attention starved had been downsized. Now, anybody could get on the air, if only for a moment. All a person had to do was act stupidly enough or insert oneself into a tragedy.

Progress was slow but sure in Madeline, California. The citizens of the community were no different from other Americans, and they wanted to be a part of something bigger than their own mundane lives. As people became aware of what was happening, they began to flock to the natural history museum. Why watch tragedy on television when you could see it in person? Why not become a part of history by being on the front lines? Parents brought their children, guys their girlfriends. Movie theaters emptied, and softball games were suspended.

Soon an excited mob of local people had gathered, waiting for the show to begin. Across the nation view-

ers settled in for a night of riveting entertainment.
Television and advertising executives were delighted
as ratings spiked. Even the most popular cop shows
and soaps could not compete with the drama unfolding in Madeline, a dream scenario.

At ground zero the crowds watched in surprise as
news crews suddenly bolted from their positions and
ran toward their trucks. Something big was about to
happen. One cameraman shouted to his colleagues,
"It's about to run." A reporter told his producer,
"Christ, I'm going to hate this." The question in the
producer's mind, however, was whether the reporter
was disgusted by what was about to happen—or
whether he was upset to have missed the scoop. Either
way, they all climbed into their vans and switched
their televisions to Channel Six, KXBD, Continental
Broadcasting for Madeline, California.

A promo for *The Gary Spangler Show* and its upcoming segment on "Women Who Fall in Love with
the Murderer of Their Children" faded to black, and
an edgy musical fanfare announced a KXBD Special
Report, "Inside the Siege." A moment later, a solemn-
looking Mort Dohlen came on screen and welcomed
the audience. "We now bring you this exclusive report. Max Brackett is . . . Inside the Siege."

Brackett appeared in his shirtsleeves, his tie slightly
askew. It was a look meant to convey a serious man
hard at work under difficult circumstances. Brackett
faced the camera gravely and began his introduction,
solemn but compassionate. "Your name is Sam Baily.
You're a loving husband and a devoted father of two.
You've got a mortgage, car payments, medical ex-
penses, food bills, electricity bills, gas bills, clothing
bills. Oh, and by the way. You're fired."

Sam performed as he had been directed. He exuded

regret, bewilderment, and most of all—the vulnerability of a victim. "I used to complain about my paycheck. Seemed to get smaller every week. Then all of a sudden, it was gone and I realized that little piece of paper was the only thing holding my life together."

Across America worried fathers and mothers were surprised by what they heard. They had expected the despicable ravings of a madman. Instead, they stared at a guy who looked something like them and seemed—well, kind of—nice. What's more he did not have a radical agenda. He was not protesting American involvement in some part of the world. He was not a fame-obsessed lunatic looking for a place in history. The crazed gunman holding those kids hostage somewhere in California was concerned about exactly the same matters that kept them up at night. Who had not wanted to strike back? In living rooms across the country, families decided to hear the man out.

Sam kept his eyes directed toward the camera lens. Brackett wanted him looking into the eyes of the audience. Otherwise Sam would seem shifty, as though he had done something wrong. Sam told his tale. "I'd see people living on the street and I thought, just junkies. Bums. But one day I saw a man and a woman and a few kids sitting on some cardboard behind this building. And I realized there were whole families on the street. I thought about my babies sleeping in a box and it made me crazy."

At a coffee shop outside Detroit the working-class clientele watched Sam as they finished their late-night dinners. They had worked for generations in the great automotive factories of the Rust Belt. Now their jobs were threatened and the security they once enjoyed lost forever. Some had seen homeless families; some shared the fear of losing their homes and the dreams for their kids' futures. They put down their forks and stopped talking. Expecting a lurid scene that presented a monster whose demise they could root for, they were dumbfounded to hear a man who seemed to speak for them.

No one spoke as Sam went on. "I watch TV. And I dunno, people are always flashing guns, and it gets people's attention. It wasn't like I was going to shoot anybody. I wasn't stealing money. I just wanted my boss to listen to me for five minutes. That's all."

Every man and woman in the Detroit coffee shop had entertained fantasies of shotgunning their employers. That was the way of the world. While they had never done anything about it, it was clear this Sam Baily had been pushed by a boss who did not care. Sam had not wanted to hurt anyone. He only wanted to make a point—then things had spun out of control. They watched some more.

"There's just nobody listening to guys like me anymore. It's like I'm supposed to just lie down and say, okay, run over me. Because no one cares. I'm just some guy who goes to work every day."

Outside the natural history museum, journalists allowed the crowd to watch the interview over their monitors as Sam went on. "I come from a good family. I do. No drugs, no trouble, we go to church. But I don't think we're going to make it. I really don't."

Within the besieged building a troubled Brackett watched Sam finish his statement. "And I don't think anybody cares. If me and my family fall off the face of the earth, does anybody care? Is anybody listening?"

At CBN headquarters in New York, Kevin Hollander watched the interview and had an idea. "Jesus. This guy shot a man in cold blood and is holding a bunch of fourth-graders at gunpoint, and I feel like I want to bring him home for Christmas dinner." Hollander's idea evolved into a plan. He turned to one of his staffers and gave instructions. "Let's run a nationwide poll on how this guy is playing. I bet he's stirring something up."

Hollander's attention returned to the TV monitor. He saw an exterior shot of the museum and the mob of media, law-enforcement authorities, terrified parents, and curious onlookers. Hollander frowned when Brackett reappeared on the screen and seemed to be talking directly to him. "Your name is Sam Baily and the full weight of the law is pushing in on you. You're trapped by an impulsive act into the fight of your life. Your sole demand is simple to the point of absurdity, yet dauntingly complex."

Sam came back on screen. "My demand is that the police, that everybody just forget about this and let me go home."

Brackett thought Sam had delivered the line well. Too bad the poor bastard didn't stand a chance in hell of ever having his demand fulfilled.

The crowd outside approved, and a murmur swept through the parking lot. Sheriff Lemke watched on a portable television and laughed ruefully. "Oh, that's beautiful," he said.

At Mercy Hospital, Diane Williams watched the interview as her husband lay in bed, still unconscious. Her arms wrapped around her husband's shoulders, she listened to Sam and tried to figure out how he could have done such a terrible thing. "I didn't mean to hurt Cliff," Sam said. "Cliff is my friend. I'm praying for him. And I know he'll forgive me when he gets better."

Jenny Baily and her mother watched as Brackett

panned his camera over to the children. They listened as Sam continued, "And the boys and girls in here, they're all fine. I would never, I swear . . . I mean, I've got kids of my own. I need a job to take care of them. And now, who's going to take care of them?"

Jenny's mother put a comforting arm around her daughter's shoulders and consoled her. Sam seemed now to speak directly to them. "I'm just saying that I'm sorry, I couldn't be sorrier, and I'm just hoping that everybody will just understand. Please, just understand the pressure I've been under here and . . . let me go. Just let me go. There. That's my demand. That's it, right there." Sam was no longer acting as Brackett had instructed him. He was sincere in his request. All he truly did want was for Cliff to be okay and for this nightmare to be over.

It was Brackett's turn. "Sam. People watching this right now, are saying, 'Yeah, right. The guy's holding a gun to a bunch of helpless kids. He should be hung.' What do you say to those people?"

Sam looked up, truly shocked. Hadn't he just explained how this had all come about? Didn't people understand him? Sam pondered Brackett's comment, then simply said, "I hope you never have to go through this." His frightened expression was more articulate than words.

Brackett wrapped up his report, giving a final spin to the story. "Your name is Sam Baily, and you're asking for the most poignant ransom of all: forgiveness. And while we all have it to give, we're not the law. Time stands still in this small corner of America tonight as we search our hearts. Reporting exclusively for KXBD, this is Max Brackett, Inside the Siege."

Across the country the ominous theme music surged, and Mort Dohlen reappeared to continue the broadcast. But inside the museum, the music and the anchorman could not be heard. Brackett turned off the TV and looked at Sam. Sam stared back, awed by how convincingly his story had been told. Brackett had delivered the goods, and Sam wanted to be told what to do next. Brackett's orders were concise. "Now we wait."

Sam shrugged and went to the window overlooking the parking lot, to see if anything had changed. Though unrealistic, part of him hoped that the crowds and police would have vanished. But, if anything, the crowd was larger. Their mood, however, was slightly altered, no longer hungry for blood. Somewhere in the crowd a person began strumming a guitar and sang a folk song. "Is anybody listening, does anybody care . . . ?"

Chapter Fifteen

As dawn broke over the California hills surrounding Madeline, Sheriff Alvin Lemke stood by the huge hangar of a private airplane leasing company. Lemke had spent the night at the museum parking lot, and the early morning chill made him shiver. As a sleek private jet landed and taxied toward the hangar, Lemke took some consolation in the fact that though the hostage incident was not over, at least it had not deteriorated. The sheriff was proud of his men and women. At the same time he was not unhappy that more experienced help was arriving.

The jet engines were turned off, and the morning seemed dangerously quiet as their turbines whirred to a stop. The door to the airplane opened. A stern and remarkably alert-looking man stepped out, walked confidently down the steps, and headed straight for Lemke. The man who had just arrived from Washington knew the sheriff's name. "Lemke?" The sheriff was surprised by the visitor's brusqueness. During his long career in law enforcement, most people addressed him respectfully as "Sheriff Lemke." Lemke detected a decline in his authority and involuntarily offered a crisp "Yessir." Lemke had not called anyone "sir" for a long time.

The new arrival did not waste time with an expansive greeting. Walking vigorously past the sheriff, the man waited impatiently for Lemke to keep up. Lemke did a double take, turned to follow, and was amazed to see a black van appear from nowhere. With Lemke just behind him, the man got down to business. "Special Agent Dobbins. FBI."

Lemke wanted to assure the federal agent that his department had done its job. "Yessir. The situation has been stable." There it was again—calling this guy "sir." Lemke frowned and made a mental note not to do it again.

Dobbins did not seem overly impressed. In fact, he seemed annoyed that Lemke felt the need to bring him up to date. "We have televisions in Washington. We know the situation." Dobbins grimaced as though he knew something more about the confrontation than Lemke did. That worried the Madeline sheriff. He looked nervously over his shoulder as the black van pursued them from a polite distance.

Dobbins led the sheriff to his Madeline Police Department car and took the driver's seat. Lemke was confused. Dobbins filled him in. "I'll drive." Usually no one drove the sheriff's car but Lemke. But he found that the special agent's authoritative tone prevented him from arguing. Lemke sat in the passenger seat as Dobbins continued, "Have the militias arrived yet?"

Militias? What was this guy talking about? Lemke wanted nothing to do with militias, and he replied timidly, "Jesus, no. At least I don't think so." He handed over his keys.

Dobbins was hardly reassuring. "They will." The special agent started the car and floored the accelerator. Lemke was thrust back in his seat as the police car pulled a U-turn and raced off to the siege.

*   *   *

At the same time, Kevin Hollander stepped from underneath the canopy outside his Upper East Side co-op building and into his chauffeur-driven town car.

His regular driver, like many in New York, was an immigrant who was proud to have clients like the world-famous CBN anchor. Hollander often discussed current events with the driver, who in turn believed that his proximity to celebrity validated his dreams. The driver was listening to talk radio. A caller was siding with Sam Baily. ". . . Judges can't handle it all. This guy, he's never broken a law in his life, he's under pressure we can all understand—I say let him walk."

Hollander was impressed. He was looking forward to talking with Merton and Frank. His suspicion that Sam Baily had touched a nerve looked like it was going to pan out. Hollander wanted to see the results of the overnight polls he had requested. Meanwhile, he listened as the program host took a more traditional view. "But who's going to monitor that specific point at which a passable offense becomes a crime?"

Hollander thought this was an excellent point. While it was fine to sympathize with Sam Baily—how could a society based on law function if he was forgiven? Hollander had a feeling that the man on the street was not interested in the details. He tested his theory on his driver. "This situation is a shame, isn't it? A man takes children hostage."

That was the bottom line—Sam Baily was a kidnapper. But that was not the point for the driver. "Mr. Hollander, I've been driving for fourteen hours, just trying to feed my family. This America—it can make you crazy."

Hollander listened. Here was a guy who worked

himself to the bone, and yet he was rooting for some moron with a gun who stepped outside of the rules. That had to mean something. Hollander made a decision—and the network was going to have to go along with him on this one.

As Hollander arrived at CBN headquarters, a number of executives already had been working for hours. High above Manhattan in an executive boardroom, Merton, Frank, and their staff were discussing a Madeline strategy. Merton, who was senior person in the room, used a remote to fast-forward a videotape. He was briefing the others on the bitter relationship between Max Brackett and their star anchorman.

The images moved too quickly for the others to get the whole impact. It was just as well, for the footage was the gruesome record of a tragic airplane crash from several years before. The men and women in the room watched images of burning debris on black ocean water, flotillas of fishing boats heading to sea, Coast Guard personnel giving interviews, and finally a casually dressed, somber Kevin Hollander.

Merton slowed the tape to regular speed. As the executives watched, Merton explained the bad blood between the two men who had once been allies and co-stars of the CBN pantheon. "Brackett got there first and hopped a fishing boat that was going out to the crash site. Hollander arrived in the morning just in time to grab Brackett as he came off the water. They were live—on the air."

The videotape showed a crisp-looking Hollander greeting a weary and pained Brackett. The tape had been shot several years previously, but Brackett looked older than he did on the current feed from Madeline. Brackett had been aged by his night on the water. His clothes were rumpled, but more to the point, his whole persona seemed haunted. Max Brackett, veteran of wars and tragedy, had seen something he had never fully understood before.

Having just arrived on the scene, Hollander was fresher and unaffected by the tragedy. He was there to do his job. "What was it like out there, Max? Describe it for us."

Brackett was running on autopilot and began to deliver his report. "Uh . . . Well, it's a real mess, as you can imagine. A lot of wreckage on the water. It was—"

Hollander interrupted Brackett midsentence. "Any bodies?"

The horror of what Brackett had seen was reflected in his face. But for the first time in his professional life, he did not want to describe what he had witnessed. Something had changed for him during the night—and Hollander's question vaguely irritated him. Hollander wanted to know if there were any bodies? Brackett told him, "Yes . . . Yes, there are."

Hollander continued on, unaware that something was stewing within the correspondent. "What was the condition of them, Max? Were they mutilated?"

"Well, we were looking for survivors so—"

He was not allowed to finish. The anchorman wanted something specific—something Brackett no longer thought he could give. Hollander told the reporter exactly what the audience was looking for in the way he phrased his question. "But did they seem to have suffered trauma? Were they broken up in any way?"

Brackett felt something raging within him. He was not sure what it was, but he concentrated furiously on keeping it down. It took everything he had not to lose his composure. "Well, they fell out of the sky, Kevin—"

That was not good enough for Hollander. He knew—everyone knew the victims of the crash had fallen out of the sky. Hollander, CBN, and the great television audience wanted specifics. Brackett had been out on the ocean all night in the middle of tragedy. As far as Hollander knew, no other reporter had seen what Brackett had seen. This was an exclusive. Hollander needed Brackett to get to the point. The anchor pushed his reporter further. "Any body parts?"

Brackett never thought anything could shock or horrify him. But now Hollander was asking questions that suddenly seemed obscene. Revulsion from Brackett's stomach surged to his mouth. "Excuse me, Kevin. I didn't copy that. You're asking me about body parts?"

Hollander knew his wording had to be careful. Absolutely, he wanted to hear about body parts—but he tried to rein back a bit—knowing that he could not sound too enthusiastically ghoulish. "Well, I don't mean to be grim, but we've heard reports of sharks being in the area."

Something burst within Max Brackett. After years of seeing the horrors of the world and bearing witness on behalf of his television audience, he could no longer play along. After seeing the broken humanity from the fallen airplane, Brackett had momentary insight into what he had become, attacking himself as well as the anchorman. "Grim? You don't sound grim, you sound ecstatic, but don't let the fact that the victims' families are probably watching this hold you back, there, Kev."

Hollander tried to reel him back. "Okay, Max, I can see you've had a tough night. Let's—"

But once Brackett had begun, there was no retreat. "No, I feel great. This is my job. Me and the twelve thousand other vultures that have flocked to the seashore. Put on your sad face, Kev, I'm ready to head back out." Live, on the air, Brackett walked up to his knees into the ocean. He turned back to the camera. "You want me to grab a gaff, see if I can snag you an arm or a leg?"

The cameraman and producer were stunned. In the news van the director and technicians did not move. Hollander tried to stop Brackett and return the report to the story at hand. But Brackett was mesmerizing in his self-hatred and was a force that could not be slowed down. "Let's give the people what they want."

Brackett stormed out of the water and threw a familial arm around Hollander's shoulders. Their disgrace was almost complete. Brackett's fury surged through millions of television sets across the country. He addressed those who were watching. "Isn't that right, folks? That's what you want. A little peep show. That's what old Kev is trying to give you."

The cameraman recovered from his shock and began to pan away, but Brackett followed the lens, making sure he stayed in frame. "Hey, where you going? That's why you're all glued to the boob tube, hoping to spot a body bag."

As the cameraman tried to back away, Brackett grabbed the moving lens, captured it, and held it still. In living rooms, kitchens, bedrooms, dens, bars, hotel rooms, boardrooms, and airport lounges—Max Brackett's outraged face glared into the eyes of his viewers and condemned them. His accusation was spit out with the disgust of a mad prophet before the apocalypse.

"America and her collective car wreck. Just can't look away, can you?"

And then a merciful technician absolved the audience by cutting the feed from the crash site and returning the nation to the comforting image of the *Wake Up, America!* show. A normally perky hostess stared slack jawed at her monitor until she realized she was on the air. After a stuttering start, she quickly regained her equilibrium—offering glossy condolences to the victims' families and apologies to her viewers.

Then the tape froze as Merton hit the pause key on his remote control. Everyone in the room was hypnotized by what they had seen. Frank asked the question even though he already had guessed the answer. "That went out over the air?" Every second of it had aired. It was hard to imagine that nobody bothered to cut the feed. At the time, however, everyone at the network had been just as spellbound as people in the boardroom today.

An idea creeped into Frank's mind. It was an inevitable development, but one lurid enough to make him hesitate. "It would be interesting to see them together again."

Merton had been thinking of nothing but that since the crisis broke. He agreed. "Good for two or three points." The overnight ratings had been a windfall. Add to their continuing coverage the reunion of two rival journalists, and the other networks would be left in their dust.

Before they could go further, Kevin Hollander entered the room. He was charged up with enthusiasm and waving the results from the overnight poll. As Merton discreetly turned off the VCR and the image of an incensed Brackett disappeared, Hollander began to sell them on his idea. "Fifty-nine percent of the American people are showing compassion for an armed felon! The guy is asking for forgiveness and they are saying, 'Sure, why not?'"

Frank wanted to appear slightly resistant to the idea that was sure to follow. "But we're covering it, Kevin. Brackett's interview was brilliant."

Merton played along. "You could double-team the story. You here and—"

That was not what Hollander had been thinking of. He wanted no part of Max Brackett ever again, for any reason. "I'm not sharing time with him! Max Brackett is a loose cannon."

Merton agreed and pronounced the story of insufficient interest and unpredictable duration.

Hollander was caught. He wanted the story, but did not want the competition. Still, he knew Brackett well enough and was certain that he could keep the story alive long enough for Hollander to fly in and take it over as his own. "No, Brackett won't let it be over," he said. "This has the potential to be a huge story. We should jump all over it. This guy's a poster child for the disenfranchised."

Merton and Frank looked at each other as though they were starting to be convinced of Hollander's argument. Merton began to see the logic. "Our numbers are way down with the working class." Frank finished his thought. "If this guy ends up speaking for them . . ." Merton played his role wonderfully and then began to have second thoughts. "What about Brackett?"

Hollander had his story. It had taken a little work, but he convinced Merton and Frank that it was worth pursuing. At this stage he was not going to let any past difficulties get in his way. He would find a solution. "I'll take care of Brackett."

Merton, Frank, and their staffers all agreed and treated Hollander as though he were a genius. It was a done deal. Then Merton slapped Hollander down just a little so that the anchor would not get too carried away. "Okay, we'll get you there for tonight's show. But you're traveling light, Kevin. We're still over budget from your First Lady show."

Kevin Hollander would not have had it any other way.

Chapter Sixteen

The eye of a hurricane is a calm refuge caught between raging storms. Max Brackett was no weatherman, but he could be forgiven for thinking of his situation as reporting from the "eye." Things had been pretty wild earlier, and he was certain that they would become chaotic again. But right now inside the natural history museum was the quietest place in Madeline.

Despite the ordeal of captivity, the schoolchildren slept soundly under rough wool blankets supplied by the local Red Cross. Exhausted by the trauma of the previous day, Mrs. Banks and Kelly slept protectively beside the students. Even Brackett had eventually fallen to sleep. For him, however, it was excitement, not fear, that had kept him awake.

Only Sam Baily had stayed up through the night. Cradling his rifle, he looked at his hostages and for a moment enjoyed the thought that he was guarding them—just as he had once protected the exhibits in the building. Struggling to keep his eyes open, Sam got up and went to the window. He knew that if he did not keep moving, he would fall asleep—and then it might all be over. Brackett told him that he should not surrender until he had public opinion on his side. The previous night's interview had gone well, and Sam prayed that people across America would sympathize with him.

Peering out the window, and staying close to the wall so as not to offer much of a target for police sharpshooters, Sam was astonished to see what the morning revealed.

The parking lot and surrounding streets were crammed with the citizens of a new city. During the night people from all walks of life had converged upon the museum. Every square inch was packed with more media personnel and equipment—more law-enforcement officials and their apparatus—more onlookers and the tools that made a spectator sport easier to watch.

And to service this new community, the police provided portable toilets and vendors set up food carts. Sales were brisk as no one wanted to leave the scene for fear of missing something exciting. Whatever a person craved could be purchased: hot dogs, Mexican food, Chinese food, coffee, decaffeinated no fat latte, even sushi.

But Sam's attention was drawn elsewhere. He stared at a building on the far side of the parking lot which only twenty-four hours earlier had been a day-care center. Now it seemed a focal point. Sam guessed, correctly, that the people inside were planning on removing him from the picture.

Sam was not the only person amazed by the rapidly evolved command center. Sheriff Lemke walked its halls and tried to take it all in: a scale model of the museum in one room, another room with its walls plastered with architectural blueprints, a room full of FBI agents working a bank of radios and phones, another filled with agents monitoring television broadcasts, a commissary, a relaxation lounge, and finally a room filled with cots for napping federal agents.

Sheriff Lemke felt like a rube and was seriously puzzled. "How did you . . . ? I was across the street all night."

Dobbins enjoyed the local cop's awed confusion. "We're very sneaky."

Apparently they were. Lemke then moved on. "What's the plan, sir? I'm getting a lot of pressure out there to do something."

Dobbins grabbed a cup of coffee and brought the small-town sheriff up to speed. "Once upon a time, Sam Baily would have been in a cell or a box by now. But thanks to a little place called Waco, Texas, we're between a rock and a hard place."

A few years earlier a religious community in Waco calling themselves the Branch Davidians had shot and killed a number of U.S. Treasury Agents as they tried to arrest the group's leader, David Koresh. To some people the Davidians were victims of religious persecution. To others they were a cult that financed themselves with illegal weapons sales. What was incontrovertible was that good men had been killed in the line of duty. A long siege followed, culminating in a terrible fire in which dozens of people lost their lives. To some people, Waco had become a symbol of a government turned against its own citizens. To others, Waco was a tragedy brought upon the victims by their own leaders.

And because of Waco, federal authorities revised their procedures for dealing with potentially dangerous sieges. The new policy chose to indefinitely wait out transgressors in an armed confrontation.

Dobbins briefed Lemke on how the new policy worked. The sheriff gestured to the television moni-

tors showing a repeat of Brackett's interview with
Sam. "People are starting to like him."

Dobbins was not concerned. He had seen how these
standoffs worked in the past. "That'll change. They'll
get bored or he'll do something to make them turn
on him. By then we'll be in position to take him out."

In his thirty years of police work, Lemke had
worked with the bureau several times previously. His
experiences had been positive, and he had nothing but
respect for the agents who put their lives on the line
every day to protect citizens across the country. This
particular agent, Dobbins, however, was an arrogant
son of a bitch. Lemke worried about the circumstances
Dobbins had just mentioned—that would allow the
FBI to take Sam Baily "out." "I'd hate to think what
that something might be."

But Dobbins had already taken Lemke's arm and
was steering him toward the door. "That's not your
concern. Just get yourself in front of the TV cameras
and keep saying that we're waiting as long as it takes.
We're not about to play games when kids are
involved."

So Lemke was going to be the parrot for the bureau.
Okay, he could live with that. Still, he wanted to make
sure he did not screw it up. "Anything I should be
afraid of saying?"

Dobbins was not one for empowering the people
who worked beneath him. "Like what? You don't
know anything."

As Dobbins led Lemke out the door, he handed the
sheriff a portable communications device and indi-
cated that he would be in touch when it was necessary.
Lemke was across the threshold and out of the loop
before he realized what had happened.

Chapter Seventeen

Sam Baily's eyes finally shut. After a night of watching the doors and windows, Sam Baily fell asleep, his back against a wall and the gun cradled in his lap.

Just as he did, however, the museum telephone began to ring, jolting everyone in the building awake. Sam's nerves detonated and brought him to his feet. As he moved, his finger clenched and accidentally pulled the trigger of his rifle. A single shot fired straight up into the ceiling was deafening. Plaster rained down, and everyone, including Sam, began to panic.

The phone continued to ring—and the tension level grew exponentially. Panic swept everyone within earshot. Food vendors, observers, reporters, police, and medical personnel were all shaken by the noise, and adrenaline began to flow. Cops pulled their weapons and ran to their assigned positions. Technicians turned on their video cameras. Photographers flipped on their auto-winds. Reporters turned on their laptops and checked their reflections in car windows, fixing their hair quickly for on-camera duty. Lemke spoke into the communication device that Dobbins had given him. "There's a shot."

Within the command center no one could hear the gunfire. An FBI agent assigned to a listening post was jolted to attention by Lemke's panicked shout. The agent passed word along the FBI frequency. "Gun!" Flack-jacketed federal agents leaped to their feet and grabbed their assault rifles. Dobbins ran to his observation post and stared at the scene, using high-powered binoculars. He saw nothing out of the ordinary and ordered his men to stand down. Grabbing a headset, he listened in to his agents and continued to watch the museum.

Meanwhile, Sam was trying to restore order among his hostages. The children were frightened, and so were Mrs. Banks and Kelly Rose. Sam's efforts were futile. He began to lose his cool and shouted angrily for everyone to shut up.

The phone was still ringing, but Sam did not answer it. Instead, he stood frozen near the window—his eyes darting back and forth between his hostages and the telephone. Brackett caught his attention and gestured for Sam to stay away from the window. Sam ducked down, scrambled along the floor, and grabbed the telephone off the security desk. Mrs. Banks watched him with growing dread—the sudden burst of activity, shattered nerves, and lack of sleep made Sam angrier than she had ever seen him. Mrs. Banks flinched as Sam shouted into the phone, "What do you want?"

A worried Sheriff Lemke wanted to know what had just happened, not realizing that his phone call had triggered the shot. He assumed that Brackett had misjudged the gunman and that Sam was more dangerous than the reporter suggested. An overwrought Sam assured him that nothing disastrous had happened and not to worry. Lemke was not assuaged. "Don't worry? Has anyone been hurt?"

As Sam's panic eased, he became more convincing.

"No, no one's been hurt. It was an accident, okay? Just an accident."

Sam looked to Brackett for approval and found only a neutral stare. The reporter could see that Sam wanted advice, but decided to withhold any new ideas for the time being. With a curious smile Brackett crossed his arms and watched the gunman. He wanted to see what Sam Baily could do on his own.

Lemke was relieved. As long as the gunman was not overly agitated, Lemke felt they could talk him out. "Look, you fire guns off, and we're going to have no choice but to storm the place. And neither one of us wants that. Right?"

Sam agreed.

Lemke continued, "Okay. Now, look, Sam. We had a deal. We let the interview run. We kept up our end of the bargain. Now it's time to end this."

At the FBI control center, Agent Dobbins was called into the monitoring room and listened in on Lemke and Sam's conversation. Overall he was pleased with how events were unfolding. No news was good news. It was Dobbins's plan to string Sam along until public opinion turned against him. Then he would be freer to settle things more efficiently.

As he listened, Dobbins tried to gauge Sam's mental state. After a while the federal agent was not sure he liked what he heard. While Sam did not sound dangerous at the moment, he was raising a difficult question. "What about my demand? Can we forget all this?"

On the one hand Sam's demand was simple and unthreatening. He did not want much. On the other hand Sam's thinking showed a bothersome disconnection from reality. Dobbins listened in as Lemke tried to reason with the gunman. "Come on, Sam. You know you're not going to be allowed to walk away from this."

In the museum Brackett's nonchalant attitude faltered when he saw Sam react badly to something he had just been told. Brackett had not seen Sam look truly dangerous before—panicked, angry, frustrated maybe, but no bloodlust. Now, however, the gunman had a killer's eye. Brackett could not hear the other end of the conversation, but hoped that whoever was talking to Sam would lighten up a bit.

Lemke, however, thought that the time to talk turkey had arrived. A tragedy had been narrowly missed with the accidental gunshot. The sheriff wanted Sam to understand the seriousness of his predicament. He hoped that the truth could convince Sam that his efforts were futile. "Sam, your only option is to give up."

Brackett thought the voice on the other end of the line was not helping much. Sam roared back into the phone, "I'll decide what my options are! You're going to have to do better than that!"

Sam slammed down the receiver and whipped open a drawer in the security desk. Finding a bottle of pills, he opened it and greedily swallowed a few.

Brackett prayed that Sam was swallowing Valium or some sort of anxiety suppressant, but doubted it. Brackett asked what the pills were, and Sam handed him the bottle explaining, "I used to pull night duty in the air force. Didn't fall asleep once."

Brackett saw this as an ominous development. "I had this shit in the seventies. Be careful, Sam. You don't want to lose control."

Sam grinned too broadly and assured Brackett that he could handle the pills.

Taking the bottle back, Sam became aware of a

child's sobbing, and his aggressiveness diminished. Turning around, Sam found eight-year-old Katie Wilson in tears as Mrs. Banks stroked the little girl's hair to comfort her. Sam took a step toward Katie, but the girl recoiled in fear.

Sam's personality shift was pronounced, and Brackett saw that it was as if Sam's moods were now controlled by a manic pendulum.

His smile was genuine, however, as he tried to let the girl know that he meant no harm. "Hey, it's okay. I'm sorry. I didn't mean to scare you."

Sam sat down next to Katie and put a friendly arm around her shoulders. Mrs. Banks and Brackett watched as Sam began a friendly conversation. Mrs. Banks was not surprised to see this gentle side of him. This was the Sam she knew. Nevertheless, she was concerned about his increasing instability. Similarly, Brackett feared that Sam's widening mood swings could mean serious trouble in the future.

Sam talked to the girl as though there were nothing unusual about their circumstances. He spoke as a loving father would to his daughter. "Did you sleep okay?" Katie guessed she had slept well enough. But now she was hungry. Other children were listening and began to chime in that they, too, were hungry. Sam looked at the students, and the last hint of his anger receded.

Mrs. Banks watched the change in Sam and thought the time had come to trade on his goodwill. "You have to let them go now, Sam."

Mrs. Banks might be right. The fight gone out of him, Sam looked around at the children, hoping to find an answer. No matter how big his problems, Sam knew he was wrong to make the kids suffer.

Brackett recognized that Sam was about to give up,

sidled up to him, and whispered something. Whatever his suggestion was, Sam clearly liked it. He smiled at the students and told them to stand up and follow him.

The children did as they were told, and Sam herded them out of the room. Mrs. Banks and Kelly were overwhelmed by a sense of relief. Both women thought that Sam was releasing them. It was all over.

But they were wrong. Sam did not lead the children toward the exit, but into a small concession alcove where visitors could buy candy, snacks, and sodas. Mrs. Banks's spirit sank, and she glared angrily at Brackett who had given Sam the idea. Sam stood in front of the candy machine, grinned at the kids, and performed like a favorite uncle. "Okay. Who knows the magic word?"

The kids' mouths dropped open with anticipation. One boy yelled out "Open sesame!" and Sam obeyed. Loading the vending machines had been one of his responsibilities, and Sam showed off a key to his audience. Then he unlocked the door and revealed the treasures within. The children cheered and pushed a laughing Sam out of the way as they descended upon the free junk food. Wrappers flew as they ravenously attacked their loot. Sam enjoyed watching the kids. For one of the few times in his life, Sam Baily could be generous and give something away. He got a kick out of the students' delight, and for the moment the kids forgot that Sam was holding them against their will.

Brackett also felt relief as he observed the feeding frenzy. He was not certain, however, what it was that was making him feel better. Was he relieved because the tension had broken, or because Sam had not given up and surrendered? He realized that while he was pleased no one had been hurt, it was more important that his story still was in play.

Mrs. Banks watched the scene with a different attitude. She saw the look of admiration in the children's eyes—a look that showed boundless affection for the amazing man who gave them free candy. Nowadays the Pied Piper carried a shotgun and a vending machine key instead of a flute. So that was progress. Mrs. Banks eased her way over to Brackett, asking quietly, "Whose side are you on, Mr. Brackett?"

"The good guys."

Mrs. Banks was beyond anger. A few minutes ago she had almost talked Sam into letting everyone go—and then Brackett had intervened. "It doesn't look that way to me."

Brackett was aware that Mrs. Banks was tough and smart, but there were few people in the world whom he could not bullshit. "Sam's stuck. He needs all the help he can get. It could be the difference between one and ten years in prison."

Mrs. Banks did not accept his explanation for a second. "I can't help but note that Sam's insanity benefits your career."

Brackett stared at the curator a little more closely, as though appraising her as a more capable enemy than he anticipated. If she truly understood the nature of his "opportunity," then she could also appreciate the way it might profit her. "I hope it does. It benefits you as well. After tomorrow you'll run the most famous little museum in the world. You'll have dodos and dinosaur bones up the wazoo."

Mrs. Banks wanted to hit him. Her outrage toward this man, who was willing to risk the lives of children for the benefit of his career, disgusted her. He was more dangerous than Sam.

But just as she was about to tell Brackett what she thought of him, Mrs. Banks understood what he was proposing. Her words stuck in her throat, and she blinked. She looked at the reporter, and his expression told her to think about it.

Quickly, the possibilities became clear. The awful hustler of a man was not so terrible after all. In fact, he had a point, and she had not realized it until this minute. The Madeline Natural History Museum might have just been given its greatest endowment since her great-grandfather founded it. It was ironic. A security guard who had been fired for budgetary reasons might be about to become the museum's benefactor. Her great-grandfather had created the museum with his fortune, and now his beloved institution would continue to live into the next century, thanks to a windfall of the new currency—publicity.

Then, after a moment of indecision, Mrs. Banks resisted temptation. Still, the horse was out of the gate. And while she would not cooperate with Max Brackett or Sam Baily, it was nice to know that something good might come out of this unfortunate affair.

Chapter Eighteen

The circus outside the museum had grown, and new performers were arriving to entertain and peddle their ideas. The press served as ringmaster, and a dozen cameras gathered around the interview of the moment.

Field Commander J. Q. Statz of the Western Minuteman Militia had driven all night in his mobile command center along with his support staff. The old Winnebago had broken down several times crossing the Sierra Nevadas, but the men were resourceful and jerry-rigged it with the most unlikely of parts. Dressed in combat fatigues and battle ribbons of uncertain origin, Statz displayed a fine military bearing. His tone was reasoned, if slightly menacing, and his logic well articulated, but of questionable direction. "We're here to prevent trouble. We are here to provide the American people what they were denied at Ruby Ridge, and at Waco: witnesses to the action of the so-called law-enforcement establishment."

Like Waco, Ruby Ridge was another flash point in the ongoing confrontation between the government and the militia movement. An armed standoff deep in the woods of Idaho during the early nineties had led to tragedy. People on both sides were killed at Ruby Ridge, and accusations were traded. The only thing that could not be disputed was that families from each perspective grieved for their losses.

As Statz made his case, Laurie asked her camera operator to pan away from the speaker toward something else. As she did, Laurie realized that her life was changing. She no longer *was* the camera operator—but was actually directing the segment. Laurie decided that given this opportunity, she was going to make the most of it.

And what was becoming clear was that this story was growing beyond Sam Baily's simple gesture of failure. Instead, others were arriving to make use of the standoff, to turn it into something that would advance their own agendas. Laurie asked her cameraman to focus on the members of the Western Minuteman Militia as they documented every move made by the police and FBI with their own video cameras.

Statz announced his declaration of intent. "This time if innocent American children are slaughtered at the hands of government stormtroopers it will be documented."

Laurie was amazed by his language. It seemed to her that the police were there to do exactly the opposite of what Statz was suggesting. She marvelled that someone would try to benefit by the impending catastrophe in the museum. Then, she looked around at the others—the army of press, food vendors, spectators, and hawkers—Laurie realized that Statz was not alone.

Within the command center Agent Dobbins watched the interview of the militia leader and scowled. A reporter asked Statz if he agreed with the police in calling for Sam to surrender peacefully. Statz acted as though he had been insulted, and he postured a bit self-righteously. "What is that, a trick question? Of course we don't approve of his putting little children in harm's way. But the story of Sam Baily is telling—is the story of a working man, a family man, thrown out of work by racial quotas."

Watching his TV inside the museum, Sam turned to Brackett with a look of confusion and anger. "Racial quotas? What is he talking about?"

Brackett could only acknowledge that somebody had been bound to bring this up. Sam was not pleased to hear this twisting of his motivations, and as the speed kicked into his system, he began to look wild again. Sam wanted to set the record straight. "It makes me look prejudiced. I have to go on TV again. I have to answer this."

Brackett had not expected Sam to consider television his personal forum. He tried to explain that neither the cops nor the networks would let Sam have any more airtime. But Sam was outraged. How could people say shooting Cliff had been racially motivated? It hadn't had any motivation at all. It had been a terrible accident—that was all. Sam told Brackett that he would trade another hostage for more airtime. When the reporter shook his head no Sam offered two kids and then five.

Brackett needed to calm Sam down. He tried to show Sam that another television appearance could work against them. When Sam demanded to know why, Brackett got worried. His story depended upon Sam being a nice guy—and if he engaged the militia in dialogue, his image would be tarnished. Brackett performed the best damage control that he could. "The public is fickle. They keep their sympathy on a very short leash. We built an image they like. Great. But we're in a very narrow window of opportunity. We have to pick the right moment."

Sam did not understand. "Right moment to do what?" he asked.

"To end this thing. To free those kids."

Brackett took a deep breath and tried to focus on the climactic moment he had in mind for *his* story. Everything depended upon a happy ending. He already had an exclusive interview on national TV, but if he wanted to stay on national TV once this crisis was over, it would have to be resolved peacefully. Brackett could not let this scoop be tainted by disaster. He explained further. "Don't engage these white supremacist guys. You'll just legitimize them."

Sam did not want to legitimize anyone, much less people who were making him look bad. What he was worried about, however, was that these people were on television, assigning ideologies to him, and viewers might be listening. But Brackett dismissed the importance of Statz with a sarcastic remark. "Television loves neo-Nazis. They give great sound bite."

Genuinely annoyed, Sam did not laugh. Once again he felt powerless. Not only had people told him what to do all his life, but now people who knew nothing about him were making him out to be something he was not. "It's not fair. You could put my wife and my friends on TV and get 'em to say good stuff about me." Sam's anger was spent, and now he was pleading.

Brackett agreed to try to get Jenny onto the phone. He thought it would be an excellent ending to the whole affair. It would make great TV for Jenny to meet Sam—and Brackett—at the top of the museum steps. She could then lead the lovable gunman to a peaceful surrender.

Although it was Sam's own idea, he hesitated once Brackett put it into play. "She's going to yell at me."

Brackett did not think Sam was serious and offered

him the phone. "Come on. She must be worried sick about you."

But Sam was not kidding and backed away from the telephone like a scared child. He had ruined his family life and did not have the courage to speak to his wife. "No. You see her first. Then I . . ."

In the parking lot matters had quieted down somewhat. Fatigue and the heat of the morning overwhelmed most of the participants. After a night of excitement, the day was becoming downright dull. News reporters delivered their stand-ups, and the law-enforcement officers guarded the building.

Then, unexpectedly, the front door to the museum rattled and opened. On the police line, dozens of cops sprang to life. One man shouted over the communications system, "We've got movement!" Guns and cameras were locked, loaded, and aimed toward the top of the steps.

A moment later, Brackett stepped awkwardly out the door and made his way down the steps. Concerned about looking like a serious reporter as much as he was about being accidentally shot—Brackett mastered his fear and approached the sidewalk with as much gravitas as he could muster.

Sheriff Lemke's heart beat a lot faster. Why was Brackett coming outside again on his own? Why had the gunman let him go? It could only mean one thing. Lemke scrambled to meet the reporter, hoping to be the first one to receive the good news. "Tell me he's coming out."

Brackett shrugged as though he had nothing to do with Sam's request. "He wants another story."

Lemke was not buying. He had already stretched the limits of propriety. Now the son of a bitch wanted more?

Brackett pressed Sam's case. "He'll let five more kids go. He just wants to talk to his wife and a few other people. Five kids, Lemke. He wants people to understand him."

Lemke rejected the offer out of hand. "I don't want him understood. I want him out of there!"

Brackett knew the cop had a point, but the possibility of interviewing Sam and Jenny Baily on live television represented the coup of a lifetime. Brackett was not going to back down and knew that he could talk circles around the sheriff any day. "Prison terrifies him. He's not ready to quit. TV keeps him calm. I'll interview his wife right in front of you. You can shut me down anytime."

Sheriff Lemke was infuriated and began to swear. There already had been more than enough show business in this case. It was time for police work—serious, tough negotiating. Besides, how was Brackett able to move so easily as an intermediary? "No way! And you're supposed to be a hostage! You can't just keep walking and—"

Lemke stopped talking as though he had been shot. He appeared to be listening to an unseen person. Brackett squinted at him with alarm before realizing that the sheriff was receiving instructions through an earpiece. Dobbins ordered Lemke, "Let him do it."

The sheriff frowned and did as he was told, although he clearly did not approve. "You can do it. But you and Baily better not be playing games with me."

Despite the admonition, this was great news, and Brackett was thrilled. "Hey, Sam Baily's making you the most famous cop in America. You should thank him."

Lemke was beginning to dislike the TV reporter

more than he thought possible. "Try your bullshit out on somebody else, Brackett."

Brackett had never been magnanimous in victory. Instead, Brackett always liked getting a rise out of somebody he defeated. He leaned closer to Lemke's face than the sheriff would have liked and grinned. "Who's the FBI? Maybe I know him. No? Shy, huh?" Brackett walked off to arrange the next interview.

The old-fashioned cop watched the reporter saunter away, and his anger boiled.

Then surprisingly, Lemke's temper waned, and a new feeling began. For a moment, Lemke did not understand, then realized he was attracted to the idea of fame—*Nightline,* maybe even *The Tonight Show.* Lemke had worked hard all his life and received little enough attention for it. Now he began to imagine the image he presented as the senior lawman on the scene. He wasn't exactly Gary Cooper or Harrison Ford, but if he sucked in his gut some and kept his hat on to hide his bald spot . . .

It would be the highlight of his career if he could lead the schoolchildren to safety—on national TV. Lemke imagined himself holding one child in his arms and holding the hand of another. For all of it, Lemke was a traditionalist, and while the fantasies of television were appealing, he was most enticed by the notion of making the cover of *Time.*

Sheriff Alvin Lemke liked the idea, enjoyed the fantasy, and then dismissed it. But now he knew a little more about himself and everyone else. He almost had been seduced. Lemke sighed and pulled up his trousers in a nervous gesture. He faced a more dangerous enemy than he previously realized.

Chapter Nineteen

It took some time for Jenny Baily to arrive at the museum. At first she did not want to go. Camera crews surrounding her house since the news broke that Sam was in the middle of this crisis were bad enough. Jenny did not want to be on TV for any reason. What's more, she worried that something she said could be used to hurt her husband. Finally, Brackett convinced her that Sam wanted the interview. In fact, he needed it.

The broadcast time was near. Brackett and Laurie performed a pre-interview in a yard by the side of the museum. Brackett was trying to get background that would help him ask better questions and to familiarize Jenny with the process. As other news crews and curious onlookers watched, Jenny tried to answer truthfully. "Sam tries real hard. Sometimes he screws things up because—"

That was not a direction Brackett cared to follow. He interrupted, steering the conversation away from analysis and toward a more human perspective on the gunman. "What kind of husband is he?"

Laurie watched with compassion as Jenny struggled to defend Sam. "He's a good husband, as long as you keep him pointed in the right direction. I don't understand this. This isn't like him."

*　　*　　*

And it wasn't. Jenny and Sam had known each other since high school. She had never known him to act violently toward anyone or to break the law. Not that Sam was a Milquetoast who would not stand up for himself or those he cared about. Like anyone, Sam had a temper. But for as long as they had been together, he only displayed it in appropriate circumstances. Certainly, he never hit Jenny or their two children. They might argue, but she had never seen him lose control. During their years together, Jenny knew of only one fight that Sam was involved in—and that was when he tried to stop a drunken brawl in a bar. Sam was in many ways exactly what Jenny thought a man should be—kind, slow to anger, but not one to be pushed around either.

The only exception to this rule was his career—or lack of one. Sam had taken a lot of hits in his working life and never fought back—until now.

Sam joined the air force after an average high school career and worked hard to become an aircraft mechanic. After two tours of duty, Sam was cashiered when military budgets were cut. His plan to return to Madeline, marry Jenny, and get a job with an airline somehow never materialized. The economy slowed, and Sam took lesser jobs to put food on the table. Still, he kept his applications up to date at the airlines and figured his luck would turn.

Unfortunately for Sam, deregulation of the airlines had led to consolidation of the industry and massive layoffs. Sam waited patiently, and then he waited hopelessly. After several years Sam realized that he was no longer middle-class, but slipping down the economic ladder. In the best of times Sam was not overly aggressive, preferring to do his work and take his fair share. But years of underemployment took its toll and the time came when something within him died. Sam's dreams of a good house, college educations for his kids, and travel around the world with Jenny were put on a shelf.

Other men might have been ruined by the change in fortune, but Sam's laid-back personality helped him get through the rough times. Though he maintained his equilibrium, he also lost his sense of initiative. He was a good man who needed guidance.

The museum job was meant to be temporary, but Sam quickly learned to find value in it. It paid enough and provided the benefits a young family needed. Sam genuinely cared for the museum and was particularly fascinated by certain exhibits—particularly the vanished Miwok Indian tribe. Sam was never going to be rich, but his lifestyle allowed him a peaceful existence, and he felt wealthy in ways that had nothing to do with money.

Like the Jimmy Stewart character in Frank Capra's *It's a Wonderful Life,* Sam did not have a fortune, but he had friends. In some ways, he was the character downsized for the nineties and reacting to the stress of modern life. Unlike the movie character, however, Sam had not been rescued by a benevolent angel, and he broke under the pressure. Instead of his neighbors rushing to save him in time for the closing credits—they came to eat hot dogs and watch him perish in a ghoulish spasm of voyeurism.

Such was the age of television.

Max Brackett was not persuaded by Jenny's description of her husband. His turbulent behavior was out of character? How much did she really know about him? "So, tell me, Jenny, did you make his lunch the last three days?"

To Jenny Baily the question seemed irrelevant. "He makes his own lunch," she answered.

Brackett made his point and astonished her. "Okay. He'd already been fired. Did you know that? But he made his own lunch every morning, got into his uniform and pretended he was going to work. How do you feel about that?"

Jenny had no answer. Brackett wanted to use her expression and instructed his cameraman to roll tape. Brackett asked again, "How do you feel that Sam was afraid to tell you he got fired?"

Jenny found the obvious answer. "He didn't want to worry me."

Brackett, however, had a different interpretation. "He was scared. You think that's a sign of a good marriage?"

Jenny never doubted that her marriage was the greatest asset in her life. This slick reporter could do nothing to convince her otherwise. "We have a good marriage. Did he tell you we don't have a good marriage?"

While the pre-interview was not going out over the air, they were still being watched over various monitors. Inside the command center Agent Dobbins was impressed by Jenny Baily's strength, made a decision, and spoke through his headset. "Grab her. We'll put her on a line with Sam. See what she can do."

Lemke received his instructions and watched more of the pre-interview. Brackett was prodding Jenny, trying to stir a forceful emotional reaction—something that would defend her husband—something that would make good television. "You have a good marriage but you treat him like a child."

Jenny did not bother to deny it. That was what Sam had become. It did not mean she loved him any less. "He is like a child sometimes. He likes to call himself my third child."

That was not exactly what Brackett was hoping to hear. Whatever the cause, a man who acted like a child was not sympathetic. If Sam's actions in the museum were a noble last stand gone horribly wrong— that would be acceptable. If Sam's behavior was nothing more than a temper tantrum, however, the viewers across the nation would turn off their televisions. For the first time during the siege, Brackett felt frustration. He was close to delivering the story of a career, but he was unable to steer Jenny Baily in the necessary direction.

"Do you still love him?"

Brackett knew immediately that this was exactly the right question. He wished he thought of it. Instead, he whirled around and looked with surprise at Laurie, who found the way to elicit the response they wanted.

Jenny looked at Laurie, and immediately her sturdy facade melted. A swell of emotion overwhelmed her, and she answered the compassionate young woman's question. "Of course, I do. Sam is the most gentle, honest man I know. I want the parents of the children in there to know that. He would never hurt a child. Never."

Just as Jenny was giving Brackett the heartrending performance he needed, Sheriff Lemke stepped forward and interfered. "Jenny, we'd like you to talk to him. Let's try to end this thing."

This was not what Brackett wanted, not why he convinced Sam and the police to bring Jenny to the museum. He needed the two of them on the air—for his interview. Brackett defended his turf with a warning. "I'd be very careful."

Having almost been tempted by Brackett, Lemke knew all too well what the reporter was up to, and wanted him out of the picture. "Brackett, this has nothing to do with you."

Brackett was not pleased. How could the siege have nothing to do with him? Whose story was it? Who had been inside? Who negotiated the release of hostages? Brackett turned to Jenny, hoping to convince her not to speak to Sam without using him as an intermediary. "Jenny, Sam is in a very nervous state. There's no telling how he'll react." He could see Jenny pause and struggle over what she should do. Brackett seized the opportunity and tried to get Lemke back on his side. "Sheriff, don't do this. He's sensitive about his wife."

It did not work. Lemke thought it was good news Sam was worried about Jenny. The more he cared about her, the stronger ammunition she was in their arsenal. Lemke exchanged a look with Jenny, and they walked off together, leaving the news crew behind.

Brackett seethed for a moment and tried to think of his next option. He decided to stay near the action and followed the sheriff back toward the parking lot. Laurie walked with him, and Brackett did something he rarely did—he complimented someone. "You asked the right question."

Laurie had worried that Brackett would be angry when she interrupted the interview. When she saw Jenny's response, however, Laurie knew she had done the right thing. Still, a veteran journalist might not take such interference especially well. Laurie was relieved that Brackett was not upset. He even seemed pleased, although he did not dwell on the matter.

Instead, he led Laurie and their cameraman back to

the museum steps and staked out a position right in front of Jenny. Other news crews got wise to what was about to happen and rushed to stake out their own angles. Lemke dialed his cell phone, and the lights of the cameras were all switched on.

Lemke handed Jenny the phone when it was answered inside the museum. No one said anything. A look of pain crossed Jenny's face as she called Sam's name several times. Finally, he answered with a casual "Hi, Jen."

Jenny's voice was firm, but desperate with fear. "What are you doing, Sam?"

As always, Sam was honest. But it did not seem like much of an explanation. "I don't know. I guess I got myself in kind of a bind here."

Jenny tried to keep her tone reasonable as she went directly to the bottom line. "You gotta come out now, Sam."

But Sam did not want to talk about surrendering yet. He was more interested in his children. He knew the mess he created had to be tough for them. "How are the sprouts?"

"They're wondering where their father is—is how they are."

Hearing Jenny, there was nothing Sam would have liked better than to have put down his rifle, give up the siege, and walk out into her arms. He wanted to be with her in their home and with their children more than anything. But he knew that was not going to happen. "They want to send me to prison, Jenny. I can't go to prison."

Jenny was distressed by Sam's tone. He was not thinking clearly. If the beginning of the hostage crisis had been a colossal error, the current pressure was making him lose any perspective. She had to get through to him. "Sam! I don't want any more argument. I want you to come out."

Normally this would have worked. When Jenny spoke with authority, he knew that it was best to do as he was told. Sam might have responded positively if at that moment he had not noticed the television screen. KXBD's live feed, showed Jenny surrounded by police and reporters—talking to Sam on the phone. Sheriff Lemke stood by her side and urged her on.

Sam got angry. He began to flip the channels and found that different shots of Jenny and Lemke were on every station. Sam shouted over the phone, "What are you doing!? You're all over the TV!"

Sam looked back at the screen and saw Jenny react to his furor. That made him all the angrier. Holding the phone at his side, Sam roared at the TV screen, "Get away from her!" He raised the receiver back to his mouth and continued, "Get away from them! Where is Brackett?"

Jenny shouted back desperately, "Forget Brackett! Put down that stupid gun and come out here!"

"I won't go to prison! You can tell them that! I won't go to prison! Now go home, Jen!"

Jenny tried to calm him, but Sam was still demanding that she leave. He slammed the phone onto its cradle and then dashed it off the counter. The clamor of the phone crashing onto the floor made his hostages flinch. Everyone who could hear the noise was frightened—including Sam.

In all their twenty years, Sam had never hung up on his wife. Jenny knew that in a predicament he looked to her for guidance and support. If he did not want to talk to her, then he must have been more despondent than she ever thought he could be.

Clearly, Sam was approaching the point of no return, and she had to do something to stop him.

Jenny threw the cell phone back to a surprised Lemke and stared past the cameras toward the museum. "I'll get him out of there."

It was great theater. The crowd was thrilled. Journalists were delighted. In media centers across the country, executives sitting in advertising and broadcasting agencies high-fived each other. In the living rooms of the nation, people stopped crunching their Cheez Doodles and moved closer to the edges of their seats.

Millions watched as a forthright, dedicated woman started up a flight of granite steps in a heroic effort to save her husband's life and liberate a classroom of hostage children. Lemke stopped her, but only briefly. He gave Sam Baily's wife a microphone that was attached to a bullhorn. Jenny pressed the trigger, and her voice bellowed out over the scene. "Sam! Sam Baily!"

Brackett could see both his exclusive and his future going down the drain as Jenny climbed the steps. He wanted her to back off, and the best way to accomplish this would be to frighten her. "Jenny, don't do this!" Sheriff Lemke grabbed his shoulder and told him to shut up.

Jenny stood near the door to the museum and tried to talk Sam into surrendering.

The pressure inside the building grew to an intolerable level. Sam watched as his wife berated him on national television. It was humiliating, and he did not want her anywhere near the siege. Sam wanted his wife at home with their children. The surreal combination of watching Jenny shouting to him on TV and the enormous sound of her amplified voice echoing through the building pushed Sam closer to the edge of sanity.

"Please listen to me. You've got to stop this nonsense."

Anguished, Sam tried to block the sound of her voice by covering his ears and muttering, "Shut up. Shut up. Shut up. Shut up."

He did not how to make her stop, and Jenny continued, "You've got to come out, Sam. Please. Come out now. Now."

Everyone told Sam what to do. That was how it had always been. And now the whole country was witness. Sam could no longer tolerate the degradation, and he imploded. He screamed for Jenny to shut up, then leapt to a window—smashing out the glass with his rifle and opening fire across the parking lot above the heads of the crowd.

Chaos erupted as the bullets flew. Onlookers screamed. Some dove for cover, while others ran off into the night. Sharpshooters scrambled into position, looked for a target, and waited for a command. The news crews hit the ground, but still managed to keep taping.

Jenny stood where she was—dazed. As he fired, Sam shouted to her, "Jen! I know what I'm doing. Go home!"

As the bullets whizzed overhead and the crowds panicked, Brackett kept his cool. He saw disaster looming and knew there was only one way that he could save Sam's life—not to mention his story.

As Laurie and the other news crews looked on in horror, Brackett charged up the museum stairs. He was shouting as he went, and Sam leaned out of the window to hear what he was saying. Sam was a wide-open target for the sharpshooters, and Brackett knew that he had only seconds in which to keep his boy alive. Now Brackett was hollering at the top of his lungs, "Sam! Get out of the window!"

Sam did not understand. Either that, or he did not quite hear Brackett. He wanted Brackett to repeat himself. Brackett could not believe the gunman had not been picked off. "The window! For God's sake!"

In that instant Sam realized the danger. As dozens of sharpshooters were given the command to open fire, Sam fell back into the museum, and their target disappeared. The sharpshooters lowered their weapons, and Brackett pushed his way through the heavy brass door and back into the building. The scoop was still alive.

Alive but enraged. As soon as Brackett crossed the threshold, Sam sprang on him, pushing the reporter aside as he slammed the door shut. "How could you do that? How could you let her say those things with all these people around her?"

Brackett was not in the mood to be pushed around. He met Sam's rage with his own. "I didn't! And that is not a good reason to start shooting over people's heads."

Sam felt that he had been betrayed. He did not understand why Brackett had changed the rules on him. "We said you were the only one who'd be speaking to her."

Brackett told him that the additional cameras had been Sheriff Lemke's idea and added, "Can't you see they're goading you?"

Sam did not know what "goading" meant.

Brackett took him through the events step by step. "People were starting to like you, but you start shooting out windows and we're back to square one, your image is down the drain."

Sam had been pushed around again, and he had not even known. His fury faded into remorse, and he tried to tell the reporter why he behaved so badly. "It's just that it drove me crazy to see her there . . . what have I done?"

Brackett stared at him. Sam was not angry and not dangerous, although Brackett knew this could change minute to minute. Brackett thought Sam might cry. He needed to soothe Sam's ragged nerves and wanted some assurances about his future conduct. "Tell me you're not going to start throwing dynamite out of the window."

Sam promised Brackett not to do anything rash. He was numb. "You know I won't do that again. But it's too late now, I screwed it up again." Sam looked like he was ready to open the doors and call the whole thing off.

Brackett recognized surrender when he saw it and knew that something had to be done. Brackett gave Sam's shoulder an encouraging squeeze and tried to cheer the dejected gunman. "Don't worry, I know just the thing. Let me go out again, I'll try to do some damage control."

The gunshots occurred less than fifteen minutes before, but already the crowd had returned to their favorite viewing positions. Brackett walked back down the steps toward the parking lot and was pleased. If the crowd had stayed away, they truly feared Sam—not a good sign.

As it happened, the gunshots were not so catastrophic after all. After a long, quiet night, they added fresh excitement to the event. Since no one had been hurt, most especially Sam, it could turn out to be a good thing. Ratings could go up. That would be great—as long as more people viewed Sam positively than negatively. Brackett was riding a treacherous wave of viewer opinion, and he was leaving the museum to make sure that Sam's public image remained sympathetic.

Laurie met him as he reached the bottom of the stairs. Her admiration for Brackett grew by the hour. His bravery under fire set him apart from the other journalists covering the story. Laurie wanted to stay by his side and learn everything she could. Brackett had other plans, however. "I've got to send you out into the field." Laurie was surprised. Brackett continued, "I'll provide you with all the questions you need."

Laurie became flustered. She had not expected to be on her own. Unnerved, she protested, "Why can't you . . ."

There was no time for long conversations. This was how it had to be. Brackett laid down the law. "I have to stay close to Sam. He's getting a little wiggy—"

Brackett stopped midsentence. Something bothered him, and he could not mask his dismay. "What is that?"

A small tractor trailer eased through the crowded parking lot. Brackett knew it did not belong to the FBI or the police. Laurie shared the good news. "It's for Hollander. Kevin Hollander is coming here." Brackett was astonished. He had heard nothing about the CBN anchor coming to Madeline.

He was also a little shaken to see the look in Laurie's eyes. Clearly, she idolized Hollander. Things were getting complicated. Brackett complained as he walked toward his news van, "Terrific. Now we've got to protect the story from him."

Laurie did not understand. She thought Brackett would be thrilled with the arrival of the network's top anchor and the story clearly established as the most important on the news. That had to be good for them.

Brackett carried on. "He's the man America trusts, and he's going to try and freeze us out. It's called 'being big-footed.' "

Laurie was more puzzled than ever. "But it's not about us, right?" The story of Sam and the hostages was the important matter here—their position in the journalistic hierarchy was secondary.

Brackett did not agree. He looked at her carefully and wanted to laugh. Even when he was young, Max Brackett had never been quite that nice or naive. From the beginning he knew what the game was about—and that knowledge had served him well. Up to a point. On the other hand, what did he expect from a kid in Madeline, California? He needed to keep Laurie happy. "It's not about Hollander either. Look, I need this done before he gets here. Here's who I want you to talk to."

He handed her a clipboard with extensive notes about the material he needed. Laurie was silent, overwhelmed by the responsibility. Brackett could sense Laurie's uncertainty and knew she needed some confidence. Grasping her shoulders, Brackett gave her a quick pep talk. "We are the A-team on this story. We have exclusivity, it's our story, we have power. Use it."

Still astonished that someone like Max Brackett would entrust her with such an important mission, Laurie nodded. Moved by his faith in her, Laurie would have stormed castles or struggled through natural disasters. As it was, her assignment was not that melodramatic. Laurie Callahan ran toward the news van, eager to prove her worth.

Brackett watched her go and, despite himself, felt a slight sense of pride and affection for his eager protégée.

Chapter Twenty

Laurie Callahan was on her own, covering the first major story of her career. Her nerves were taut. While the enthusiasm that came with Brackett's little speech sent her dashing off after her first interview—she found that the farther away from her mentor she went, the less confident she felt.

Laurie checked Brackett's notes. He wanted interviews at a bowling alley. That was no problem. Madeline had several bowling alleys, and Laurie chose Bernie's Bowlerama in a slightly forgotten part of town.

When she walked in, a beautiful young woman leading a camera man with a video setup, the sparse activity in the bowlerdrome came to a halt. The few people who were bowling had chosen to ignore the hostage crisis and were rewarded with uncrowded lanes. It surprised them that with all that was going on—someone from television was interested in them.

Initially, Laurie was shy and felt like an imposter. Fresh out of college, and here she was covering the top story in the United States. The Madeline hostage crisis was leading off every newscast, sat at the top of every paper, and Brackett's live segments were the envy of the nation's media. The men and women in Bernie's Bowlerama looked at her warily, and she felt her pulse race. Laurie overcame the butterflies in her stomach and asked if the bowlers wouldn't mind talking to her.

Much to Laurie's surprise, they were happy to be interviewed. Laurie remembered Lou Potts's telling her about the incredible power of a camera—how people were captivated and would gladly answer even inappropriate questions. Laurie had not believed him entirely, but now she did.

Relying heavily on questions that Brackett had written out, Laurie interviewed two young working-class men. They had known Sam growing up and described him as a normal kid—decent and likeable, someone who got into the usual trouble, but nothing serious. They knew he had joined the air force, married Jenny, but had not heard much of him over the past few years. They did not approve of holding kids hostage—but figured that someone must have really screwed Sam for him to react this way. They guessed that Sam had been pushed too far, and Laurie was surprised to learn that they did not see the standoff as a crime, but a tragedy.

Laurie got what Brackett wanted and thanked the men. Walking back to the news van, she could feel their eyes on her, and Laurie thrilled in the success of her first solo mission. She drove to her next assignment, knowing that her work would soon be influencing people's opinions nationwide. For a moment, Laurie savored the power of the press. Then, arriving at Ryan's Recession, she went back to work.

The Recession was a bar catering to ordinary guys—Budweiser, Coors, a pool table, and a TV permanently set to ESPN. It was a low-key place with a warm atmosphere. People came to the Recession to talk with old friends, not to impress anyone or pick someone up. The heavy set, genial bartender, Bill Kovich, was cleaning the bar. People in Madeline did not drink during the middle of the day, and he was preparing for the evening crowd. Laurie said hello and noted that Kovich was probably the only guy in town who did not have his TV set to the hostage crisis. The bartender laughed and said he had no intention of changing channels—if someone wanted to watch Sam Baily holed up in the natural history museum, they would have to go elsewhere. He had no interest in watching an old friend get killed on live television.

Still, Kovich was pleased to have Laurie walk into the Recession. Last night's business had been slow. A lot of people stayed home to watch the hostage crisis or went to the actual scene. Bad business always depressed Kovich, and it gave him a lift to have a young woman as attractive as Laurie asking him questions for the news.

Laurie had gone to the Recession because Brackett listed it as Sam's favorite hangout in his notes. She had her doubts about the interview, however. Suppose Sam was an alcoholic who spent his days and nights slugging down whiskey and wallowing in his misfortune? But Brackett knew Sam well enough, and his instincts were accurate. Kovich had only good things to say about Sam. His only character flaw was that he *did not* drink enough. Sam spent time at the Recession to catch up with friends, watch sports, and play some pool. Sam rarely had more than a beer or two and a sandwich. And no matter what he had, Sam always tipped generously.

The interview was pure gold. Laurie wanted to rush the tape back to the network truck and its editing bay, but Kovich insisted that she stay long enough for a bowl of homemade Polish stew.

Afterward, a newly confident Laurie handed off her tape to Brackett, who began cutting right away. Laurie was excited by the process, and Brackett immediately sent her back into the field.

Next on his list was a fishing hole just out of town. Apparently, Sam was a fisherman. Laurie admired the setting—a wooden bridge over a gently flowing stream. Did Brackett actually know it was a perfect backdrop, or was it just luck?

Laurie found an elderly fisherman who knew about Sam's predicament, but chose not to believe that his friend could actually be mixed up in something like that. After they talked for a while, he took Laurie by the arm and showed her Sam's weathered name carved into the bridge's railing, clearly carved there many years before. It was impossible not to be moved by his loyalty to the spot—it spoke of someone with sturdy values. The fisherman shook his head, unable to comprehend that Sam could be in trouble.

As though to explain that the incident must be a terrible mistake, he assured Laurie that Sam was the best fisherman he had ever met. The message was loud and clear—Sam was a patient, considerate man, not the sort who lost control.

Later, back at the editing bay, Brackett watched the rough footage of Laurie's interviews with pleasure. He had not expected much. In truth, he assumed that Laurie would be clumsy on camera and that the material would stand out only because of his choices and questions. He would have to make do with whatever she could provide.

Not a man given to smiling easily, Brackett could not help but grin as he watched Laurie's footage. There was no doubt—she was good—and she was making his story all the stronger. Brackett did not want Laurie to grow overly confident, however, and offered only a steady "good job" before sending her back into the field.

Then he went to work, cutting the tape, and editing the material into a well-structured narrative.

Laurie's next stop was an air force base twenty miles outside of Madeline. There she interviewed a sergeant who knew Sam. Sam had been a decent soldier although he had never possessed the killing instinct that would have made him a warrior. Instead, he did reliable work on the aircraft support staff. The sergeant recalled how much Sam enjoyed his overseas posting. Sam Baily was a good man, and it was a shame that his fortunes had declined since leaving the air force.

After leaving the base, Laurie went back into town and visited Sam's church. The building reflected its congregation—modest and straightforward—no stained glass windows, no sweeping architectural designs, no lavish decorations. Just a box construction, circa 1970, that was lovingly maintained.

Minister Willoughby had been praying for a peaceful resolution to the hostage crisis when Laurie walked into the sanctuary. Seriously distressed by the situation, Willoughby knew two of the children being held—and he had known Sam since childhood. The elderly minister's faith was sorely tried—how did a good person like Sam Baily make such a dreadful error? How could a man who was kind aim a gun at a child? Many platitudes should have comforted Willoughby, but they were not working.

Still, the minister found some consolation in speaking with Laurie. Knowing that most people would assume Sam was a monster, he wanted to set the record straight. Laurie's sympathetic approach surprised Willoughby, for he expected the press to indulge their blood lust in tearing Sam apart. Instead, Laurie let the camera run as Willoughby talked on about Sam's faith. Not all was going to get on the air, but Laurie knew she was giving Brackett a lot to work with.

Everything was quiet at the museum as the crisis entered a relatively tranquil period. There was no more shooting from Sam, and the police and crowds were content to enjoy the lull.

But inside the network truck editing bay, Max Brackett was stumped by an unwelcome development. He had sent Laurie to interview Sam's high school principal. Though Sam had graduated many years before, if the same principal was still in charge, he might feel nostalgic about the past, even if he had not liked Sam.

Unfortunately, Brackett had miscalculated.

Brackett pressed a button, rewound the interview, and played it again. An older gentleman, looking every bit the trusted village elder, stood in front of Madeline High School and shared his opinion of Sam. "He was not a remarkable student. I'm sure you'll find someone who will say we've failed Sam Baily, that somehow the system isn't set up anymore to provide a safety net for men like him. But I feel the only person accountable for this situation is Sam Baily."

That was not what Brackett wanted to hear, and he swore at the monitor. "Uncompassionate bastard."

Brackett could have chosen not to use the principal's footage. He could have cut it out of the segment and no one would have ever known about it. But the image of the wise old man was irresistible. If only he had said the right thing—Sam's image would have been given a real boost.

Brackett thought a moment and rolled the tape back. Hitting a few buttons, he programmed half a dozen new edits into the system's computer. Then Brackett hit play and watched his new masterpiece.

It was the same interview. Only now several important words had been deleted and the corresponding video replaced with a reverse angle shot of Laurie listening attentively. The principal shared a "new" opinion of Sam Baily and his recent actions. "We've failed Sam Baily. The system isn't set up anymore to provide a safety net for men like him."

Brackett was pleased with his work and laughed. "That's what I thought you said." Then he punched another button that locked in the new edit and continued on assembling the program.

Before he could enjoy his triumph, the phone rang. Laurie was calling from a farmhouse on the outskirts of Madeline. She had a problem and needed advice from Brackett. "Max, the parents won't talk to me."

Brackett did not consider this a serious problem because there was no choice but to succeed. He had to have the parents for the broadcast. There could be no excuses. Brackett's tone was calm, and Laurie sensed that this was more important than those issues he yelled about. "I'm holding a hole open for this," he said quietly.

He did not seem to understand. Laurie had not wanted to call him with bad news. Some things could not be made to happen. Laurie laid out the facts for Brackett. He had to understand that mere willpower was not enough. "The mother's crying, and the father has a stutter. They won't speak—"

Brackett cut her off. "Do not come back without it."

Laurie was left with nothing but dial tone. She knew

she would have to come up with something quickly. The consequences of failure appeared to be dire.

Laurie had no way of knowing that Brackett was not mad at all. In fact, he had a hopeful smile on his face, knowing that his protégée would not let him down.

Given the choice between disappointing Brackett and upsetting Sam Baily's mother, Laurie hesitated. She looked apprehensively at the farmhouse and knew that if she wanted the interview, she would have to cross an uncertain moral border. Laurie could well imagine that Sam Baily's parents wanted only to be left alone. Still, she had a job to do, and if she failed, she could be unemployed.

That realization made the decision easier, although it left Laurie uneasy. As she led her cameraman across the Bailys' lawn toward the back yard, she began to weave a rationalization. If she could find something that made Sam look good, it could only help him. Any good mother would want to help her son if he was in danger.

Nora Baily was pulling clothes off a line when Laurie rounded the corner of the house. Sam's mother was a frail, tired-looking woman with unkempt white hair. She had the stunned look of an ordinary person caught in extraordinary events. Normally, her white hair would have been clean and neatly brushed back and she would have worn freshly ironed clothing. In Nora Baily's world one maintained a certain level of dignity and that carried over to how one presented oneself in the community.

All that had changed. Nora was bewildered by the catastrophe that had descended upon her family. She stumbled through routine chores, hoping somehow to reassert normality into a world gone mad.

Laurie approached Nora gingerly. She was afraid of being reproached. When she said hello to Nora, the older woman was surprised and displeased. "Please, I asked you to leave."

Laurie took a shot. "Ma'am. I'm sorry to bother you, but we really are trying to help your son. Would he still have a pet here, maybe a dog or a horse?"

Nora Baily had been brought up to be polite even under trying circumstances. Yet, she was being pushed too far by this intrusive young woman. Nora had half a mind to chase the reporter off the farm. She might well have done it, too, but she was just too tired.

Laurie waited nervously for a response. Getting none, and avoiding outright rejection, Laurie tried to explain that she really had Sam's best interests at heart. "To show people Sam can't be all bad if he had a dog he loves."

The explanation sounded a little too glossy to Nora Baily, but she was willing to try anything. Since the incident began, and before she had turned off the TV for good, Nora thought the coverage made Sam look like a madman. All of it was negative except Max Brackett's reporting on Channel Six. The young woman standing before her worked with Brackett, and that made Nora more willing to take a chance. She did not say a word, but simply gestured for Laurie to follow.

Nora Baily introduced Laurie to Rex, a large, handsome Airedale terrier whose muzzle was now gray and his legs hobbled by arthritis. Like most terriers, Rex still had a strong heart and an unerring sense of who was good and who was not. Nora half expected the smartly dressed young reporter would try to get a quick picture of the old dog and leave. She also half hoped Rex would give Laurie a dismissive growl—and confirm Nora's own doubts.

But Laurie was clearly a person who loved animals. Ignoring the possibility that her attractive clothing might be ruined, she knelt on the grass next to Rex and took off her tweed blazer. Nora was surprised. Laurie said hello to the old dog and began to pet him, politely at first, and then with warmth. Rex looked at her for moment and passed judgment. This young woman was all right. Nora noticed and was as convinced by the dog's opinion as she was by Laurie's genuine kindness.

Nora Baily was not one to discuss family matters in public, but Laurie's gesture had engendered a sense of trust—and so she began to talk. "Rex has been with us since Sam was in high school. The old boy is almost fifteen years old now."

Laurie showed her surprise, and that comforted Nora Baily all the more. She liked it that Rex appeared younger than he was, for she could not bear the thought of losing him. Nora's eyes filled as she watched the old dog enjoy Laurie's attention.

Her vision obscured by tears, Nora Baily never saw Laurie gesture to her cameraman to begin rolling tape. Nora continued to talk. "We almost lost him last year. Sam was a wreck, stayed up all night with him, making sure he kept warm."

An hour later, Brackett was watching the footage in his editing bay. He marvelled at the intimacy of the interview and Nora's priceless commentary. "He really is a sweet boy. He's confused, but all he's trying to do is get by."

Brackett laughed out loud. "You got his sweet country mother saying that he loves his dog! You're brilliant."

It was a dazzling moment of heartrending drama. Later, if she bothered to watch the broadcast at all, Nora Baily would be embarrassed to see herself talking about such private matters on the air. Laurie had drawn her out in a way that even a more experienced journalist like Brackett might not have been able to accomplish.

Laurie had traded on the sincerity of her manner and the innocence of her face. It worked wonders, and she knew then that it would take her far. Laurie Callahan beamed with pride, for she had just left the amateur leagues and was now a journalist.

The phone in the editing bay rang, and an assistant picked it up. He turned to Brackett. "It's Lou Potts. They're here."

Brackett's good mood instantly vanished. Their moment of victory was short-lived, and now Brackett and Laurie were going to have to defend their turf.

Chapter Twenty-one

The crowd outside the museum was excited by the arrival of an elegant town car with tinted windows. Rumors had been flying for some time that CBN anchor Kevin Hollander was on his way to Madeline to take over as chief correspondent. Not only the locals were thrilled as the sleek car pulled to a stop by the network truck. Even the press and the police were thrilled. The appearance of a living legend elevated the status of everyone associated with the story.

A producer jumped out of an escort car and opened Hollander's door. After a pause intended to add drama to his entrance, the great anchorman stepped out to bask in the crowd's idolization. While newsmen could not indulge in the sort of obvious fan pandering that movie starlets and athletes enjoyed, Hollander clearly relished his fame. With a humility that always shocked the people who knew him best, Hollander graciously gave a quick wave of the hand and a nod of the head. The gesture acknowledged his lofty position without appearing to need the adulation.

There were, however, one pair of eyes watching the anchorman that decidedly did not favor his arrival. Max Brackett knew that Hollander was there to steal his exclusive and thus ruin his best chance in years to return to the network.

Hollander saw Brackett's frown and was slightly intimidated. He was still the anchorman, however, and Brackett just a local boy. It was Hollander's call, and he was not going to be pushed around by a has-been. He led his entourage to a network motor home and got ready for business.

Inside the motor home, sitting around a crowded table in the living room, Kevin Hollander led the discussion. Sitting with him were several network staffers, Brackett, Laurie, and Lou Potts, who was ostensibly in charge of the story. Hollander discussed his vision of what was going on. "I see a great underlying theme. Sam Baily is tapping into something the working class can relate to."

Brackett watched Laurie listening to Hollander. She was awed by the great man. Brackett tried to keep the contempt out of his voice, but failed. "What's the matter, Kevin? Your numbers taking a dip?"

Laurie was startled. Lou Potts held his breath. The staffers laughed nervously, then hid their amusement by pretending to cough into their hands. Everyone waited to see how the great anchorman would respond. Would he laugh? Would he storm out? Would he demand that Brackett be fired?

Hollander surprised them all. He simply smiled, then talked turkey to Brackett—no anger, no threats—just the bottom line. "Let's cut the crap. I know we haven't gotten along in the past, but you want the network to take you back. Well, you're talking to it, buddy. Be a team player and this will be your ticket back in."

Brackett could not look at Hollander. His eyes darted to Lou and then briefly to Laurie. But it was her gaze that was the most difficult to match. In the end, Brackett could only stare down at the table. He was ashamed to be in this position, humiliated to look like a supplicant in front of Laurie and Lou, but he could not ignore what had just been offered to him. Brackett hated himself, but he was sorely tempted.

Hollander enjoyed himself tremendously. He was making Brackett eat humble pie, and at the same time moving in on the story of the year. There was little in this world that would give him more pleasure than to watch Brackett beg for his old job. Hollander began to play with his former nemesis. "When can I meet with Baily?"

Brackett could not reply.

Hollander kept right on, sparing Brackett nothing. "The network wants him to do a one-on-one. With me."

That was precisely what Brackett was determined to prevent. If Hollander got to do a solo interview with Sam, Brackett knew that he would be left by the wayside. The one piece of ammunition in his arsenal was that he alone knew Baily. The others did not, and as far as they knew, Sam might be a cold-blooded killer.

"Sam won't accept that. The guy's in the middle of committing a crime."

Hollander took another approach. He tried to win Brackett over by complimenting him for the fine work he already had done—good interviews with revealing, honest material.

Brackett parried by pointing out that he had already spent a day and a night with Sam trapped inside the museum. He had established a relationship. Sam had faith in him.

But Hollander did not buy the argument. He knew that years behind the CBN desk counted for a lot.

"He'll talk to me. I'm 'the man America trusts for news.' "

Brackett began to lose his self-control. Hollander could not uncover a real news story if it bit him on the ass. "That's a marketing slogan, Kevin. You shouldn't let it go to your head."

It was a standoff. While Hollander would normally have won hands down, taking a scoop away from a veteran journalist—even a disgraced one—was an undeniable complication. The two men glared across the tiny table at each other, years of animosity burning toward the surface.

And then before she realized she was speaking, Laurie interrupted the stalemate. "Maybe you both could speak to him on-air, make it more comfortable for him."

The blaring silence suddenly terrified Laurie. Why had she opened her mouth? The conflict between Brackett and Hollander was none of her business. Brackett shot her a look of fury, and Laurie swallowed hard. Simultaneously, Hollander looked at her curiously, and then he recognized her from the initial CBN broadcast. "You're the one who saved the guard."

Embarrassed to be the focus of his attention, Laurie admitted shyly that he was right.

Hollander recognized an easy target, and knew then how he could get what he wanted. Turning on his considerable charm—which was meant to convince Laurie that this great and experienced man admired the quality of her work—Hollander went for the kill. "I understand you've been working on a new piece about Sam Baily."

"Well, yes. But it's Max's story."

Hollander did not waste time with diplomatic niceties. He turned to Brackett. "I want to see it."

Brackett hesitated, but could not fight Kevin Hollander and win. If America's leading news anchor wanted to see the footage, he was going to see it.

Twenty minutes later, they screened the rough cut. Brackett watched himself proudly as he delivered the conclusion. "Sam Baily holds firm to his appeal for clemency. The law says no. So the waiting continues. This is Max Brackett reporting."

The crowded editing bay fell silent as everyone deferred to Hollander. Once they knew where he stood, they would feel free to agree with him. Then a comment came from an unexpected source. During the battle of egos, Lou Potts had become a forgotten man. Now, having watched the tape, the local news director did not like what he saw. Something was wrong. "This is a testimonial to the man," he said.

Brackett defended his work. "We're not here to try Sam Baily. That's for a court to do."

It was a facile response Lou could not accept. Had everyone forgotten that there were hostages inside the museum—innocent women and children who could be killed at any second? "This man is committing a felony."

Brackett was surprised when Hollander disagreed with Lou. "We're just packaging what people who know Sam Baily say about him. I'll take care of the felonies in the lead-in."

Brackett slammed his hand on the table. "Wait a minute! This is my story."

One of the CBN staffers stood up and laid down the law. "This story belongs to the network."

The lines were drawn, and the decision left to a miserable Lou Potts. However, it was not his decision at all. The network merely allowed him to appear to make the decision—to assuage the feelings of the local affiliate. Had Potts defended his turf, CBN would have taken over anyway. Everyone knew he was trapped, but Lou Potts still had to make it official.

Brackett scowled at the local news director. Lou tried to find a way out of the mess, then weakly signaled for Hollander to take over. Hollander wasted no time. "Great. Laurie, we're going to need to do some cutting. Let me see your outtakes."

Laurie's thrill was unmistakable. Brackett dully noted her shifted loyalty and got up from his chair to leave. Before he was out the door, however, Hollander caught him off guard again. "So when can I meet with Baily? To prepare for this one-on-one with me?"

Brackett would have liked nothing better than to smash Hollander's perfectly symmetrical smile with his fists. Instead, having learned the lessons of the past, he headed for the door, hoping to clear his head and think about how he could get back in control. In response to Hollander's question, Brackett confessed that he could not guarantee that Sam would cooperate. Hollander was of another opinion. "Oh, he'll jump at the chance. They all do. Play nice, Max. It could work well for you."

Brackett frowned as he left the network truck. Hollander was now firmly in command, and the scoop of a lifetime was threatening to slip away.

Hours later, as dusk began to fall, storm clouds gathered over the suburban sprawl of Madeline, California. Rain began to fall lightly, and in the distance lightning flashed.

Brackett left the KXBD news van, where he had been waiting. Lou followed the reporter back to the museum steps. Lou's sense of unease was growing. "What are you doing, Max?"

Brackett knew what he was doing, even if a small-time operator like Lou Potts could not understand. Brackett was saving his ass, doing whatever he could to save his future. "It's called journalism. I'm creating a sense of danger while maintaining an image of intimacy with my subject."

Lou knew bullshit when he heard it. "I guess I went to the wrong school."

Brackett loved to hassle people who had journalism degrees. He wore his lack of an education as a populist badge of honor. "Hey, at least you went."

But Lou was not distracted by Brackett's bootstraps bluster. Lou knew the whole deal stunk and wanted to register his opinion. "I learned you don't sleep with someone you're doing a story on, but I guess the oldest profession is alive and well. It's getting you back on the network."

What a sanctimonious jerk Lou could be. Brackett's hide was pretty tough, however, and he mustered up as much sincerity as he could. "Believe it or not, I'm not thinking that far ahead."

"You're right. I don't believe it."

As they walked, the two men passed a truck from Food-Star Supermarkets parked between the media and the police line. The side of the vehicle was placed in such a way that any camera taping the museum would get a lensful of logo as its workers unloaded food for the hostages. Next to the Food-Star truck was a van, from which workers unloaded boxes of Nike sneakers and sleeping bags for the hostages. A huge banner in a camera-friendly position read "Shoes—and Prayers—Offered by Coach Bob's Sporting Goods."

Brackett smiled at the stores' campaigns to help the children and their own images at the same time. It was crass consumerism at its most shameless.

Lou Potts was not so easily diverted. He focused on issues of right and wrong in the crisis. "what about the kids, Max?"

Brackett was not worried about the kids. Maybe they'd rather be home with their families right now, but Sam was certainly not going to hurt them. If they had to spend a night or two away from their bedrooms for Brackett to get back on the network, so be it. "The kids are okay. The kids are going to have a great tale to take to show and tell." If Brackett was not concerned about the children, he was certainly distressed about the greedy anchorman from New York. "I'm worried about Hollander. You could help by keeping him off my back."

Lou sighed. There was not much he could do. And at this point he was not sure there was much he wanted to do for Brackett anyway. "No I can't keep him off your back. I can't wrestle three-hundred-pound gorillas, either."

Without saying good-bye, Lou headed back to the news van. As heavier rain began to fall, umbrellas popped up everywhere amidst the circus. Television crews rushed to protect their electronic gear from the storm. Lou had no umbrella and did not care to have one. As he walked through the rain, he hoped it could somehow cleanse him. For the first time in his long career, Lou Potts felt dirty.

At the same moment, Brackett was figuring the angles as quickly as his mind could work through the possibilities. As it stood, he was still the only newsman Sam knew and trusted. That meant a lot. Kevin Hollander's reputation and ratings would mean nothing if

Sam was loyal to Brackett. So, Brackett was more determined than ever to keep Sam in his camp. One way would be to help maintain Sam's equilibrium. Anything Brackett could do to keep the hostages and their keeper happy could only be good. Brackett went to the rear door of the Coach Bob's Sporting Goods truck and gathered gifts to carry into the museum. With his arms full, he turned to make his way back up the granite steps.

Brackett was so focused upon his machinations, however, that he never bothered to look into the truck itself. If he had done so, he might have seen something that would have prevented him from losing control of his story later on.

The veteran reporter violated one of the most basic tenets of his profession: know what's going on better than anyone else.

Staring at Brackett from their positions hidden behind merchandise in the truck were three FBI snipers—faces blackened, well armed, and ready to kill.

Chapter Twenty-two

An hour later, the children finished their well-publicized dinners catered by Food-Star. Revitalized by a warm meal, they were burning off excess energy by running around the museum in their well-publicized new sneakers. Coach Bob had been generous. He could have sent nameless footwear and still gotten his airtime. But Coach Bob wanted the kids to talk about his store when the event was over and had given them expensive Nikes—complete with lights that flashed when the children's heels hit the floor. Coach Bob would be known throughout Madeline as a good neighbor—someone there for you in a pinch.

His accountant predicted a ten-percent increase in sales over the next six months. It was the most efficient advertising dollar he had ever spent. Coach Bob just hoped that the crazy son of a bitch with the gun did not kill anyone. Coach Bob's image would surely be tarnished if his footwear clad the feet of little corpses as they were rolled away on gurneys.

It was a risk. But that was business.

But the kids were not thinking of risk, business, or the danger of their predicament. Instead, they charged around the building and savored the chance to defy the traditional rules of order.

As the storm settled over Madeline, lightning

flashed and thunder rumbled. Some children shouted with delight, others squealed with fear—their nerves more on edge than the adults realized. Kelly Rose glanced at Sam, afraid that the noise might trigger another outburst. So far it had not, and she tried to calm her students before anything changed.

Sam looked at Kelly, Mrs. Banks, and then the rambunctious kids. The pandemonium did not bother him, but he was tired and the amphetamines he swallowed were making him increasingly anxious. Brackett wanted to keep Sam loose and tried to make a joke about the clamor. "Kids find museums boring as hell. Imagine being trapped in one."

Sam did not respond. Shaking another pill out of his bottle, Sam gulped it dry. He sat silently for a moment, then cocked his head as though he had heard something. Brackett tensed and looked around. What was going on? Sam listened intently and then shouted, "What's that?"

Sam walked to the center of the room, trying to isolate the sound that was bothering him. Brackett was puzzled. He had not heard anything. "What? What's going on?"

The children fell silent as they sensed trouble. Kelly and Mrs. Banks moved in front of the kids to protect them in case matters spun further out of control. Sam ignored Brackett and held up a hand, admonishing everyone to stay silent. "Did you hear that? There it is again!"

The adults exchanged glances, and each felt deep-rooted fear. So far Sam had been relatively rational. If the crisis itself was an act of madness, or more accurately carelessness, Sam had never been intent upon doing anyone harm. What they feared was accidental violence. If Sam was now hearing things, how-

ever, that could change everything. A deranged Sam
Baily could kill them all—quickly and easily. Brackett,
Mrs. Banks, and Kelly had all prayed that this moment
would never come. The children quickly felt the
grown-ups' fear and remained still.

Events seemed to degenerate rapidly toward chaos.
Sam started to herd the children to the wing of the
museum where the nineteenth-century exhibits were
kept. Brackett watched him carefully. Sam did not
shout and seemed quietly amused by what was going
on—as though he were involved in a private joke.
"Quick. Everyone this way. Hurry!"

Sam stood on the threshold of the nineteenth-
century wing and ushered everyone inside. The children were confused. Kelly and Mrs. Banks struggled
to restrain their growing sense of terror. Brackett was
the last one into the room and tried to read Sam's
eyes. But Sam turned away from him, walked past
the children, and approached the life-size statue of
an Indian.

The statue of the Miwok chief presented a contradiction, for he was simultaneously regal yet sad.
Dressed in buckskin ceremonial clothing with elaborate designs, beautiful accessories, and dignified feath-
ers in his hair—the Indian's right arm was raised in
greeting. The Miwok chief stood before a diorama of
an Indian village made up of tepees and a natural
environment designed to re-create the hills of Madeline from more than a century in the past. His round
face could have been kind, strong, and even fierce.
But the people who had built this statue gave him a
melancholy air—as though he were resigned to the
fate that awaited his people.

Holding his rifle, Sam walked up to the Indian in a
crouch, a suspicious look on his face. Sam cocked his

head again as though he had just heard something.
Then he spoke to the Indian in a familial tone that
chilled the blood of everyone who was watching. "Was
that you again, Big John?"

Brackett's pulse started to pound. He was overwhelmed with disbelief and fear. The pressure had
finally broken Sam, and he was now experiencing a
psychotic episode—hallucinating and not recognizing
the distinction between reality and imagination.

Mrs. Banks and Kelly were also horrified by what
they observed. Both knew that matters were now on
the edge of catastrophe. Each woman wanted to save
the lives of the children, but neither knew what they
could do. They stood, unblinking, staring at Sam, paralyzed with dread.

The children were less upset by Sam's breakdown.
They were used to talking to inanimate objects from
their own play. While it was odd that an adult would
engage in such activity, they did not perceive the in-
herent threat.

Sam turned an ear to the Indian, a smile on his
face. He listened carefully, then spoke to the statue.
"You want me to tell them? Are you sure? All right,
then, I will."

Fear and sadness overwhelmed Brackett's disappointment that his scoop was about to go bad. This
would probably be the end of the line for some of the
hostages and Sam as well. Brackett was not especially
worried about his own welfare. He had been in worse
jams, and he doubted Sam would kill him anyway. If
he did, who would be left to tell Sam's story?

Turning away from the Indian, Sam spoke gently to
the kids. "This here's Big John, he's a friend of mine.
You all sit down."

The students did as they were told. Mrs. Banks and

Kelly looked at each other curiously. Suddenly, Sam did not seem like such a threat after all. More than anything, Sam talked to the students like . . . a teacher. "Big John is a Miwok Indian. Can you all say that? Miwok."

The kids responded, and Sam was pleased. He stepped into the diorama, stood next to Big John, and continued. "Good. His people used to own this country. All this country. This was their home. Right here. Did you know that?"

One boy raised his hand as if they were still in school. Sam asked him what he wanted. The boy had once found a Miwok arrowhead. Sam leaned forward with a mock warning. "Shhh. Don't say that. Or Big John'll come and take it back."

The boy swallowed hard, and the others laughed nervously. Sam smiled broadly and began to tell the children about the Miwok Indians.

Brackett watched the transformation in Sam and realized that this hearing voices had all been for show. The kids had been bored, and Sam was offering a little entertainment and education.

"The Miwoks lived off the land. They hunted. They raised crops. They tended to their kids—kids just like you. And Big John, he was their chief. Anybody know what a chief is?"

Half the children shot up their hands in a friendly competition to provide the answer. Sam called on a girl, and she answered, "The chief is the boss."

"That's right. The chief is the *good* boss." Sam shot an accusatory look over to a startled Mrs. Banks. "He's supposed to take care of everybody." Sam walked over to a rheostat and dimmed the lights over the Miwok display.

Everyone's attention was on Sam. No one noticed

as lightning flashed through the skylight and illuminated three pairs of legs as they rushed past. As thunder rolled over the town, a blackened face appeared against the skylight, looking down into the nineteenth-century room. The man's eyes locked on Sam and followed him as he continued his story to the spellbound children.

"But the white man wanted this land. So one day, he came through and he killed everybody. He killed Big John's family. Kapow!"

Sam was getting into the spirit of storytelling. To emphasize the drama of the Miwok saga, Sam pointed his rifle harmlessly at different children each time he said "killed" or "kapow." "And he killed Big John's friends. Kapow! Just like that. Kapow! Kapow!"

A sharpshooter squinted through the rain-soaked skylight, trying to see more clearly. It appeared that Sam was threatening the children as he swung his rifle from kid to kid. He reported back to the command center. "He's got his rifle drawn on the students."

Agent Dobbins watched the museum through night-vision equipment. His view of Sam was obscured, but when he heard the report, he gave the order to open fire. "Take the shot. Now!"

The sharpshooters on the roof went to work. One man used a glass-cutting tool and a suction cup to remove a large pane of glass from the skylight. Two other sharpshooters crept into position and aimed their weapons at Sam. Both men hesitated. Sam was too close to the children to risk a shot.

"And Big John was way up on a hill overlooking his valley. He watched as everyone he knew, everyone he loved was killed. And it made him so sad—that his heart turned hard. It froze him up, just like a statue. Just like this."

The kids were astounded. What they were looking at was not a replica of Big John, but Big John himself. One boy did not bother to raise his hand to ask, "He's still alive?"

Sam smiled broadly. "You bet he is."

A sudden crash of thunder and lightning caused everyone in the room to look up at the skylight. Many kids giggled with excitement.

Brackett was not giggling. In the instant he looked to the ceiling he thought he saw a figure move away from the skylight. Was there someone up there watching them?

Sam walked away from the children and back into the diorama. He pointed to Big John's arm as it was held frozen in the air in a gesture of greeting. Sam had a different explanation, however. "Now, when the museum found him, his arm was down here." Sam pointed to Big John's side, where the Miwok chief would have held his hand if he were relaxing. "And when I started working here, a long time ago, it was up here." Sam raised his own arm to waist level. "So I started watching him, see, and darned if his arm didn't keep moving, so slowly that you'd hardly notice it. And I watched him, year after year, and one day I figured out what he's up to."

Sam paused dramatically. The adults were just as captivated as the children. Sam saw that he had their attention and finished his tale. Standing next to Big John, Sam slowly raised his arm to match the Miwok chief's wave. "I think Big John, the last chief of the Miwok Indians, is trying to wave good-bye."

No one in the room spoke or moved. While it was against his nature, Brackett found that he was touched. Sam Baily—an ordinary guy with an ordinary job, ordinary bills, ordinary family—had extraordinary problems. At that moment, Brackett could see that people like Sam—and Sam most especially—were succumbing to the new pressure of society and would soon be extinct. Sam's affinity for the display-case Indian was based upon their common fate.

Lightning exploded directly above the museum and cast a colossal shadow of a sharpshooter onto the wall behind Sam Baily.

One boy, who had been particularly mesmerized by Sam's tale, saw the shadow and assumed the Miwok chief had arrived in the form of a spirit. He pointed to the shadow and shouted, "Big John!"

Sam spun around and saw the immense shadow towering above him. Instinctively, Sam fell to his knees and looked up with awe. Just as he hit the floor, two gunshots were fired from the skylight. Instead of killing Sam, they hit Big John. One struck his shoulder, and the other blew off his raised hand.

Sam jumped to his feet and placed himself between the sharpshooters and the children—hoping to protect the students any way that he could. Mrs. Banks and Kelly shouted for the kids to follow them. They ran screaming out of the room and into a hallway, where there were no windows for anyone to shoot through.

From his position outside the museum, Dobbins saw that Sam was unharmed, and watched as he ran from the room and out of the line of fire. Dobbins swore and shouted his orders over his microphone. "You missed him. Pull back. Now!"

Near the front door, Sheriff Lemke stood waiting with a SWAT team, ready to rush inside. Lemke heard the bad news and Dobbins's further order. "Lemke, it's off. Stand down."

Lemke raced back to the police barricades to see

what had happened. His cellular phone rang, and Lemke grabbed it.

Sam shouted over the phone, "What the hell is going on? There are children in here!!"

Lemke lied as well as he could. "That wasn't us, Sam. That was some wacko. He got through the perimeter, but we'll take care of it. Everything will be under control, okay?"

While Sam was talking with the police, Mrs. Banks went after Brackett and demanded that he deal with Sam now. "You could end this."

"Don't be so sure."

For the first time Brackett was unsettled by what had just occurred. No one had been hurt, but it was still a closer call than he would have liked. Control in an unstable situation could be elusive, and Brackett began to wonder if he had pushed his luck too far.

Mrs. Banks would not leave him alone. "You're using this situation for your own self-aggrandizement."

Brackett snapped back, "None of us would be here if you'd taken an hour of your precious time to listen to what the guy had to say."

He turned and walked away before the curator could continue her harangue. Sam was on the phone. When he saw Brackett, he covered the mouthpiece and explained, "Lemke says it wasn't them."

Brackett was not in the mood to mess around. He reached for the phone, and Sam was only too happy to give it to him. Brackett did not buy the official story for a minute. "Listen to me, Lemke. You pull another stunt like that and I'm calling a parents' conference to let them know you're taking potshots at their towheads. And tell the FBI guy in your ear I said so." Brackett slammed down the phone.

Chapter Twenty-three

It was almost midnight, and the storm clouds were gone. As the children and the two women slept on the floor, Sam and Brackett sat up watching television. Both men were as relaxed as they had been since the crisis began. Perhaps both were just too tired to be anxious anymore. Sitting by the security desk, Sam could almost imagine that he was pulling a night shift with another guard. The silence was interrupted only by the TV sound and their conversation. Otherwise, if Sam did not look at the floor and see his hostages, or look out the window and see the circus, everything could have been normal.

The two men watched *The Tonight Show* as Jay Leno completed his opening monologue. "Then up there in Madeline, California, we've got this Sam Baily using the Steve Martin defense, which hasn't been used since the late seventies: Well, excuuuuusee meeee!"

The television audience in Burbank laughed raucously. Brackett glanced at Sam to see how he would react, but Sam took no offense whatsoever. In fact, he was delighted. "Jay Leno said my name."

Brackett was not sure the affair was worth the talk show host's attention. "How about that."

"Jay Leno knows who I am." That fact seemed to

provide some satisfaction for Sam. Brackett saw a look of contentment spread over the gunman's face—as though he had now accomplished something in life.

Brackett, not wanting to spoil Sam's mood, followed the direction of the conversation. "He's a nice guy."

Sam sat up and looked at Brackett differently. He had never imagined that anyone he knew would have ever met someone like Jay Leno. Even though Sam trusted Brackett with his life—and that implied a certain degree of respect—this new knowledge raised Brackett a few giant notches in Sam's estimation. "You met him?"

Brackett had met Jay Leno once long ago. They discussed old cars. Sam wanted to know who else Brackett knew. The most famous person Sam had ever met was a state assemblyman—and they had not actually met—Sam saw him from a distance at a rally near the air force base. Brackett knew notables from the pope to Tom Cruise—and the order in which he mentioned them did not necessarily indicate who was more important. Sam wanted to know what Tom Cruise was like.

"Who knows? I gave him softball questions, he gave me softball answers. You don't really get to know these people."

Sam thought this made sense. "But he plays softball, huh?"

Brackett was not sure if he should smile at Sam's naiveté or be annoyed. Both men were feeling relatively mellow, however, so Brackett chose to keep things light. "Bet your wife didn't know she was getting a celebrity when she married you, huh?"

The memory of Jenny made Sam sigh wistfully. "I think she knew what she was getting. Thirty-five years old and the best I can do is find a museum to guard for eight bucks an hour. And I can't even keep that."

Brackett asked how long Sam had been at the natural history museum.

"About five years. I was in the air force before that. I would have stayed in, too, but they wouldn't let me fly. No college. I don't know why you need a college degree to fly a plane."

"Why didn't you go to college?"

Brackett was amazed to hear no trace of bitterness in Sam's voice. "Rich kids go to college. Besides, all the results aren't in yet, but it appears that I'm not too bright."

Sliding closer to Sam, Brackett tried to make him feel better. "Guess what? I didn't go either."

"Get outta here."

Brackett had never even finished high school. He had quit and gone to work when he was fifteen years old. Sam did not understand. "How'd you get to be so smart?"

"Well, all the results aren't in yet, but I always got by on my personality. Just like you."

"So I could be on television and people would respond to me?"

"Sure. You're already famous."

"I'm famous in a bad way."

Brackett found himself encouraging Sam Baily to consider a career in television. It struck him as bizarre, and Brackett was suddenly not sure what he was doing. Here he was sitting up in the middle of the night—telling a gunman that he too might someday find fame and fortune on TV. But his words seemed to comfort Sam, and the reporter did not have the heart to disturb the fantasy. "Doesn't make any difference for TV."

Sam wanted to believe, but could not quite make the breakthrough. "Of course it makes a difference: people see it on TV and they know it's true. Look at me, I learned fishing on TV, and now I can do much better than those guys on those fishing shows."

"Oh, yeah, I heard you were a great fisherman."

Sam imagined a different life for himself—a life that did not have to end here in the Madeline Natural History Museum. "Man, I'd love to get paid to fish all day on TV. Traveling to all the best spots. Trying out the newest equipment. Man."

Perhaps it was the sheer impossibility of Sam's dream that brought Brackett back to reality. What were they talking about? What did the gunman think was going to happen here when the last cards were dealt? Sam was never going to have a fishing show. Chances were that he would never get out of prison or a mental hospital.

Yet, Brackett still needed Sam on his side, so he was not going to tell him the truth and upset him. The bottom line for Brackett was not Sam's survival, but airtime. If Sam got angry with Brackett and joined forces with Kevin Hollander, then Max Brackett would spend the rest of his career in Madeline. He was not going to let that happen. If Brackett could give Sam some peace of mind, earn his loyalty, and string him along for a while longer—then that was a price he was willing to pay.

Brackett knew what he had to say, and as outrageous as it sounded, he made it seem credible. "Tell you what, when this is over, I'll recommend you to my station."

Sam did not believe his ears and laughed. It was too crazy to even think about. However, after a moment, he gradually became thrilled by the possibility.

If Max Brackett—friend of Jay Leno and Tom Cruise—backed him, how could he fail? Then his spirits sagged, remembering that he was surrounded by hundred of cops and held a classroom of school-children hostage. Sam gestured around the room sadly. "It's over for me."

No. It wasn't over until Brackett said it was over, and he was not going to let Sam give up. "Hey. Things are bad, but we've got people sympathizing with you."

"Am I gonna get out of here without going to jail?"

Allowing no despair or negative thinking and defying reason, Brackett created a future for Sam to believe in. "Best case scenario; we put enough spin on this thing, you'll get a little time plus probation. Then: *Sam Baily's Catfish Corner.*"

Sam did not buy it.

Brackett used an old standby—the personal testimonial. "Stranger things have happened. Look at me. I used to work for the network."

Sam wanted to know what had happened, but that was territory Brackett would not explore. "The point is I was down and now I'm up. Thanks to you. You never can tell, Sam. You might be back in your woman's lovin' arms sooner than you think."

Sam thought how lucky he was that Brackett stumbled into the hostage crisis. Brackett helped him negotiate with the police, and now Sam felt that Brackett was becoming a friend. For what else was a friend but someone who stood by you and selflessly faced down danger?

But Sam knew nothing about the reporter's life, so he asked if Brackett was married. Brackett had been married. When Sam asked if he had any kids, Brackett laughed ruefully. "Three out of four." Sam did not understand. "Three kids out of four wives. They're scattered all over the country. I have to do a grand tour to visit them all."

Brackett's marriages had all been short, but none of them sweet. As a young reporter, Brackett was obsessed with climbing to the top. That cost one marriage. When he arrived at the top as a network correspondent, Brackett's obsession increased as he fought to remain where he was. That cost two more wives. And while on the skids, he reached out to a woman to slow his fall. But he still fell. His bitterness cost him the fourth marriage.

Brackett's children, seventeen to six, knew their father only from dynamic, if frenzied, visits. Brackett would sweep into their lives, feed them, offer banal encouragement and hurried apologies, then depart without noticing they were family.

Like any good journalist, Max Brackett did not get personally involved.

But Brackett shared none of this with Sam. Instead, he yawned and stretched as Jay Leno said good night. Sam yawned, too. His exhaustion was complete, for he had not slept since the whole business began. Brackett saw Sam look enviously at the sleeping children. "Look, why don't you get a few hours sleep?" Sam was tempted, but skeptical. Brackett tried again. "Nothing is going to happen. I promise."

Sam looked at Brackett, wanting to believe him. Then he remembered the sharpshooters in the skylight and realized that not even Brackett could control everything. He turned down the offer with regret.

Brackett shrugged and climbed into a sleeping bag.

Sam watched Brackett, then turned his attention to his TV. Soon he was transfixed by another late night talk show and quickly forgot his problems.

Chapter Twenty-four

Early in the morning Sam paced through the building. Fatigue and cumulative amphetamines translated into a myriad of little twitches and nervous apprehension.

Some children were already awake and were watching television at the security desk. Sam joined them briefly and saw Kevin Hollander delivering a description of his life to the *Wake Up, America!* show. For a second, Sam's tired mind registered that the reporter knew everything about his life, and talked about its detail with an amazing ease. And then he stumbled away again and haunted the halls.

Meanwhile, in another part of the museum, Brackett sat alone, speaking into his cell phone. He had been watching *Wake Up, America!* and was not a happy man. While keeping his voice down, Brackett spoke angrily to his agent in New York. "You tell them this is my story. Hollander's snatching it away."

A continent away, Marty Young was crowing over his client's recent success. For some time Young had given up Brackett's career for dead. Now with Brackett in the middle of the hottest news story of the year, Young was fielding offers left and right. At the moment, however, he had to convince Brackett to let the Madeline story go. Considering what the networks were offering, it should not have been difficult. "They know that's what Hollander's doing. They approve. And in exchange they're offering you your own show. A magazine *Sixty Minutes* format. Investigative. In your face. They say, and it remains to be seen, that you will have editorial freedom, whatever that means. But it will be national, and they are talking about real money."

This was the news that Brackett had been waiting for years to hear. Actually, it was even better than he could have hoped. Brackett had been aiming to return as a network correspondent. And now he was being offered his own program!

And it was all due to Sam Baily.

Brackett wanted to shout at the top of his lungs. He even wanted to hug Mrs. Banks for being such a tight-ass, and Lou Potts for his petty, vindictive assignment.

He should not forget the cops, either. They didn't bother to find out that Sam Baily was harmless and that this business was an accident. If they had not wildly overreacted by calling in the FBI, sharpshooters, helicopters, the works—Max Brackett would have had no story to ride to greater glory.

Nor could Brackett forget to thank the crowds. He should embrace every one of the vultures who gathered to watch *Bloodshed Live!* Without their presence, the hostage crisis would have been less of a mass-market event. Because they left their homes and jobs for entertainment, the networks saw an outpouring of concern that was irresistible television.

Could Brackett forget to thank the network? All those smug suits who had let him rot for years in a backwater affiliate? Yes, he thought, for without their cooperation, Sam Baily would have been no more than a local blip. While their self-righteous trumpeting of obligations and ethics annoyed him, Max Brackett knew they were wonderfully gifted carnies standing at the freak show gate.

But most of all, Max Brackett wanted to hug his new friend, Sam Baily. Without Sam's clumsy entry into the pantheon of America's disaffected, Max Brackett would still be covering the opening of shopping malls and local pooch parades. Brackett had grabbed innocuous Sam Baily's coattails and was being dragged back into the world of the living. Brackett had no intention of letting go, even at the cost of his—Sam's—life.

Anything could happen now, all to Brackett's advantage. The museum as a slaughterhouse would be good TV—as long as the correspondent on the spot survived to describe it. Brackett hoped the siege could be played to its breaking point. Just before the guns opened fire, Brackett wanted to lead Sam Baily to surrender. He had imagined it over and over during the long night. Kevin Hollander could host a live national TV broadcast as Max Brackett delivered captive children to their parents—and record-breaking ratings to the network.

Brackett's reverie continued as his agent rattled on about his negotiating triumph. "They're making an interesting request, however. And you did not hear this from me."

Brackett listened, but also watched as Sam opened his bottle of amphetamines and realized he was out of pills.

"They are suggesting that if you have any control over the situation—I insisted that you don't—it would be a good idea if Baily were to surrender in the evening."

The reporter gasped. "Prime time." At that moment, Max Brackett could not have said whether his reaction was one of triumph or disgust. Quite possibly it was both.

"Their Thursdays are particularly weak."

"Christ, Marty."

But business was business. They were not in television to earn a halo and wings. The agent needed an answer. "I know. I know. Should I lock the deal down? What do you say?"

Brackett did not have to consider for long. "Just tell them to be ready to move their gear in."

He hung up the phone and looked at the TV screen. Hollander was anchoring a broadcast from a hastily assembled news desk in the parking lot. Brackett felt a twinge of envy. As though he could feel his friend's discomfort, Sam switched to Channel Five and found a psychologist giving his assessment of the affair. "Sam Baily's story strikes a chord with a populace fearful of becoming redundant. Companies are downsizing. Technology is passing them by. People are afraid. And fear can turn to anger in a heartbeat. They see a Sam Baily snap, and they feel justified in their anger. Somebody is taking a stand for them."

Sam switched stations again and found a man-in-the-street interview from a neighboring community. "Sam Baily's right. This is one of the best college towns in the country, but I can't afford to go. We don't have a future."

Less than twenty-four hours earlier Sam had fired shots over the crowd in despair and disappointment. Now, watching TV, he was beginning to think that things might not turn out so bad after all. People across America did not think of Sam Baily as a common criminal. To the contrary, Sam was being embraced as an icon of the embattled ordinary American.

People nationwide were not only sympathetic, but viewed him as something of a hero. To many, Sam was standing up for them, their futures, and that of their families.

Sam watched his transformation with amazement. All his life he had been among the great unnoticed. Now he became intoxicated with his new status and could not get enough of the shows that discussed his life. Sam turned back to the on-air psychologist who raised a new question. "Of course, everything would have been different had the young man who was shot died."

Sam did not want to think about this less appealing perspective. He flipped again and found himself watching an interview by reporter Nat Jackson from Cliff Williams's hospital room. Sam smiled when he saw Cliff. Soon, he hoped, his friend would be out of the hospital. Sam owed Cliff big time for what happened and planned to make good.

Jackson stood beside a sleeping Cliff and wrapped up his report. "What about Cliff Williams? He cannot know that his attacker, Samuel Baily, has become something of a folk hero, his words tapping into a nationwide mood of discontent among the public."

As Jackson spoke, Cliff's eyes fluttered open. Disoriented enough by his medical trauma, he was confused further when he saw a live image of himself broadcast on the television set mounted onto a wall. Cliff looked to his right and saw a tall man standing next to him, speaking into a microphone. Cliff looked up at the TV and saw the man there, too. He listened as the man spoke solemnly. "Baily seems to be asking 'What about us?' The people who support him are asking the same question."

Certain that he was hallucinating, Cliff wiggled his fingers, and was dismayed to see the man on the TV doing the same thing. Nat Jackson never noticed that Cliff was awake and distressed. Instead, he stared at the camera with as much empathy as he could manufacture and made a plea to his audience. "But what about Cliff Williams?"

Cliff could not believe what he was seeing and hearing. It was easier just to avoid the whole business, and he closed his eyes while shaking his head. Even his nightmares could not be as strange as this reality.

Sam switched channels again. CNN was live from the parking lot. The circus continued to grow as people from all over the country began to congregate at the museum to espouse a variety of agendas. An anchorwoman asked the on-site reporter to comment upon a disturbing schism that had developed. As Brackett had predicted, playing the race card produced a "black" camp and a "white" camp.

White men and women chanted, "What about us?", while only several feet and a few police barricades away black men and women shouted back, "What about us?" Neither group was particularly inspired to eloquence.

The stupider ones among the crowed chose to blame people with a different skin color for their own misfortunes. The police had to intervene in small but desperate skirmishes that broke out between some of the black and white factions.

Kevin Hollander strolled through the turbulent crowd and descended on Laurie, who was talking to Lou. Hollander spoke as though he were recruiting Laurie to a noble crusade. "I need a sidebar to do in case Baily isn't ready to talk. Can you plug me in out in the field, be my eyes and ears?"

Laurie looked astonished to be asked for assistance. Hollander explained himself. "You've been on the story from day one."

Lou listened as Hollander bewitched Laurie. The anchorman used the language of a suitor. She was the one person who could help him. She was unique. He needed her.

With all the journalistic firepower on the scene, Lou had been considering assigning Laurie to another story, one she could make her own. If she stayed with this assignment, she would be lost in the crowd. But once Hollander began his flirtation, Lou knew Laurie would be lost. Still, he tried. "They tried to cut a deal in the Foothill Bank fraud last night."

The bank fraud story had been Brackett's. He uncovered it and ambushed the bank president just before Sam Baily took his hostages. Laurie was surprised to hear there had been such rapid progress. "That was quick," she said.

"They figured no one would notice with this circus going on. I need you. We could free you up to work on it. Hundreds of people have lost their life savings, and no one's covering the story."

Lou's offer would have been a huge step forward in Laurie's career. A few days earlier she had been an assistant, a Jill of all trades, getting coffee, shooting an occasional piece, doing whatever had to be done. And now here was the news director offering her a major story of her own. Laurie was about to take Lou's offer, but Hollander interrupted. "That sounds like an important story, but it's no ticket to the network. You should think about that."

Things were going too fast for Laurie. It should

have been enough that Lou just gave her the first big assignment of her life. Now, Hollander raised the stakes exponentially. A chance at the network was not an opportunity that came along every day. Yet, she felt a loyalty to Lou Potts, the man who had mentored her career. Ambition versus fidelity—it seemed an easier decision framed in those terms.

An hour later, an uncertain Cliff Williams sat up in his hospital bed, stared into a television camera, and said, "My name is Cliff Williams."

An impatient member of a television crew adjusted the microphone clipped to Cliff's hospital gown. The crew member checked the equipment and spoke to Cliff, his annoyance unmistakable. "It's not the microphone. You have to talk louder."

Chastened, Cliff apologized.

Outside the room, standing in the corridor, Cliff's wife, Diane, was being lobbied by two different people. Dr. Madison was a large, kindly-looking man with a trimmed beard and glasses. His firmness could not mask his concern. "Mrs. Williams, I really must advise against this. Your husband isn't strong enough yet."

Laurie Callahan cut the doctor off. "I saved his life! His first interview should be with Kevin Hollander."

Laurie had made her decision for the network. She knew this must have disappointed Lou Potts, but rationalized that since he was a friend of the family, he would have her best interests at heart. Anyone would know that a shot at the network was in her best interest.

Now she had to deliver. Short of Sam Baily, the only scoop worth having was an interview with Cliff Williams. She had saved the man's life, and he was giving his on-air appearance to someone else. How could someone do something like that?

Diane Williams's answer was apologetic. "They're paying us fifteen thousand dollars."

"*Crime and Punishment* is a tabloid show. Do you know what kind of sleaze they do?"

This time Diane Williams's response was firmer. Her family was in trouble, and she did not need the added aggravation of this holier-than-thou reporter. "We really needed the money."

Dr. Madison watched this interchange and was appalled both by Laurie's audacity and Mrs. Williams's foolish decision to cash in while her husband was still a sick man. He knew, however, that neither woman was going to listen. Dr. Madison threw up his hands in exasperation and walked away.

Crime and Punishment was about to go on the air with an exclusive interview from Cliff Williams's hospital bed. Since the deal had been struck hours before, the upstart network that broadcast the syndicated tabloid show had inundated the airwaves with promos. All across America viewers tuned in for their best glimpse at the unfolding tragedy in Madeline.

Hovering over Cliff's bed was *C&P*'s star reporter, Angelica Sierra. An assistant checked Sierra's makeup while the glamorous and tenacious correspondent cleared her throat and gave the bedridden patient last-minute instructions. "Okay, we'll go again. In five-four-three-two . . . Cliff. Sam Baily—the man who shot you—has been pleading for forgiveness. How do you feel about that?"

Cliff had given this some thought and discussed it with his wife. Despite his bullet wounds, he found it difficult to think that Sam had been trying to kill him. Cliff took a deep breath and spoke weakly. "Well,

I've known Sam for a long time, and I really don't think he meant to hurt me."

He paused to regain his strength. Angelica Sierra conjured up her "worried, sympathetic, and isn't this terrible" look over the airwaves. Across America, men, women, children, and unusually perceptive dogs watched Angelica Sierra and were worried. They felt sympathy for Cliff and thought, Gee, isn't this terrible.

Cliff felt ready to continue, and defended his old friend. "The doctor says it looks like I'm going to be okay. Insurance is covering the hospital bills. Everything's fine on my end. Hey, I've got no problem with Sam."

Sitting with Sam at the security desk in the museum lobby, Max Brackett was thrilled. They were watching *Crime and Punishment,* and Brackett could not believe the good news. "Jesus. You've got his blessing." If Sam Baily's victim, still lying in a hospital bed, could forgive the gunman, then how could the rest of America not? It might just be that Sam Baily was going to be saved by public opinion.

Brackett saw that Sam was not equally excited by Cliff's statement. In fact, he was preoccupied. He turned to Brackett. "They get paid for that show, huh?"

"It's a tabloid. They buy up exclusive access."

"How much?"

"I don't know. Ten grand."

Brackett's discomfort grew when Sam said, "If they'd pay Cliff ten grand, they'd pay me, what, maybe fifty? I'm the whole deal here."

Brackett had to kill this catastrophic development as quickly as he could. He had not put his life on the line and labored furiously to keep this business from deteriorating—just so Angelica Sierra could steal it from him. He tried the high road, hoping to appeal to Sam's basic decency. "I thought this wasn't about ransom."

But Sam, suddenly more sophisticated, had been watching the whole process carefully and was learning. He was a different man from the one who walked into the museum, hoping just to be heard. Brackett swore at himself. He had created a monster. He knew what was coming next.

Sam agreed with Brackett. "You're right. It's not about ransom. It's about show business."

Brackett had to move quickly before Sam made any rash decisions. Although beginning to like Sam, Brackett had to risk angering him. "You shoot a guy, you take a bunch of kids hostage and your checkbook gets fat? How do you think that's going to look to those people out there?"

Sam's brief rebellion stalled, and his spirit sank. He tried to hold out for what he deserved. It was all his idea, his doing. If he had to go to jail, or was going to be killed—he should be compensated. "I should get my family some money. . . ."

Brackett was magnanimous in victory. The best way to keep Sam in his place was to increase his obligation. "Look, if this thing keeps building, there might be money later on, from a book or a TV movie or whatever. I know people who will help you."

But Sam did not accept this new defeat graciously. His anger quickly flashed in rejection. Brackett was making vague promises, and this was not what Sam had expected. Sam had spent a lifetime waiting to receive the rewards of similar promises. He invested himself in the American Dream. For all of it, he had nothing, and his future was grim—quite possibly very short. Sam was tired of waiting. "That's in the future.

It wouldn't hurt to at least see what these other shows are offering now."

The dying embers of Sam's insurrection had to be put out. But before Brackett could do so, his cell phone rang. Brackett could hear the nervousness in Lou Potts's voice. "Hollander needs to see you out here. Something's come down from New York."

Brackett knew the bad news. The network would order him to hand Sam over to Hollander—and that would be the end of his participation in the story. He hung up the phone, turned to leave, then offered Sam some last advice—a shot at turning a setback into an advantage by taking credit for a decision that had nothing to do with him. "You want money? Go ahead, call the tabloids yourself. Kevin Hollander's out there. I'm taking this to the next level. You stick with me and you'll sit down with the top anchorman in America. If not, then good luck with whoever pays you the most."

As a self-righteous Brackett stormed out of the museum, Sam was astonished. Brackett was going to put Sam on the air with Kevin Hollander. The gunman began to feel bad for threatening to take his story away from the reporter. He had threatened the one man who helped him through this disaster. Not only did Sam feel like a jerk, he also might have jeopardized his chance to be on TV with a legend. Tabloids and their money were one thing. But Kevin Hollander, the most trusted man in America, might actually be able to set things straight for Sam and help him get his life back to normal.

Sam vowed to make things right with Brackett.

Brackett rushed down the museum steps and headed for the news van. As he moved through the crowd, he sensed a growing tension. The circus atmosphere—festive, if garish—had become darker. The crowd was becoming a mob as fatigue and impatience wore people down. Brackett listened to a reporter file a live report. "Madeline, California, is now experiencing an unfamiliar fury. And it appears that Baily is not anymore a source of wish fulfillment for a number of Americans."

A young woman stepped in front of Brackett and blocked his path. She was the mother of one of Sam's hostages. "Mr. Brackett, please. My son, Daniel, is in there. Sam has made his point. Why doesn't he let them go?"

Brackett tried to pull away from her. "I hope it will be over soon."

But she would not let him get away that easily. The woman grabbed Brackett's arm and begged him to do something. "When? When? Please tell Sam to let my son go!"

Her husband nodded to Brackett and led his wife away. Brackett moved on through the mob, passing a group of amateur folksingers playing guitars, and singing something known as "Sam's Song." Their words, "Is anybody listening, does anybody care . . ." should have delighted Brackett. It was favorable coverage, and was it not the truest test of a person's folk-hero status—to have odes written about them? Brackett was not sure he cared anymore. If he could hold onto the story, fine. But if Hollander stole Sam Baily, then Brackett did not care how many earnest songs were written.

Wading through the tightly packed crowd, he passed a group of young African Americans performing an embittered rap piece. "What about Cliff? He's the one who got shot. Does anybody care? I don't think so. What about Cliff? He got gunned down. Is anybody listening?" Once again, Brackett was not impressed by the creative effort. But it was impossible not to feel the anger.

Buffeted by the throng, Brackett began to be genuinely disturbed by the ugly atmosphere. People were angry, and violence only a reckless comment away. The smallest provocation could set this horde to fighting. Shepherding the account of Sam's life onto the network was difficult enough. Brackett did not need any more excitement.

As he passed a CNN crew preparing for broadcast, a producer fell into step with Brackett. Word had come in from the executives in Atlanta. "Larry King wants to make you an offer. The full hour tonight. Just your boy and you."

Brackett did not stop to discuss the matter. "I got something going," he said.

The producer from CNN made a convincing argument. "We're talking global, Max. The networks can't compete with that."

As the two men reached the CBN truck, Kevin Hollander glared at them from the doorway and sternly gestured for Brackett to get inside. The CNN producer saw this, smiled, and took a last shot. "You know where to find me!"

Hollander led Brackett into the truck's editing bay, where they found a worried Lou and a solemn Laurie. Hollander did not waste time with niceties. "The network wants you to turn Baily over to me. We're offering him an expanded segment in prime time tonight."

No surprises here. Brackett knew there was a certain inevitability about the whole deal. Still, he saw no point in being a good sport about it. "Maybe you could get him his own variety show."

Pushed nearly to the limit, Hollander would have

hit Brackett, but still needed the reporter to hand Baily off to him. "Listen, you fuck. Get off your high horse. Hand Baily over to us now, and you'll be back at the network."

"Baily belongs to the network, Max."

Brackett stared at Laurie—disbelieving her words. Brackett was disappointed. Not in Laurie. For if he had been in her position, he would have sided with the biggest dog in the kennel, too. But Brackett was discouraged by his own naiveté.

The man who prided himself at having seen it all, someone who witnessed the basest actions of the human species, a person so cynical that he could not be hurt, was still wounded when a fresh-faced kid went over to the other side.

Perplexed, Max Brackett had never felt this way before. What was happening?

Chapter Twenty-five

Sam Baily stared out a window at the melee in the parking lot. The arc and frequency of his mood swings grew as the pressure of the siege continued unabated. When Brackett had gone, Sam felt bad about mistreating his one ally. Then he felt better, cheered that at least someone was looking out for his best interests. Watching the turmoil surrounding him, however, Sam was became agitated again.

He never heard Mrs. Banks walk up behind him. He turned when she called his name softly. For the first time since he had been fired, Sam did not see her as the enemy. He did not understand his feelings, but for some reason her presence calmed him. Maybe a familiar face posed less of a threat than the churning crowd.

With Brackett out of the building, Mrs. Banks decided to approach Sam. She could no longer predict the behavior of anyone involved, but was certain that Brackett had steered Sam away from several opportunities to end the siege. Aware that her rebuke had provoked Sam into his outlandish conduct, Mrs. Banks softened her approach. "How is this going to end, Sam?" she asked.

"They'll let me go. Or—"

Mrs. Banks was not happy to hear Sam start down

this path. He did not seem to fully understand the trouble he was in. "Or what, Sam? Because they're not going to let you go."

"Max said—"

Mrs. Banks interrupted him a second time. But she did not scold. Rather her tone was firm and sad. "Max Brackett is not your friend."

This was a revelation to Sam. What did she mean? She had fired him. The police were trying to shoot him. Max, on the other hand, helped him survive. Sam was tired, and he did not have the energy to try to understand Mrs. Banks's point. He just wished the whole business had never taken place. "If you had given me five minutes."

Mrs. Banks was practical, and while she had her regrets, wallowing in them would achieve nothing. "I wish I'd listened to you. But this is bigger than you and me now. You're forcing them to do something drastic. I don't want to scare you, but they are ready to kill you, and Brackett cannot stop them."

Sam listened to the wildly different perspective from Brackett's, and that confused him. Brackett talked of TV shows and interviews with Kevin Hollander. Mrs. Banks told him that there would be no media canonization for him, no happy ending—the police wanted him dead. It was as simple as that. Sam wished it did not have to be this way, but he knew in his heart that Mrs. Banks's version was true.

In the CBN editing bay, Hollander wore down Brackett's resistance. While Brackett wanted to maintain control over Sam, Hollander knew he had the trump card. Brackett could have taken Sam to another network. But Hollander understood that Brackett's vindication could only be complete if he went back on the airwaves of CBN. Returning to his old network would prove that CBN had made a mistake—and that Brackett had been wronged. "Come on home, Max," Hollander said. "It's where you belong. Even I'll admit that."

A phone rang, and Laurie grabbed it.

Brackett thought through his options. Exhausted, he wanted to be especially careful. Having examined all the possibilities, and having enjoyed watching Hollander practically beg, Brackett agreed. "All right. You'll get your show."

He got up and headed for the door. Lou Potts offered bitter congratulations. Brackett stopped where he was and looked back at a smiling Hollander, then stayed to listen as Laurie handed a telephone to the anchorman. The network statistics department had just called the executives. Laurie beamed and looked at Hollander with admiration. "You were right. They've turned."

Hollander listened to the call from New York. "It's flipped. Fifty-nine percent positive down to thirty-two percent and sliding." Hollander tossed the phone back to Laurie and shared the news with the room. "The polls've turned against him."

He turned to Laurie with new instructions. "We need a new opening. I want stuff on the guy in the hospital—the footage where he's shot on camera. I want grieving mothers, frightened children. I want racists singing Baily's praises. Go."

Laurie pushed past Brackett and out the door. "See you in New York, Max!"

Brackett stood where he was. An empty feeling overwhelmed him. He must need sleep. Somewhere deep within, Max Brackett felt something he had not experienced in years. When Brackett spoke to Hollander, his voice sounded hollow, and he did not recognize himself. "You're going to sink him."

Hollander was neutral. He stated the facts. "He's sunk. I'm just riding the wave."

That strange feeling surged in Brackett's chest. He still could not identify it—anger, disgust, sadness? Not sure, he registered his protest anyway. "You can't do this."

Hollander replied scornfully. "I can't? Haven't you learned anything in your forty days in the desert? It's not a big tragedy. Go prime your guy for me. And don't forget, you work for us now."

What would be the point of responding? Brackett did not want to give the leering anchorman the satisfaction. Instead, Brackett left the truck and walked through the crowd. Passing the CNN producer, he said pointedly, "I'm thinking about it." Then he made his way wearily back up the steps to the museum. Before he entered, Brackett turned to the parking lot and gazed at the insanity.

In the command center people were feeling different. Agent Dobbins got off the phone with Washington, stood up triumphantly, and gave his men an order. "Get ready."

As his sharpshooters picked up their weapons, Sheriff Lemke awakened from a nap and wanted to know what was going on. He was chilled by Dobbins's enthusiastic reply. "Looks like John Q. Public has come to his senses."

Brackett found Sam in bad condition. Frightened by what Mrs. Banks had told him, Sam sat, cradling his gun and rocking back and forth. He hoped he might have overlooked something. Nothing came to Sam.

Once again his anger began to brew. He never noticed Brackett in front of him, and stared. When Sam did realize someone was there, he reacted with a start. "What? What is it?"

As gently as he could, Brackett delivered the bad news. "It's time to give up, Sam."

Sam did not want to hear this from Brackett. CBN and the anchor were his one last hope. Brackett could not take that away from him now. "What are you talking about? I'm going back on TV with Kevin Hollander."

Even as he spoke, Brackett was not sure what he was going to do. Should he talk Sam into surrendering, or do something else? Did he have the right to talk Sam into quitting—and spending the rest of his life behind bars? Or should he encourage Sam to enjoy a last shot at the limelight? Could a good conversation with Larry King turn around his negative numbers? Could a successful interview get Brackett a job at CNN? Brackett was tired, but the more he thought about Larry King's offer, the more excited he became.

Max Brackett decided that Sam's future lay with the king of talk himself. They would screw Kevin Hollander and CBN before they themselves were screwed. Sam would take his exclusive to *Larry King Live*. But Brackett had to get Sam to go along.

And then complicating matters, there was this nagging new sensation he felt. In the past Max Brackett never considered people's lives more than a commodity. The good, the bad, the joyful, and the tragic were nothing more than product that filled a time slot. Now, having been as close to Sam as he had been to any person in a long time, Max Brackett felt a hint of human emotion. Naturally curious about his response,

Brackett did not recognize the feeling and chose to ignore it since he had too much on his plate anyway.

All he was certain of was that Sam had to switch allegiances to CNN immediately and abandon the notion of talking to Kevin Hollander. Brackett went to work. "Hollander's going to destroy you."

Sam shook his head. That did not make sense. People on TV said everyone loved Sam. That's why a celebrity like Kevin Hollander would fly clear across the country to interview him. He was a hero. Strangers wrote folk songs about him. "Why would he do that?" Sam asked.

Brackett did not explain the details, choosing instead to make it an issue of trust. "Believe me. He's going to make you look bad."

"I can take care of myself!"

In the past a man like Sam could have taken care of himself, but now he faced extinction. Brackett knew it as certainly as he knew that tomorrow morning's talk shows would be broadcast from the East.

And there it was again—that unfamiliar feeling. Was it compassion? Why did he care? He never did before. Or was Max Brackett simply beyond exhaustion?

Fortunately, Brackett's need to warn Sam worked in tandem with his desire to get him to take his exclusive to Larry King. "No, Sam. You can't take care of yourself. Not with Kevin Hollander."

"I'm not afraid of him."

Sam was not going to listen. He was caught somewhere between the defiant spirit of a frontier American and a six-year-old's temper tantrum. "I'm not afraid of anybody," he said. "I'm going back on TV. The people respond to me. If you won't help me, I'll go to Hollander myself."

Brackett sighed. He was too late. Sam believed what he heard on TV. He thought he actually had a rapport with the people. Little did Sam know that his favorability ratings had plummeted overnight. Sam had no idea that he had slipped from hero to terrorist between *Nightline*'s good night and *Wake Up America!*'s good morning. Clearly, Sam no longer felt that he needed the reporter's help.

Brackett's options were limited. Sam had to switch allegiances, but Brackett no longer had a certain way to manipulate the gunman's decision. Instead, he decided to appeal to Sam's ego. "All right, but not Hollander. We get somebody else."

Sam was wary. "As big as Hollander?"

"Bigger."

"Set it up, newsman." For a moment it seemed Sam had already acquired the swagger of celebrity. Then Brackett saw Sam's grin and knew that he was kidding. Sam was on top of the world and having a good time. Both men knew there was only one man bigger than CBN's Kevin Hollander, and to appear on his show was the ultimate endorsement of having arrived.

The mood was not so celebratory inside the CBN truck. Kevin Hollander was on the phone to New York, and no one nearby could bear to look at him. The legendary anchorman was pale, his humiliation public. He had just lost his exclusive interview with Sam Baily, and Al Merton, back at network headquarters, screamed at him so loudly that everyone in the room had an idea of what was being said. "You get there and lose the only exclusive all the networks dream of. You make the network look preposterous after announcing all day long your exclusive one-on-

one with Baily. Now you'll look stupid, and worse, you make the network look witless."

The local staff were astounded that someone would talk to Hollander like that. Hollander did his best to pretend that no one else could hear his excoriation. Then Merton added the definitive insult. "You come back immediately. It's all Brackett's now."

That was war. Kevin Hollander would not accept that kind of degradation from anybody. He was not going back to New York, and he was not about to give Sam Baily back to his nemesis. "I'm staying. I'll take care of Brackett. Nobody'll be able to say I did anything to harm the network's image."

Hollander slammed down the phone, stalked through the truck, and locked himself in the bathroom. He started putting together a plan.

Chapter Twenty-six

The seconds were ticking down to Sam and Brackett's live appearance on TV's most influential show. Brackett aimed an unmanned camera at Sam and an empty chair, then ran to join Sam on their makeshift set beneath the dinosaur skeleton. As he tried to look comfortable, Brackett noticed Sam's rifle, out of camera view at his feet.

A voice in their earpieces told them they were moments away from show time. Then the cheerful voice of Larry King offered an introduction and got down to business. "How are the kids, Sam?" he asked.

Sam was on Larry King. It did not seem possible, yet here he was. Sam adopted the glib tone of a movie star without a care in the world, shilling his latest picture. Sam's smile had a winner's charm as he repeated Larry's question with good-natured confidence. "How are they?"

Turning to the children on the "set" behind him, Sam addressed them like a beloved camp counselor, beaming with the satisfaction of having taken good care of his charges. "How are you guys?"

The kids reacted perfectly—roaring their delight at being on *Larry King Live,* jumping up and down and waving to America through the camera. They hardly resembled hostages. Instead, at their tender ages, they had already fulfilled the new American dream—they were on TV. The enthusiastic children made Larry King smile, and he carried on with his interview. "You've got a couple of your own, don't you, Sam?"

"Sure do."

"Are they friends with any of these?"

Sam's kids did not know the hostage children. They were younger and not yet in school.

Larry King opened up the show to telephone calls. "Okay, Van Nuys, California. You have a question for Sam Baily?"

Caller One had a serious voice. "Mr. Baily, what would you say to the people of the former Soviet Union, who are suffering under hardships even greater than your own here in the United States?"

Brackett had no idea what Larry King thought of the query, but the notion of Sam Baily counseling other countries was ludicrous. Sam gave it some consideration, then answered honestly. "I don't speak Russian."

That sounded a little flippant, so Brackett tried to make Sam look good. "I think Sam has a normal complement of compassion."

Larry King changed the focus of his interview. "Max Brackett, veteran newsman. Why are you here, Max? Why have you chosen to stay with this volatile situation?"

"I'm just here to help, Larry. Sam wants me here, so I'm here."

Sam shot Brackett an uneasy look as Larry King went on to the next caller. "Wichita, Kansas, you're on the air with Sam Baily."

Caller Two spoke with the flat accent of the Great Plains. "Sam, we got liberals saying how guys like you show why we need more gun control laws. Why don't you tell them to shut up?"

It was a kick to have people interested in your opinion. Few people had ever asked Sam Baily what he thought about anything. Now, people were watching him all over the world—ranchers in Argentina, bankers in London, entrepreneurs in China—all were waiting to hear what Sam Baily had to say about gun control. He had not thought much about it, but was willing to answer off the cuff. "Um, well. I guess everybody's got their own point of view, but—"

Brackett interrupted and tried to steer Sam away from contentious subjects. "This isn't about gun control. Mr. Baily is not taking sides on such a controversial issue."

Sam was not pleased that Brackett had broken in and spoken for him. Brackett had gotten him on the air, but people wanted to hear what Sam had to say. Sam was news, Brackett simply a delivery system. Larry King stepped in with another caller before tempers flared in Madeline. "Lubbock, Texas. Go ahead."

A sleepy drawl got to his point quickly. "How long you gonna hold out, Sam?"

Mrs. Banks and Kelly Rose leaned forward, anxious to hear his response. The children couldn't decide which to watch—Sam in person, or Sam on TV. Most shifted back and forth between the man and the image. They, and everyone around the world, waited to hear Sam's response.

"I—"

Brackett cut him off again. "Setting deadlines at this point would be counterproductive and—"

He had gone too far. For the first time, Sam cut Brackett off. "The man was talking to me," Sam said, furious. At long last he had achieved something, and

Brackett was getting in the way. Sam addressed the camera. "I'm not sure people are taking me seriously out there, but I'm telling you, something's gotta happen."

Trying to assert himself, Sam unwittingly gave the law-enforcement agencies an excuse to swing into action. Agent Dobbins watched from the command center and issued new orders. "Things are breaking down in there. Let's go on alert."

Larry King wanted to give Sam a chance to explain himself. "You want to elaborate on that, Sam?"

"No, just that. That's all."

A new attitude in Sam's voice suggested that he should not be pushed. The ominous tone was a revelation to Brackett, who looked at Sam with a new sense of respect.

Another caller was holding. "Okay, from right there in Madeline, I understand we have the mother of one of the children being held. Are you there, ma'am?"

A young woman who sounded both fatigued and angry made Sam and Brackett apprehensive. "I am here, thank you, Larry. And thank you for giving me a worldwide audience to address what a travesty this whole situation is. This man has been pointing a gun at my child for three days now!"

Sitting behind the "set," six-year-old Jackie Burton began to cry as she heard her mother's voice. A moment before, everything had been a wonderful adventure. But now, hearing her mother, the little girl realized how much she missed her family. Her sobbing could be heard on the air, and Brackett prayed it did not set Sam off.

Larry King challenged Sam as nicely as he could. "What about it, Sam? Why do you deserve our sympathy after what you've done to these hostages?"

It was a hardball question, and Sam squirmed, unable to answer. Brackett was also unprepared and stumbled a moment, trying to respond. But before he could, Sam threw him a look of warning and answered. "Look, first of all, I didn't ask for this. This wasn't what I was trying to do."

"What were you trying to do?"

"I just . . . I was just . . ."

Brackett came to his assistance. "I think what Sam's trying to say—"

Sam lost his self-control and lashed out. "I'll say what I'm trying to say! I was just watching out for my own, that's all. I was just doing what anybody would do."

Larry asked if Sam felt any guilt for what had transpired. "Of course I do! But I didn't set out to hurt anybody. I never meant for any of this to happen. It's not my fault!"

He was not off the hook. The talk show host kept after him, politely but firmly. "Whose fault is it? Who are you mad at?"

"I'm not mad at anyone."

Jackie Burton's mother had enough. "We don't care about his excuses. But people like Max Brackett and the media are turning him into some kind of hero!"

The discussion was getting inflammatory, and Larry King defended the show's integrity. "Ma'am, we found this to be an opportunity to present all viewpoints of the—"

Mrs. Burton lost her patience. "Since when do we need all viewpoints of a crime?" Her voice escalated toward hysteria. "Please, let my child go. Let them all go. Be a man for once in your life."

She hung up, leaving a deadly silence. Larry King

gave Sam the chance to have the last word. "Sam, a response?"

There was little Sam could say. He searched for words, but could not find any. Shaken, all he could manage was, "I'm sorry."

Larry King could sense that he had lost his guest. It was time for a break. "We'll be right back."

As the program went to commercial, the host told Brackett that they were back on the air in two minutes.

Brackett leaned toward Sam and whispered tentatively, "For this next segment, maybe you should—"

He never got to finish his sentence. Sam was indignant. His temper was building to an eruption. "Don't tell me what to do. And don't answer questions for me!"

Brackett stated what he thought was obvious. "You need help sometimes." There was nothing shameful in that. Most people did.

Sam was not interested in listening, however. "The people want to hear from me, to know what's on my mind." Just like everybody else in Sam's life, Brackett was patronizing him. Sam had enough of being underestimated. "You don't need to be sitting here anymore."

This was a major shift in their relationship. As Brackett tried to recover from his shock, he wondered how the moment of his triumph had deteriorated so quickly. Looking at Sam, he could see the man was not kidding. Brackett tried to placate him, but Sam wanted him off the air. "I'm doing this on my own now."

What could Brackett say? There was no room for argument. He stood up and headed for the door. "Fine. I'll be out front."

Sam stopped him before he had gone far. "No. I don't want you leaving here anymore."

Trying to remain steady, Brackett acted as though he was not going to tolerate any nonsense. "What?"

"I don't want you out there cutting deals behind my back, like this CNN thing."

He was not making sense. Setting up the Larry King interview was exactly the kind of service Brackett could provide for Sam. Brackett wanted Sam to remember who his friends were. "Hey, this CNN thing is getting your story out."

Sam gestured for Brackett to join the children. He was as angry as Brackett had seen him. "Then everybody's gonna know about it if I get mad. Sit down," Sam said.

It took a stunned Brackett a moment to realize that Sam was serious. Half an hour ago Sam had been eating out of his hand. The man of experience was going to rescue Sam from the hole he had dug for himself. Now it was over. All his hard work and careful planning were wasted. Sam had gone over the edge and turned on his last ally. Brackett's return to the network had just been torpedoed, and now even his life was in danger.

Max Brackett was just another hostage.

Chapter Twenty-seven

The Larry King interview was over, and Kevin Hollander had devised his plan. He was about to go live with his own broadcast and a new angle on the story. As the time for the telecast grew nearer, a makeup artist applied pancake base to his face. Laurie waited with him in his private trailer. Hollander could not disguise his anticipation. "Our Mr. Brackett is about to find himself on the wrong side of the news camera."

He handed Laurie a videotape that he had edited. "Go to the truck. Put this transcript up on a graphic, next to his picture. Hurry."

Hollander left the makeup artist without saying thank you. A few steps behind Laurie, he walked across the parking lot to his temporary news desk. Laurie continued into the network truck to deliver the tape. An apprehensive CBN producer caught up with Hollander as he readied himself for a live feed. "New York's not happy that you haven't cleared this with them. All the other networks are leading with the Larry King stuff."

If the purpose of the producer's visit was to intimidate Hollander, it did not work. The anchorman was supremely confident. "And tomorrow they'll be leading with mine."

A technician counted down to airtime, and Hollander's gleeful expression became intensely solemn. "Good evening from Madeline, California, where the eyes of the nation remain on the events going on inside this museum behind me."

The technicians, local people, and network representatives standing inside the CBN truck's control room watched their monitors without knowing what was coming next.

Laurie knew, however. The tape she delivered to the segment director had been put together by Hollander and her. When he had arrived on the scene, Hollander invited Laurie to the network if she would help him. After losing the exclusive with Cliff to *Crime and Punishment,* Laurie had to give him something else. When Brackett beat Hollander with the Larry King interview, Laurie knew exactly what she had to give him. If that decision bothered her, no one would see. Laurie Callahan watched Kevin Hollander's live feed calmly, and apparently without a pang of conscience. As far as she was concerned, it was the price of success.

Hollander continued. "But the real story I have uncovered here is even more troubling, at least to me, a veteran newsman. It concerns the reporter inside that building, a reporter whom I used to call a colleague."

Although he was now a hostage, Brackett still had a certain authority within the museum. As he watched the beginning of Hollander's broadcast, Brackett shouted at the children playing their noisy games, "Quiet!"

Even Sam was startled by the reporter's outburst. Everyone fell silent, and Brackett stepped closer to the television screen. Suddenly, he was filled with a sense of dread. What was Hollander up to?

Inside the network truck the director followed Hol-

lander's written instructions and cut to a tape that
Laurie had shot for Brackett when he had first sent
her out on assignment. The first person to appear was
Sam's mother. "He is a sweet boy. He's confused, but
all he's trying to do is get by."

Jenny Baily was next. "Sometimes he screws
things up."

A neighbor of Sam's was next. His interview had
been sold to CBN by a reporter with network ambitions. The boorish Trevis Bartholomew added his two
cents worth. "Yeah, he's kind of weird, you know. . . .
I have seen him lose his temper . . ." When asked if
Sam was dangerous, the neighbor, who had been hoping to provide something of interest, gave an uncon-
vincing yes.

Sam joined Brackett and watched the program. He
did not understand what he was watching and felt increasingly lost. Hollander revealed his unique take on
the siege story. "This confused, dangerous man who
'screws things up sometimes' is under the control of
Max Brackett, a reporter so driven to further his career that he has misrepresented and perpetuated a
tragedy for his own good."

Sam was getting angry, although he could not figure
out what Brackett had allegedly done.

Hollander played the dismayed anchorman to the
hilt. "I hoped my suspicions were wrong. Sadly, they
were not." The broadcast cut to two photos—one of
Brackett and one of Lou Potts.

Brackett's mind raced as he desperately tried to sort
out what he was seeing. What did Hollander have on
him? And then he heard his own voice in a conversation with Potts from several days before. ". . . Lou,
this is going to turn into a big thing. Right now it's
our thing . . ."

Lou's picture was replaced by Sheriff Lemke's. Once again, Brackett heard himself talking—but now to the local cop. ". . . I think I can guarantee that Mr. Baily is sincere. I also think this is going to become increasingly unstable if you don't grant him his interview . . ."

The television screen switched to videotape of the two young girls who had been released, as they ran down the museum steps. Hollander continued his accusation. "Two little girls were set free, supposedly at the behest of Sam Baily. But the truth I have uncovered tells a far different story."

Sam and Brackett's photographs were back on the air. Brackett was sickened as he heard a conversation go out over the airwaves that should never have been made public. It took place during the first twenty-four hours of the crisis. Sam was choosing a girl to release. "Maybe her," he said.

Brackett listened to himself agree. "Good." Then came the devastating part. The world listened as Brackett coached Sam. "Now let's give them two."

At that moment, millions heard Brackett's explanation—by the next morning the number would be up to tens of millions. "Look, you shot a black man. Some people are going to make an issue of that. You show kindness to a black kid and it'll be harder to play the race card against you."

His stomach cramped, and he felt light-headed. Brackett could not look away from the television screen that condemned him before the world. He did not understand. Had Laurie accidentally left his mike open when he reentered the museum? Was his camera rolling? Did Laurie help Hollander put the compilation tape together? Or had the anchorman taken the raw footage away from her?

The details of Max Brackett's destruction were really not important, however. In the past he would have fought back and tracked down the conspirators who shattered his career. But Brackett knew too well that there was nothing left. Hollander had destroyed him. More accurately, the CBN anchor had annihilated his character. And this time, Max Brackett would never again entertain dreams of returning to any news broadcast, must less a network.

Brackett sat silently, with no inclination to laugh or cry. Either would have taken more strength than he had left. Breathing was about as challenging a hurdle as he could meet.

Ever since his humiliation at the hands of a self-righteous Max Brackett, on a beach thousands of miles away, Kevin Hollander dreamt of returning the deed. Now he had Brackett exactly where he wanted him. Brackett was on his back in the arena. The anchorman did not wait for the crowd's judgment before turning his thumb down. Hollander finished Max Brackett off. "A reporter, scripting the events of a story to conform to his agenda, and playing games with children's lives. It is the most vile perversion of the journalistic code that I have ever encountered. There is a man inside that building, holding children at gunpoint. But inside that building there is also the truth. The facts of this story are being held hostage by Max Brackett. And I submit to you that they are at great risk."

Throughout the crisis, Sam had been slow to understand many things. This duplicity, however, he understood immediately. He looked at Brackett. "What have you done to me?"

After days of tension and moments of unbearable fear, the hostages and their captor reached a new level of dread. Sam had been betrayed by the person closest to him. The two women in the room were silent. Aware that anything was now possible, they feared Sam might end the situation in a grisly spasm of bitterness.

Sam Baily said nothing now. He turned down the volume on the television and stared at the screen. Sam did not look angry. Nor did he look sad. Instead, Sam Baily's expression said everything he was, and could have been, was obliterated.

Max Brackett was the most upset. He had been so close, he had done everything right, and yet it was all over. "Sam, you were a bad story, and I made it good television. You're in a better position now than when you pulled the trigger. I'm the one who's screwed."

Sam wanted to know what happened next. Not that he was looking for direction, however. He was finished. He just wanted to know how his story was going to end.

"You give up now. You free the kids. It's over."

Resentment surged within Sam Baily. Faced with a bitter reality, he clung to the exhilaration he had known only minutes earlier. Sam Baily had been the hottest thing on television. People sang songs about him. People came from all over the country to stand vigil outside the museum. Larry King gave him an hour of airtime. Sam did not want to let go of his moment of glory. He had waited too long, and once he was in it, he found it infuriatingly elusive. Sam wanted his public to defend him. "No. I won't give up. I've still got people out there who want me left alone."

Brackett could do nothing more with this story, so he spoke bluntly. "Sam, goddammit. You said you've seen these things on TV before. Didn't you pay attention to how they always end? The guy ends up in jail . . . or dead."

Reeling, Sam absorbed the blow. Then, in an instant, he turned on Brackett, shoving the rifle into his face. "You used me!"

His long, slow burn ignited into something more lethal. Finally, something horrible seemed about to happen.

Welcome to the world, Sam, Brackett thought, suddenly annoyed by the gunman's ingenuousness. And yet, the nagging sensation that had bothered him earlier fought to be heard. The emotions within Brackett battled to a stalemate, and he spoke to Sam with a neutral, blank tone. "If you kill somebody, it will be prison for life—at least."

Sam did not flinch, nor did he put down his weapon. Instead, his eyes bore wildly into Brackett's. Of all the raw deals Sam had been dealt, this was the worst. He wanted Brackett to feel at least a taste of his pain.

Brackett thought in that moment he was about to die. But his eyes showed nothing. He benefited from too many close calls over the years, and if there was now an embryonic conscience within, Max Brackett could not express it. It was too late. His empty stare was that of a predator after killing the food it needed to survive.

And then Sam Baily gave up.

He had given no indication that he was planning to do so. Until he put down his rifle, Mrs. Banks thought he was going to open fire and kill as many people as he could. But like many of Sam's moods during the last three days, this one swept over him abruptly. Faced with life in prison and confronted by an unrepentant Max Brackett, Sam knew that he was hopelessly trapped. He shrugged, gave a rueful laugh, and set down his gun on the floor.

The room was silent; no one moved. Sam turned to the children and offered a grin that he hoped would put them at ease. It was over, and he felt guilty for having frightened them. The same thought raced through his mind over and over. He had not wanted to take the children hostage. He had not wanted to hurt anybody. He had simply wanted to talk to his boss and try to keep his job.

The quiet of the museum was interrupted by the ominous sound of helicopters drawing near. Sam and Brackett looked up at the ceiling, as though they would see what was happening. Then the amplified voice of Agent Dobbins began to give orders. "Samuel Baily. This is Lawrence Dobbins with the FBI. You are to free your hostages, lay down your weapons and surrender. Now."

Sam smiled wearily. Something else had just gone wrong in his life. Now no one would believe that he set the kids free on his own. He turned to Mrs. Banks. "Shoot. I wanted it to be my idea."

"Wait a minute."

The voice was tense. After years in the news business, Brackett had developed a sense for how a situation felt. There was something wrong about what was unfolding. Why had the FBI decided to make a move now? Brackett suspected a major problem had developed and gestured for quiet. He dialed Lou Potts on his cellular phone. "Lou. What's going on out there?"

Sam went over to the TV and watched a reporter corner Sheriff Lemke. "Why have you chosen this moment to take action?"

Lemke's manner was solemn and determined. "The situation has changed."

Brackett listened to Lou's explanation, his expression grim. He turned to Sam, but was too late. Sam had already seen the news delivered on the TV.

Nat Jackson was reporting live from Mercy Hospital, a frenzy of reporters and publicists behind him. "Cliff Williams went into cardiac arrest at six-fifteen this evening. Doctors worked feverishly to revive him."

The broadcast cut to a swarm of reporters hovering around Diane Williams at the hospital. Her face smeared with tears, she controlled her emotions and put up a dignified front. "I want people to see what this is all about. I want all the people who've been worrying about Sam Baily's side in all this to start thinking about my child. Her father is dead. My husband is dead."

In that instant, Sam Baily knew he had lost everything. The long line of miscues that made up his life had finally spiraled out of control. It did not matter anymore that he had not intended to harm anybody.

Sam Baily became the victim of an equation he never knew existed—the latest American downsized to the fringe of society. With more free time, the unemployed watched more television, and networks and syndicators had more customers. With the punishing demand for new material, the only requisite was that programs grab an audience's attention.

As people stayed home to watch their favorite shows, the American community changed. People did not know their neighbors. Generations did not sit together any longer to talk. Instead, human interaction was replaced by illusion. The American community, once held together by common values, now shared instead a common bond of prurient voyeurism.

People were no longer burdened by the problems facing their neighbors, family, and friends. For a problem in the new community, simply switch channels. If two hands clasped represented an earlier, idealized image of the American community, a hand on a remote channel changer was the image of the new television community.

Sam Baily, and not someone from the media, put a hunting rifle into a bag and set off to the Madeline Natural History Museum three days previously. Yet, as he went to plead his case and get his job back, Sam Baily was swept away by a cultural tidal wave. His destruction and Cliff Williams's death were not solely Sam's fault, nor Max Brackett's. The media and the conglomerates that ran them could not be condemned absolutely. Instead, everyone in a nation of channel surfers shared the blame—those who switched away from their responsibilities and instead sought out the lurid.

Such was the state of the American family in 1997: Parents ate their young and then bragged about it on TV talk shows.

Brackett stared at Sam. Lost in thought, Sam rocked slightly on his heels as he tried to digest the latest news. Brackett recognized Sam's instability and wanted to get the gun away from him. He spoke kindly, but with determination. "Sam, you've got to finish it now."

Agent Dobbins's voice filled the museum again. "Samuel Baily. You have five minutes to lay down your weapons and surrender."

Brackett gestured for Sam to hand him the rifle. The museum lobby was silent as everyone watched.

Suddenly, Sam began to shout, "Everybody out! Now!"

The surprised hostages hesitated before running to the door. Mrs. Banks paused and spoke sincerely to the man whom she had unintentionally destroyed. "I will pray for you, Sam." A little girl ran back to Sam and thanked him for letting them go. Sam smiled sweetly, then sent her on her way.

Chapter Twenty-eight

The mood in the museum parking lot had deteriorated with the news of Cliff Williams's death. Parents looked with increased concern at the museum. Now that Sam was a murderer, there was less reason for him to surrender peacefully.

People who had gathered from all over the country to support Sam were now embarrassed by their misplaced allegiance. As unobtrusively as possible, they packed up their signs, their tents, and their trailer homes and made a quiet exit. Sam Baily had been their hero, and now he was just another killer.

Tension built between antagonistic groups. People who supported Sam glared warily at those who sided with Cliff. A racial divide festered beneath their angry looks, and the climate became oppressive with the suggestion of imminent violence.

They were so consumed by their grievances that few noticed the doors to the museum open, and a classroom full of young students raced down the steps and into the arms of their deliriously happy parents. Moments later, their exhausted teacher came out after making sure all of her kids were free. Kelly Rose's parents, brothers, sisters, and boyfriend were all there waiting for her.

Mrs. Banks was next. But before she could make

her way down the steps and into her husband's embrace, she was surrounded by reporters. Even the feisty curator was no match for the press. She stood on tiptoe and tried to spot her husband, but it was clear that for the moment she was not going anywhere. Mrs. Banks had been freed by one captor and was now hostage to another.

Soon, all the families were interrupted by various news organizations desperate to get the best pictures. The rule of thumb was that if there couldn't be any bloodshed, the next best things were crying kids and family reunions. There were plenty to go around, and producers hustled the families, hoping to line up guest appearances on tomorrow's programs.

Sam and Brackett watched the happy kids on the TV at the security desk. For the first time in his life, Sam knew he had done something right.

The crisis was not entirely over, however. Sam still had a gun and explosives. Brackett tried to talk Sam into surrendering. "You treated them well. The court will remember that."

It did not matter to Sam, though. "I killed a man."

"It was an accident. I'll testify to that."

Sam stared at Brackett in disbelief. "Who's gonna believe you?"

Brackett was startled by Sam's comment. Not that his feelings were hurt, but the gunman's comment emphasized his downfall. Though he had lost everything, Brackett was surprised by a feeling of liberation that accompanied his freedom from professional obligation.

In the vacuum of thwarted ambition, Brackett at long last resolved to do something entirely selfless. He was determined to help Sam through the upcoming ordeal. "Let's get your wife on the phone. Would you like to talk to her?"

All Sam could do was nod vacantly. As Brackett dialed the command center, Sam flipped channels and watched a live feed showing the police moving into position to arrest him.

The call went through to Sam's house, where Jenny was praying for him to return. Outside, a pack of frenzied reporters pounded on her doors and windows, hungry for an interview or just a glimpse of the gunman's wife. Jenny heard Sam's torment and tried to keep herself from becoming frantic. "Sam," she said, "I heard about Cliff."

Sam started to weep. He cried for Cliff, Jenny, and both their families. "I killed him, Jen. I didn't mean to, but I killed him."

"Sam, I want you to give up, right now. You've still got our kids to think about."

He was thinking about them all the time. Sam would never see them again except in the confines of a prison visitor's room.

"How are they?"

"They miss you. They want you home."

Sam faltered. He could not go home.

Jenny sensed his despair. "Honey, it's time to get this over with."

"I know." And he hung up the phone, slowly and sadly.

Brackett had never seen Sam this low before and did his best to shake him from his gloom. "Sam, let's just get everybody to stop pointing their guns at you. Then we'll figure out what's next."

The gunman's eyes were locked on the television screen. CBN was rerunning Laurie's footage of Cliff being shot. Sam winced as he saw Cliff slide down the steps. Brackett scrambled to keep Sam on track. "Come on. Let's get out of here, Sam."

To his surprise, Sam put up no resistance. "Yeah. Okay. Could you go out first?"

Sam was afraid of stepping outside and getting shot. Brackett could not blame him and decided to do as Sam asked. He would get the cops to call off the sharpshooters. "Sure. I'll make sure everybody's calm, and then you'll come out."

Sam nodded his head, said nothing, and continued to stare at the live coverage on TV. He watched SWAT teams approaching the museum, and cops moving the crowds back to a safe distance.

While there was no longer anything Brackett could gain by it, he drew closer to the frightened man and tried to comfort him. "Hey. So who do you want to play you in the movie?"

A few hours earlier Sam would have seriously considered this an important question. Now, he knew it was Brackett's way of saying good-bye. Once Sam surrendered, he doubted Brackett could do much for him. Sam suggested Mel Gibson.

"Gibson doesn't do television."

Sam smiled back sadly. "Story of my life."

There was nothing more to say. It was over. Time for Brackett to get the police to lower their guns and let Sam give himself up. He gave the gunman a last supportive pat on the shoulder, made his way across the lobby, and out the door.

In the parking lot everyone watched the disgraced reporter emerge. Brackett squinted under the harsh lights set up by the FBI and police. He looked up to the sky and saw helicopters hovering—their high-powered searchlights crossing each other as they were directed onto the museum. Looking down the steps, Brackett noticed a dried puddle of Cliff Williams's blood.

Grimacing, Brackett saw dozens of guns pointed at him. He held up his hands to the crowd and tried to get them to lower their weapons. "His guns are down! He's coming out!"

Sam watched Brackett's performance on his TV. The reporter was dwarfed by the scene, his presence small in comparison to the army of cops, media, and spectators. "It's over!" Max called out.

And it was. Sam switched off the TV and stared at the black screen. There was nothing more to watch. Sam knew there was nothing more for him to do.

After a few minutes, Sam stood up. The noise of helicopters buzzing past harassed him. Their intensely bright searchlights beamed through the skylights. The effect was hallucinatory as brilliant shafts of light jumped around the lobby. More poured in through the windows—media and the law waited for Sam to walk out.

At some level, Sam understood that the lights had changed his life. Before he had walked into the museum, and before the press had arrived, Sam had been an ordinary man. The attention and the glare transformed him. Over three days he had become both celebrity folk hero and public enemy number one. He was neither, but he could no longer control the image people had of him. He had been molded and recast by the disparate and contradictory needs of a medium that introduced him to the public. And once the arc of his story line was complete, it was time for Sam Baily to go off the air.

Sam did not want to die, but did not know how he could go on living. Not many things in Sam Baily's life had he been able to govern. But now, as all of the insanity wound down, he knew one final course he could follow to control his own future.

Sam realized that his troubled and precarious life was more wonderful than he had appreciated. He wanted to return to Jenny, his children, his small house, his fishing, his friends, and his job. But that could never happen, and he saw no reason to go on.

Sam walked out of the lobby and into the nineteenth-century room. There, Big John, last leader of the vanished Miwok Indian tribe, held out his remaining hand in a melancholy farewell. Sam lifted his hand to say good-bye and then raised his rifle to his forehead. For a moment, nothing happened, because Sam could not bring himself to pull the trigger. Then, knowing that there must be something in his life he could accomplish successfully, Sam Baily pulled the trigger.

A hollow click reverberated through the room. The gun was empty. Sam failed yet again.

There was nothing else to do now but surrender. He had made many different attempts over the last three days, and every single one had gone wrong. Sam gave up and prepared to hand himself over to the police. He could no longer fight. He would allow himself to be pushed along in whatever direction they saw fit. As he neared the door, however, Sam noticed the canvas bag in which he had smuggled his gun into the museum.

For the last time in his life, Sam had an original idea.

Chapter Twenty-nine

Outside, at the top of the steps, Max Brackett shielded his eyes from the glare. He looked around, trying to find a figure of authority who could tell the police to lower their guns. Instead, he saw the CBN newsdesk, and Laurie standing next to Hollander. Brackett met her stare. He expected her to be ashamed and to look away. Laurie held his gaze until he was distracted by Dobbins barking over his public address system, "Step away from the building now!"

Waving his arms, Brackett pleaded with the police to be patient. "He's coming out. Please! He's coming right—"

Then he froze, realizing that Sam was not coming out. Brackett spun around and ran back to the door, but it had been locked behind him. There was nothing in it for Max Brackett but the chance to save the life of another person. He pounded on the door and begged Sam to surrender peacefully. "Sam! Wait! It's not over, Sam! The story's not over! We have to finish—"

The spectacle stunned viewers around the nation. It delivered everything that live television was uniquely qualified to handle—real-life drama, unencumbered by the dilution of time delay and editorial morality. The denouement of the Madeline hostage crisis provided excellent image and closure with biblical simplicity. The live coverage at the natural history museum illustrated the price to be paid by murderers. Better yet— it occurred during prime time.

Sam Baily had detonated the dynamite taken from his brother-in-law's toolshed.

The explosion shredded the interior of the museum, and a fire burned out of control. The blast tore open the front door and hurled Brackett down the steps toward the parking lot.

As he lay in the gutter, his head rang from the concussive wave. Then his ears cleared a bit, and he could hear excited correspondents beginning to narrate the action. Police and firemen charged past him up the stairs to do their business.

A bloodied Brackett pulled himself to his feet and staggered back up the steps. As he fell to his knees, however, he was not thinking of losing his exclusive, but of Sam Baily. Before medical attendants could arrive to help him, a pack of reporters descended upon Brackett and peppered him with a barrage of questions.

"Did you know he was considering suicide?"

"What were his last words?"

"Back it up, people! Come on!"

Paramedics arrived and began to lift Brackett onto a stretcher. He fought, however, not wanting to be taken from the scene. "No . . . let me go. . . . !"

"Just lay down. We have to move you back!"

Weakened from his injuries, Brackett fought, but could not resist. A large paramedic held him down as the others rolled him through the chaotic scene. Brackett did not give up, however, and struggled to see what was happening.

Flames poured out of the burning museum as firemen began to douse it with water. Police battled a crowd of onlookers who wanted to be closer to the action. Reporters stood as close to the inferno as they could and delivered their reports. It did not make sense to Brackett. It seemed the mob wanted to rush into the blaze itself, as if there were a collective urge toward self-destruction, as though fiery annihilation were a small price to pay for a moment of notice.

Past the bedlam and the CBN anchor desk, a grave Kevin Hollander described the scene to his viewers. A toppled vending cart lay on its side, abandoned. Lou Potts stood passively and stared at him sadly.

Away from the turmoil, the paramedics went to work. An IV was inserted to provide fluids and stave off shock. Swabs cleaned his wounds, and bandages were prepared.

As Brackett lay on his stretcher, unable to move, Laurie tried to push past a policeman who wanted to let the paramedics work without interruption. "Come on, lady! Give him a break! He's hurt!"

Laurie's concern for Brackett—her fear that he was badly injured, her panic—was clear. "I'm his friend! We work together!"

The policeman softened and let her by. When Brackett saw her, he felt overwhelming relief. She had come. Laurie was probably the only person who cared about him. He forgave her for going over to Hollander and orchestrating his professional destruction. He now saw that there were more important things in life. That was Sam's legacy. Laurie Callahan cared enough about Brackett that she would forsake the story of her career to comfort him and be by his side. Laurie's presence proved to Brackett that no one was unredeemable—even himself.

It might have been the shock or the medication now coursing through his body, but Brackett thought he was starting to hallucinate. Had Laurie pulled a camera out from a hiding place underneath a coat? She seemed to be leaning forward and talking to him in a conspiratorial manner. "You'll go exclusive for me, won't you?"

He looked at her blankly, unable to respond.

"Come on, Max."

It took all his power of concentration to speak. "What happened to Sam?"

She did not hesitate. "Sam? Sam is confetti."

Brackett began to drown in the events of the last three days. What was happening? Was this real? Was Laurie trying to get his story? Or was it a prolonged nightmare? But Laurie *was* there. She was holding his hand, pestering him, too much in his face. "How does that make you feel, Max?"

Everything was going red. Brackett looked for Laurie and her camera, but could only see through a bloody haze. Blood poured from his head wounds. He tried to wipe it out of his eyes and off his face.

"No, Max! Don't wipe it. It's good."

The light on her camera went on, and she was taping.

Blinded by the blazing light, Max Brackett tried to recoil, but there was nowhere to go. The camera lens came closer, and when he turned his head away, all he could see was chaos through a bloody prism.

Brackett's head began to spin, and his consciousness wavered. He was going to be back on the network tonight after all. And, it would be *his* story. But it would not be his story as he had once imagined. Instead, Max Brackett was now the subject, not its interpreter.

Wounded and discredited, Max Brackett had created the latest tragic news—and he was it.

LIGHTS! CAMERA! SIGNET!